Secrets in Small Towns

Also by Iza Moreau

Secrets in Small Towns

Iza Moreau

Books for people who like to think about what they read.

Secrets in Small Towns

Copyright © Iza Moreau
February, 2014

Black Bay Books
1939 Sand Basin Rd.
Grand Ridge, FL 32442

Printed in the USA
First Printing in 2014

ISBN-13: 978-1492177104
Library of Congress Control Number: 2013956278

Cover Design by Black Bay Books

First Print Edition

There is no note played on any instrument that has not been played before. That said, *Secrets in Small Towns* is sheer fiction. Any resemblance of names, places, characters, and incidents to actual persons, places, and events results from the relationship which the world must always bear to works of this kind.

The filly would draw the line and say, "Now, Martha, I'm going to tell you something; there is a line here and don't you cross it, or I'll kick up or something."

Then the rider would need to say, "Now, filly, there's a line out here and you are going to cross it."

—Tom Dorrance

That's not correct.

—Cindy McKeown

This book is dedicated to

M.F. Beal
Eve Zaremba
Vicki P. McConnell
Katherine V. Forrest

Four women who made it happen

Chapter One: Clout

"God's weenie, Sue-Ann! How do you expect me to hit something that small from way out here?"

Clarence Meekins, all six-foot-four of him, squinted out across the pasture at an empty feed bag taped to a pitchfork that I had stuck securely in the brown stubble of the field. He looked dubiously at his bow—an old Fred Bear Kodiak—and reached into his quiver for an arrow.

It was a balmy, 65-degree day in early March, one of those days that make global warming feel like it might not be such a bad thing. The blue sky was interrupted by only a few wispy clouds floating overhead and the gentle breeze inspired the broomstraw in the field to do a little shimmy. Clarence and I were out clout shooting. We were standing on the west side of my pasture; our makeshift target was 180 yards to the east, just inside the fenceline. Three horses, lounging safely behind us in the barnyard, eyed us with equine curiosity.

"You don't have to hit it, Clarence," I told him. "Just get close to it."

"How close?"

"Anything inside twelve feet scores points."

"Well, I'll try," he said, and nocked an arrow. Raising the bow, he pulled back on the string, anchored it near his right ear, and let it fly.

"Outta sight, Clarence," I said. Behind me, I heard the squeal of my weanling filly Emmy and looked back to see her prancing along the fence. She had heard the sound of bowstrings twanging her entire life, but she enjoyed acting silly.

"Did I hit it?" he asked.

"No," I laughed. "I mean it went totally out of sight. What's the weight on that bow, anyway?"

"Seventy pounds, something like that."

"Um. I forgot how strong you are. That one went over the fence and into those trees."

"I've got the feel for it now," he said confidently. "I'll aim lower this time."

"Just don't pull back so hard," I suggested.

So Clarence fired again and the result was better. I knew this from the angle of the bow and the trajectory rather than from seeing where it landed—that was impossible from the distance of almost two football fields, at least with my 37-year-old eyes. Clarence shot four more arrows, taking his time, concentrating, and watching the flight of each arrow as long as he could. I could see that he was having a grand old time and I was glad.

Clarence was the owner of Meekins' Market, a grocery store-cum-curio shop located near the edge of Pine Oak and within a couple of miles of where I lived with my horses and my black shorthair cat Kitty Amin. What with running the store, trucking in fruits and vegetables from various parts of Florida, Georgia, and Alabama, and other more personal duties, Clarence rarely had a chance to relax or do anything fun. He and I had attended high school together, but when I went off to journalism school in North Carolina, he did a stint in the Marines before returning to Pine Oak to run the family business. In the two years I had been back, working for *The Pine Oak Courier*, Clarence and I had become good friends. In fact, he had helped me solve a couple of mysteries connected with some investigative pieces I'd written.

I was carrying my Wapiti takedown, laminated with bubinga and walnut in various swirling shades of green and brown. I had purchased my inexpensive black Carbon Express arrows at the WalMart in Forester. In fact, I had bought the silver ones Clarence was using as well. Although I had once been first alternate on the U.S. Olympic archery team, my experience in shooting clout archery was almost as limited as Clarence's. I had shot a couple of hundred arrows since I had set up the field two weeks before. But any experience is better than none, and I took aim with deliberation and let my first arrow fly. Seeing it leave the bow, I knew that the distance was pretty accurate but the trajectory was off to the right some. I adjusted and shot again. This time I was rewarded with the distant sound of carbon hitting plastic and the sight of the bag shaking on its pole.

"You hit it, Sue-Ann! By golly you hit the shinola out of it! If I hadn't seen it with my own eyes—"

"Pure luck, Clarence," I told him. And it was true. In my earlier practice sessions, the closest I had come to the bag was about four feet. I shot my remaining four arrows and we began walking toward the target to collect them and see how well we had done.

"I appreciate you askin me to come shoot with you, Sue-Ann," said Clarence, his oversized brogans crushing through the brown Bahia grass and the occasional blackberry bush. In addition to the familiar shoes, he was wearing familiar clothing: blue overalls, a dark blue work shirt, and red flannel overshirt. I'm not sure he owned anything else, but the fact that they always looked cleaned and pressed told me that he had several pairs of each. "I haven't shot this bow since my granddaddy was alive. And thanks again for making me the new bowstring."

"My pleasure, Clarence. I like having someone to shoot with."

"When is Ginette coming back?" he asked. Gina Cartwright was the office manager for *The Courier*, and my best friend.

"She'll be back at work Monday," I told him.

"Is her daddy all right?"

"He had a heart attack, but evidently it wasn't as serious as the doctor originally thought. It's good that Gina got to visit, though. She hasn't seen either of her parents in years. We miss her at the office, but it's a pretty slow time and we've all been pitching in."

"You still likin bein editor?"

"It beats still being in Iraq," I told him.

"I hear ya."

We were getting close to the target now and I was on the lookout for arrows. Because of the season, the grass was low and they were easy to spot. One of my arrows had gotten hung up in the plastic bag and another was within six feet, but the others were anywhere from twenty to thirty feet away. Clarence had one within ten feet and four more scattered about, some short, some long. We picked them up and I looked into the woods beyond. "That first one of yours might be a problem," I said.

"I'll get it, Sue-Ann," said Clarence, and ducked under the electric tape fence with an agility unusual in such a big man.

Beyond the fence was a thicket of scrub oak, a few pines, one giant live oak, and several types of brush I didn't know the names of. I heard Clarence stomping around, then, "God's great gonads, Sue-Ann, I've killed somebody!"

I had been putting arrows in my quiver, but stopped at Clarence's yell. Bow and arrows in hand, I ducked under the fence—yelping a little when I didn't bend low enough and got zapped with 6,000 volts of electricity. I pushed my way through a couple of cedars and saw

Clarence standing over the body of what looked to be a young man lying face-down under the enormous live oak. I noticed with a glance that he was dressed in jeans, a dirty tee shirt, and high-topped basketball shoes with the laces undone. I also noticed something else: Clarence's arrow was stuck fast in the trunk of the oak tree. "You didn't hit him, Clarence. There's your arrow." Then I saw a pistol lying a few yards away, almost hidden in some ground cover.

Instinctively, I nocked an arrow and looked around me. "Hold on, Clarence," I said, "There's a pistol in the brush there. Has he been shot? Check to see if he's breathing."

Clarence bent down and touched the boy's shoulder. "I don't see any blood—" he began, but as he started to turn him over, the young man came alive and jabbed an elbow into Clarence's chin, knocking him backwards. The boy looked up, wildness in his eyes—wildness like a horse that has just scented a predator. Drugged, I thought. He scrambled to his knees and looked around him frantically. When he spotted the pistol, he lunged for it.

He was quick, but my arrow was quicker. I guess I could have just put an arrow through his hand, but I didn't want to hurt him if I didn't have to, so I aimed just in front of the gun. It plocked into the ground an inch from the trigger, forming a thin barrier between the boy's fingers and the pistol grip. Before he could reach around the arrow, Clarence had recovered enough to snatch him up and slam him backwards into the tree.

The whole episode had taken only a few seconds and the only sound was the "Oof" of the young man as the wind was knocked out of him. Then his eyes glazed over and he slumped down into a sitting position beneath the great oak.

"Oops," Clarence said, slightly embarrassed. "I guess I used too much strength again."

I dropped my bow and reached into my fannypack for my cell phone and an extra bow string. I tossed the string to Clarence. "I think you better tie him up," I told him. Use his shoelaces to tie his legs together, too. It's obvious he's not using them for anything else. I snapped open my cell and punched in 911, which I knew went through to the Jasper County Sheriff's Office. "Hello, who's this, Tequesta? It's Sue-Ann McKeown. I thought you worked nights. Yeah, well congratulations. Listen, I have a situation here at my farm. I found a young man passed out on my property. No idea who he is—looks kind of Latino, maybe. He was—", but Clarence caught my eye. He was pointing at the pistol and shaking his head vehemently. I nodded at him. "I mean, um, I don't know if it's a real emergency or not. I don't see any injuries and he seems to be breathing regularly, but could you send an ambulance? You have my address, right? Thanks, Tequesta, I'll be waiting."

Clarence had finished tying up the youth. "That was nice shooting, Sue-Ann," he said. "Was that just luck, too?"

"No," I replied. "I actually practice that."

"Probably saved our lives. Who knows what this fool might have done. But what if you had missed?"

"I had another arrow ready, Clarence. I practice that, too."

He picked up the automatic, then removed the clip and slipped it into his pocket. "Know what this is?" he asked, holding out the empty pistol.

"It's hard to be in Iraq for six months and not know a standard issue Berretta M9 when I see one," I answered. "But what the hell is this kid doing with a service pistol?"

"I don't know, Sue-Ann, but I didn't want you to tell the sheriff he had it until we were sure." Then he added significantly, "You know what I mean?"

And suddenly I did. "Uh oh," I said, and quickly punched in another number on my cell. "Hello, who's this? Colonel Frogmore? Who the hell is that? I've never—"

"Let me have the phone, Sue-Ann," Clarence said, and took my cell. "Colonel," he began. "It's Clarence Meekins. Right, that was Sue-Ann McKeown. . . No, she's a friend of ours . . . No, you don't have to worry about that, but we may have a situation. "We just found a kid, maybe fifteen years old in Sue-Ann's pasture. Looks like he's drugged out of his skull, but he was in possession of an M9. Have you had any break-ins out there? Okay, well, check with Ashley or Jeremy. If you find anything missing, call me back at this number." Clarence snapped the phone together and gave it back to me.

"Clarence," I demanded, "Who's Colonel Frogface and what's he doing—"

"Frogmore," said Clarence. "He's the new doctor at Torrington."

"But why didn't anybody—"

"Don't you think we oughta get this fella to the house before the ambulance gets here?" he interrupted.

"Sure. Right," I said, "But . . . wait a minute. I was working Clarence's arrow out of the oak tree when I spotted something shiny in the brush. I picked it up. A silver plastic packet with the words White Silk in dreamy script.

"What's that?" Clarence asked, lifting the boy over his shoulder as easily as he would a sack of feed. "Looks like a condom wrapper."

"I'm not . . . No, it says bath salts."

"Funny place to be taking a bath," Clarence said, his long strides carrying him across the field and toward the barn. I pocketed the packet, picked up our tackle, and hurried after him.

It didn't take us long to reach the house, but long enough for me to fill you in on a few details.

The Torrington that Clarence had mentioned was a secret compound located in the woods between my property and Clarence's. Originally the home of Pine Oak's founder, it was a fenced-in area of several hundred acres completely surrounded by miles of forest. I had stumbled on the area by accident when I was out stump shooting the summer before. I later learned that the founder's antebellum house, as well as several outbuildings, had been refurbished and were now inhabited by ex-soldiers, most of them either badly maimed or shell-shocked. The man who ran it—Ashley Torrington, a descendent of the original family—had been horribly burned by napalm in Vietnam decades before. He provided a home for soldiers who could not cope with the outside world—an alternative to spending months or years in VA hospitals. Living in Torrington gave them a chance to contribute to their own cure through farming and other activities. Clarence, a distant cousin, was Torrington's eyes and ears in the outside world. In the course of time, I had become friends with Ashley and was one of only three outsiders in Pine Oak that knew of the existence of what I referred to as The Compound. Clarence and my friend Gina were the other two. As to who Col. Frogmore was, well, it seemed that Torrington had added new personnel just when I was getting familiar with the old ones. I guess I was overdue for a visit.

Across the field we went, then through the gate and across the dressage ring to the barn. From there it was just a few yards to the house. But that's when the boy woke up again and started struggling. Clarence continued into the house as if he hadn't noticed and let him slip down onto the couch in the living room.

"Don't hurt me again," he screamed.

"Nobody's going to hurt you, I told him."

"You shut up, you *puta*!" he screamed. "You're just like all the rest of them and you almost shot me dead!" The boy's eyes were still wild, glancing around the room as if he expected to be attacked by each of the walls. He started thrashing again, legs and arms still tied, until he managed to fall off the couch onto the carpet with a thump. Then the doorbell rang and I went to answer it.

Instead of the ambulance attendant I was expecting, the large man standing at the front door, hat in his hand, was Sgt. Joey Bickley of the Jasper County Sheriff's Office. I had forgotten—stupidly, in my line of work—that any 911 call required follow-up by law enforcement. "Sergeant Bickley," I said.

"Joey" he replied.

"Sergeant Bickley," I repeated. "You got here in a hurry." For reasons you'll understand later, Joey Bickley was about the last person I wanted to see.

"I got the call from Tequesta and I was in the neighborhood," he said. Looking past me, he raised his eyebrows. "Howdy, Clarence. Didn't know you were here."

"Yeah, well. We found this kid out in the field passed out. He's gotten some bad coke or something. You can see the white around his nostrils."

From the floor, the boy rolled over and screamed at the top of his lungs, "FUCK YOU!"

"I see," said Bickley.

"You see SHIT, you cop motherfucker!" screamed the boy, trying to squirm out of his bonds.

Bickley took a few steps into the room until he stood over the boy. "You need to button your lip, little buddy," he said. "Now what's your name?"

"You tol' me to button my lip."

"Your name, boy," said Bickley impatiently.

"An I ain' no boy,"

"Have it your way." With that, despite the boy's squirming and cursing, Bickley went through his pockets. "No ID," said Bickley.

"Ha!" the boy shouted triumphantly. Whatever high he had been on, he seemed to be coming down from it. And with most of the wildness gone, I noticed that he was almost incredibly good looking. Thick, dark hair, skin smooth and almost copper-toned, dark, piercing eyes. And yes, now that Clarence had mentioned it, I saw traces of what I assumed was cocaine just around the outside of his nostrils.

Sgt. Bickley took a small notebook from his neatly ironed uniform shirt and opened the cover. He turned a few pages, then looked up. "Name wouldn't be Murillo, would it?"

"Bite me," replied the boy.

"Carlos Murillo?"

"Naw, uh-uh."

"Who's Carlos Murillo, Joe?" asked Clarence.

"Kid who escaped from Hardy a few days ago. He fits the description."

Suddenly the kid went bonkers again. "No, that's not me!"

"Suppose we just drive out there and find out, hey?" said Bickley.

"NO. I don' wanna go there!" He looked up at me, then at Clarence. "Don' let him take me there!"

"What are you on?" I asked gently.

"Wouldn' you like to know?"

"They'll find out at the hospital, you know."

"No. I don' wanna go to no hospital."

"Well, that's tough shit, kid," Joey intervened. "You hear that siren, boy? That's the ambulance. Bet you've never ridden in an ambulance, have you? But I hope you enjoy it because as soon as you get all flushed out, you and I are going to talk about Hardy."

"No, I—" but then the boy clammed up, closed his eyes, and seemed to go catatonic. I went to the door for the EMTs and watched as they placed the boy on a stretcher and wheeled him to the back of the ambulance. I watched it pull out of my driveway and was glad to see that Joey Bickley intended to follow closely behind in his squad car.

Back in the house, I grabbed a sweater. "I'm going, too," I told Clarence. "I want to get to the bottom of this. But what about the M9?"

"Ashley can get the serial number checked and we'll find out who it belongs to. If the kid got it from Torrington, no one will find out he ever had it. If it belongs to someone else . . ." He shrugged his broad shoulders. "Well, Sue-Ann, then you'll have yourself another mystery."

Chapter Two: White Silk

As hospitals go, Jasper County Memorial Medical Center isn't that easy to find. After I reached downtown Forester, I had to wait impatiently through two maddeningly slow red lights, take a right, then travel another half mile on a narrow street, which widened out to reveal the red brick complex at the end. When I finally arrived, I had to park my venerable Toyota pickup in a lot a bit too far from the entrance for my liking. I shut the door firmly, disturbing the jumble of empty Styrofoam coffee containers that seem to grow like wild mushrooms on the floor of the passenger side. I spotted Joey Bickley's squad car parked near the emergency entrance in a No Parking zone. The ambulance was there, too, so I hurried through the automatic doors and into the lobby.

The hospital is small by some standards, but bright, clean, and much more modern than the town itself. Maybe that's why they tried to hide it—so that they would have fewer patients to dirty the floors or stain the furniture. In back of the gleaming, tiled front lobby was a long receiving desk with several nurses of both sexes stationed behind it, all dressed in green scrubs. A series of elevators took up most of the space on the left while the right gave off into a much larger sitting room with comfortable chairs upholstered to match the walls— some ecru, some light brown. The flooring was the same polished tile set in a checkerboard pattern. As I walked to the desk I thought of what a comfortable place it might be to bring a cup of strong coffee and a book.

But then I did a double take. In the very corner of the room, sitting at a small table, and bent forward in his armchair over what appeared to be a tablet computer, sat a shortish man with thinning white hair. Whatever he was reading on his tablet must have been amusing because he was chuckling to himself. I knew him. His name was Benny and he owned The Best Little Bookstore in Pine Oak, which was located two shops down from *The Pine Oak Courier* offices. Benny was not only a bookstore owner, but an inventor of quirky devices (visualize a flask shaped like binoculars to sneak booze into sports events) and writer of sorts. I was a regular customer of his bookstore.

"Can I help you, Miss?"

"Oh, right." I took my eyes from Benny, who was so busy tapping on his little machine that he hadn't seen me enter, and looked around at the woman at the desk. Her ID stated that she was Rose Walker, Receptionist, although she wore the same green scrubs as the medical staff. She was a round woman in her forties with inexpensive-looking reading glasses hanging from her neck by a gold chain.

"I'm looking for that young man that just came in the ambulance. Latino teenager. I think Sergeant Bickley might have been with him."

"Um. They took him up to the third floor to have a look at him. You a relative?"

"No. I'm Sue-Ann McKeown from *The Courier.*"

"That boy done somethin bad?"

"What makes you ask that?" I asked in good journalese.

"Because *The Courier* is interested," she replied. "Handcuffs were a clue, too."

I smiled and prevaricated. "Not that I know of. I'm the one who called the ambulance. I found him passed out near my property and just want to see if he's all right." Inwardly, I was peeved that Joey had put handcuffs on the kid. On second thought, though, I realized that they may have been necessary. Whatever he was hopped up on had been weirding him out in a big way.

"That's nice of you," the woman said absently.

"Do you think I could see him?" I asked.

"Not until Dr. Morris says it's okay."

"Doctor Will Morris?" I asked.

"That's right."

"He's my doctor, too," I told her. "Listen, could you let him know that I'm here? And that I'd like to talk to him about the boy? I'll be over there in the lounge."

"I'll let the staff on that floor give him the message when he's free."

"Fine. I appreciate that."

Benny had stopped chuckling when I walked into the lounge, but was still bent over his tablet. When I got closer, I could see that he was now frowning at the screen. In fact, I heard him growling—low, like a dog when another dog comes near his food bowl. The fact that he had been chuckling to himself earlier—or that he was growling now—was not a surprise. Benny was the master of communicating without words. What did surprise me though was that he possessed a tablet at all. For an inventor—even a strange one—Benny was not just low-tech, he was no-tech.

"What's up, Benny," I asked as I approached.

"Errr, um, hey, Chief." His throaty growl turned into a welcoming smile as he looked up and recognized me. "You sick?"

"I was about to ask you the same thing."

"Mmmm. I, uh, got me a little dose of the Ted Nugent disease, heh heh."

I must've looked puzzled. "Ted Nu—"

"Cat scratch fever. Mrower. Fssst, haahh."

"That's a real disease?" I asked, sitting down across from him at his table.

"Yah, eeew. Lymph nodes swell up like marbles." He touched his left armpit gingerly. "Yowch. Gave me some antibiotics, but nothing to worry about."

"Who's running the store?" I asked. "Your wife?"

"Yikes!" he squirmed. "Couldn't allow that. Nah, me niece is there. Amelia. Nice lass. Just visiting for a day or two."

"I didn't know you had a niece," I said.

"Yah. My sister Alice's only child. Don't see her much. Get a Christmas card from time to time, though. What brings you to doctorsville?"

"Um, well, I found this teenager passed out near my horses' pasture."

"Voodoo?" Benny asked seriously.

I laughed. "Not this time, Benny. Drugs, I think. He got pretty violent when he woke up."

"Didn't have to shoot him, didja?" He mimed pulling back the string on a bow and letting it go. "Twang, swoosh!"

"Well, not quite. Clarence Meekins was out there with me, so I had him tie the boy up until we called an ambulance. I just came out to see how he was doing."

"Think there might be a story?" he asked.

"I think the biggest story might be that tablet of yours," I said.

"Oh, this? Amelia gave it to me; her mother just bought her an iPad and she doesn't need this one anymore."

"But I thought you hated computers."

"Nah, just haven't ever been able to afford one. But most of the Harry Potter books were written on a laptop. Rowling had her own table in a coffee shop in Edinburgh. Harumph. And I was kinda jealous of all that new stuff you've been getting for your office."

"Right. It's a pretty big learning curve, though, for the staff."

"In with the old, out with the new." He made sweeping motions with his arms. "Swish swish. Ouch! Damn lymph nodes, heh heh."

"What does that little thing have on it?" I asked. "You can get on line I guess, but does it have wi-fi or games or a word-processing program or what?"

"Don't know," he said. "Haven't figured out how to open anything yet. These little icons are kinda neat, though. Yuk yuk."

"But when I came in weren't you . . . I let my sentence trail off. With Benny, anything was possible. Even growling at an empty screen. I just shook my head—something I probably did more in Benny's presence than anywhere else.

My back was turned to the lobby, so I heard Dr. Will Morris before I actually saw him. "Well, well! My favorite first patient."

I looked around to see a handsome, sandy-haired man in his late twenties walking toward our table. He had on a white coat with several pencils in its pocket. "I'm your *only* first patient," I told him. And yes, it was true. In his first day as intern—almost a year ago now—he had somehow figured out that I was suffering from Graves Disease, a failure of the thyroid gland. He undoubtedly saved my life, but that's not the only reason I liked him. I always enjoyed his bright banter and his interest in what I was engaged in at the time—whether it was only my day-to-day activities at the paper or my shooting rattlesnakes in the woods near my farm.

"Love the streak," he told me. I had to blink before I realized he was referring to the highlight I'd had my hairdresser put down the left side of my hair the day before. "It's a nice look for you. Very outré."

"I like your new look, too," I told him.

"Mine?" He looked puzzled.

"No pencils in your mouth," I smiled. "I think that's a first. Very becoming."

"You got me there," he said, and smoothed his mustache. Then he noticed Benny for the first time (Benny has that non-effect on people) and held out his hand. "Will Morris," he said.

Benny took the hand and shook it heartily, looking as pleased as if Will had been President Obama himself. "Benny," he said. "Ahem, Benny Benedict, bookstore owner. Sit down and make yourself to home."

"Thanks, but I only have a minute. The message they gave me said you had some connection with a patient they just brought in."

"Right. I'm the one who found him and called 911. He looks like a nice kid, but what was he on?"

"Well, I have an idea, but he wouldn't say and unless he says something, we really can't treat him. I had a nurse draw some blood, but the results won't be in for a while. We went through his pockets, but there was no sign of anything—no trace of powder or cannabis. Where did you find him?"

"He was lying under an oak tree near my pasture."

"Did you see anything in the area that he might have dropped? A whiskey bottle, cigarette lighter, spoon, a vial maybe? Any sign of vomiting?"

"No, I . . . Then I remembered the empty packet I had found in the brush. I felt around in my pockets and located it. "I picked this up. I thought it was just trash." I held the packet out to Will Morris, who took it eagerly and glanced at it."

"Bingo!" he cried.

"What's bingo about it?" I asked. "White Silk. It's bath salts. You put it in your tub."

"It's a synthetic cathinone. You put it in your nose."

"What?"

"Got your pen? Never mind—you can look it up on Benny's thingy there. It's a legal drug—at least it is for now. The "real" name of it is a lot longer and harder to pronounce, but, depending on who uses it, it can have about the same effects as cocaine, methadone, or ecstasy. Ecstasy is a—"

"I was in Baghdad, remember?" I interrupted. "If it was there, I tried it." I shuddered inwardly—for a lot of reasons. "And it was there."

"Well, I remember you told me you were in Iraq, but you've never given me the satisfaction of telling me about it. Although you promised."

"I know, I'm sorry."

Will Morris studied the packet. "White Silk. Umm, sounds yummy, doesn't it? "This kid's not the first one we've seen who's been snorting bath salts, but he's the first one I've treated."

"It's the first time I've ever heard of it," I said.

"Used mostly by kids who can't afford coke or weed. Kind of a word-of-mouth thing."

My reporter's instinct was surfacing. "But where do they score it?" I asked.

"At gas stations," replied Dr. Morris. "Small convenience stores. It goes by a lot of different names. Let's see, I've heard Zoom, Cloud Nine, Ocean Snow, Vanilla Sky. There must be a dozen brand names, or a hundred, who knows?"

"But if they make people crazy, why . . . ?"

"Not everybody," Dr. Morris said. "Most people just get a mild buzz. And I guess a mild buzz is better than none, so they think the risk is worth taking." He stood up, "Thanks, Sue-Ann. Now at least I know what I'm looking at." Will looked at me with a little concern. "Have you been feeling all right?"

"Benny knows about my thyroid," I told him. "And, yes, I've been taking my meds."

"Good, good. And hey, I haven't heard from that blonde bombshell friend of yours, yet. She must have lost the phone number I gave her."

"In your dreams," I laughed.

"All right, all right, time to go. Nice to meet you, Benny. I'll check out your bookstore sometime."

"Ten-four, good buddy."

"Wait," I said. "What's going to happen to him?"

"Who, the teenager? I don't know. That sergeant seems to think he's escaped from a detention center. I guess he's got to be taken back, but not today. We'll keep him overnight just to make sure he's completely recovered."

"Great. That'll give me time to do a little checking."

"Checking on what?" he asked.

"I don't know."

"Damn it, Sue-Ann! Don't do anything that will make me have to save your life again. Or stitch you up again. Or—"

"Okay, okay," I laughed.

As Dr. Morris hurried away, Benny stood up too, clutching his tablet. "Gotta go," he said.

But before he could take a step, I saw Joey Bickley get off the elevator and stride toward us with an angry expression on his face.

"Who's this?" he asked. "Another of your *boyfriends*? What would Clarence say?"

Benny proffered his hand expectantly. "Benny Benedict, bookstore owner."

Joey ignored the hand and looked at him as if wondering what a book was. Then he cut his eyes back to me. "Turns out I was right about the boy," he said. "Called Hardy and gave that bitch of a receptionist the kid's description. It's him all right."

I ignored him as easily as he had ignored Benny. "See you later, Benny," I told him. "Make sure your niece tells you how to work that thing before she leaves."

"Roger wilko," he said, and waddled off without a backward glance.

Only when I had watched Benny stroll through the automatic doors did I turn back to Joey.

"What were you saying?" I said. "Something about that kid?"

"You're treading on thin ice, missy," he said.

"Not much ice in Pine Oak, I'm afraid," I told him blandly.

"If I find out that you talked that pansy doctor into letting that kid stay here overnight, you'll regret it."

"Yeah? What'll you do, ask me out again?"

"Just get fucked, McKeown." He said, and strode away, his long legs taking him through the automatic doors faster than I would have imagined.

My thoughts followed him like a contrail after a jet. "Definitely not by you, Joey."

~ ~ ~

Back at the house, I grabbed the mail out of the box and went inside for a late lunch: just some romaine lettuce, tomatoes, olives, and whatever dressing was lying around. I also reheated some coffee I had brewed before going clout shooting with Clarence. It had been a busy morning. As I ate, I looked through the mail. It was catalogs mostly: Land's End, Woolrich, Jeffers, Dover. Clothing for people and horses. I put a couple of credit card statements to the side before I found a small letter postmarked Florence, Italy. My stomach gave an uncomfortable little tug, and not from the salad.

My father, Mike McKeown, had moved to Florence just after my mother died in a riding accident while I was in Iraq, writing news stories for my previous employer. His letters had been sporadic, but always friendly. He had been practicing his artistic talents on the sidewalks and in famous museums—which he told me was a lot different from teaching the subject, as he had done for twenty-five years at Jasper High School. He met a younger woman and the two ended up not only marrying, but having a child together. The letter informing me of my half-brother's birth had come months before, and I had not replied. I don't know why. My father deserved to live out his fantasies just as I was living out mine, but every time I thought about replying, revulsion set in and I had to go out and either ride or shoot archery.

So as you can imagine, I did not really want to hear whatever admonition he might have included in this letter. But I was alone in the house with nothing else to do, so I opened it.

> *Dear Susie:*
>
> *Things are crackling around here as you can imagine! What with the little one and my new job, there doesn't seem time for anything any more. Did I tell you I was working again? No, not the sidewalk artist thing, ha ha. That was just a fad. Something to do just so I could say I did it.*
>
> *No, the new job is as a night watchman in one of the museums. Remember that I told you Maria used to work at the Uffizi? It turns out that she has an "in" with a lot of the museums around this city, so when she heard of an opening at the Museo Stibbert, she was able to put in a good word for me. Boy, you ought to see all the stuff they have there: armor, tapestries, paintings, you name it. It's not ideal, I guess, because I'm away from home most nights, but between us, Maria and I manage to keep from having to hire*

nannies or babysitters. In a couple of months, maybe, when I've been there a little longer, I can apply for a job with regular hours, like in the gift shop or the café.

Maria's okay with things. She's going to be getting another degree soon so she can start teaching somewhere, I hope. Maybe at a university. You know, it's a tough thing getting married again at my age and after so many years with your mother. I hope we don't have to relocate too much before we actually settle down into our lives.

Don't worry about my money situation, I still have a lot saved from selling that house in Forester. It was a nice place, but I never really wanted to live there. Now that it's gone I wonder how it would have been if I came back there with Maria and Sal. Water under the bridge.

Wish you could come see us. Visit us in our little apartamento. I tell Maria (and Sal, while I'm trying to get him to sleep) about you all the time. Hope she doesn't get sick of it, ha ha.

Sometimes, I don't know why, it gets lonely here.

M.M.

I folded the letter back in its creases and placed it back in the envelope. It was a strange letter, hinting at a lot but not really saying anything. I guess that was Mike's biggest problem. I put the letter with the catalogs and placed them in the trash receptacle, along with the few shards of lettuce that had been too bitter for me to eat.

Chapter Three: High-Tech

On Monday morning, the harsh screech of a police whistle shocked me out of a deep sleep. I searched with frightened eyes through the still-dark bedroom, ready to jump out of bed as soon as I knew which direction to jump.

Then the whistle blast stopped, followed by a mock-harsh voice yelling, "Up and at em soldiers! Drop your cocks and grab your socks!" I recognized the voice and realized that my radio alarm clock had fooled me again. It was Gamma, one of the scatterbrained deejays on the mysterious radio station that seemed to have no set on-air schedule or even call letters. I sank down again into the warmth of the bed and slowly exhaled.

"Listen, y'all," Gamma continued in her own voice. "I've got an idea. I mean, we've all got guns, right? Why don't we just go get em—I've got mine in a gunny sack, tee hee—and go on over to Afghanistan or wherever and just shoot all the bad guys? Who needs an army when we've got us, hey? Let's let the soldiers take a break for a while. Wish I could tell you I've got a nice recipe for gunpowder stew, but my eyebrows tell me I haven't perfected it yet. I might have a little poem later, though. In the meantime, here's some music that will make the savage beast within us seethe . . . This is Gamma, your pirate radio station girl here at WGUN, where you get more bang for your buck."

I realized that these new call letters boded me no good, so I struggled upright in the bed. I put another pillow behind me and listened as a different female voice came out of the speakers, singing,

> *With your bright yellow gun*
> *You own the sun*
> *And I think I need a little poison.*

It was a song I had never heard before, slightly depressing, making me want to sink back down and drift back into sleep, maybe forever. But I knew that there was more to come. The next song was an old protest song—probably from the sixties, which was a little before my time. It was sung by a man who seemed happy.

> *Buy a gun for your son, right away Sir.*
> *Shake his hand like a man and let him play, Sir.*
> *Let his little mind expand. Place a weapon in his hand,*
> *Cause the skills he learns today will someday pay, Sir.*

As the song went on I realized that the lyrics, blatantly ironic, would be taken literally by many of today's Jasper County parents. Or worse, would seem totally redundant. What could be a better present for a 10-year-old boy than a .22? Or a sniper rifle? Well, maybe I was being a little ironic, too.

The folk song was in its final fade-out when jangly, left-handed guitar notes from a third song came segueing through; then Jimi Hendrix' voice came over the speakers asking the perennial question,

> *Hey Joe, Where you going with that gun in*
> *your hand?*

I was sure that Gamma—or the man who ran the radio station, who they called The Creeper—could go on with this gun motif all day. What was next? "Pistol Packin' Mama," "Bang Bang?" I couldn't think of anything else. Surprisingly, when "Hey Joe" was finishing up, Gamma came back on the microphone.

"I wanted to play the version by The Music Machine because in that one, Joe decides to go to Mexico and kill himself, but that old zombie The Creeper is too cheap to pay 99 cents for the download." Gamma shifted to a husky, grating whisper, "*It's only impor-tant that he goes to Mexico, yas*," she hissed. "*Not what he does there.*" Then she giggled.

The Creeper was actually Ashley Torrington—the ex-soldier who ran The Compound. And I was familiar enough with his methods to know that he had learned something that he didn't like. He often went on single-minded musical extravaganzas to convey some kind of message.

Or, to be more accurate, to convey some kind of a message to *me*, and it took no real thought to realize that it had something to do with the pistol Clarence had taken from my property. The explicit reference to Mexico had not been hard to decipher either. But what did it all mean?

It meant that The Creeper wanted to see me.

~ ~ ~

The offices of *The Pine Oak Courier* were located at the northern end of one of the town's few strip malls. The unit next to us had previously been occupied by a small law firm, but they had recently moved into Forester, where there were presumably more clients. Next to that, a nail salon had recently opened up and seemed to be holding its own in the bad economy. Benny's Bookstore was next with its sporadic but loyal customer base. Completing the lineup on the southern end of the mall was a laundry mat, which did a regular business day in and day out. In the same parking lot, but in a building of its own, was a Piggly Wiggly grocery store, where I did a lot of my shopping.

The Courier had undergone some changes in the last few months. For one thing, I was now the editor and, maybe because I was getting paid a lot less than the previous editor, the owner had approved some renovations. Not enough, of course, but what we got was still a lot. The receptionist's desk was now located just to the left of the front door. To the right were three offices. The first, next to the door, I had given to Gina Cartwright, the office manager. The second, which used to be my own, I had assigned to Annie Gillespie, who I had made my bureau chief. She was now the "at large" writer, taking on most of the more important stories herself and making assignments to the rest of the staff. The corner office, which had once been the conference room, had become my new office, complete with new furniture.

A new conference room had been created on the left side of the room, across from a supply closet and a couple of bathrooms. And eight-foot partitions were now set in a cross-shaped pattern in the center of the building. In each of the four sections thus created stood a desk and computer. These desks were usually occupied by Randy Rivas, the sports writer, Mark Patterson, general writer-of-all-trades, Becky Colley, our intern photographer, and newly hired Corinthia Glenn—an attractive black woman fresh out of journalism school. Cori wrote obits and was learning to maintain the Community Calendar.

Betty Dickson, who put the paper together, had her own station set up in the very back of the room. Betty was kind of a loner and preferred to work off by herself.

There was another new hire, too. In fact he had only been with the paper a couple of days. His name was Robert DuPre, and I had selected the gray-haired, 60-

something gentleman as receptionist over scads of other applicants. Why? I liked the refined way he spoke and I could read his handwriting.

But the biggest change of all was our new computer system. Out with the old and in with the new. Out with the old crappy PCs and in with new Macs. Out with the old software and in with TextEdit and InDesign. Out with paste-up and in with Pagination, although Betty still set up some pages of the shopper by hand. I don't expect you to be familiar with any of this, but for a small-town newspaper staff, this technology had a pretty steep learning curve. And, of course, everybody hated it. And me for introducing it. Luckily, the paper only came out twice a week, so we had time to get everything right.

We were in the middle of our Monday morning conference, which was our most important meeting of the week. While Bobby looked after the office and answered the phone, seven of us sat around the rectangular table in the Conference Room and discussed business. Betty, a plain, middle-aged woman who seemed perpetually cross, had just finished her latest rant on the new system. Or almost finished.

"And when I try to justify columns that have long words they come out looking all stretched out."

"Get with me after the meeting, Betty," I said, "and we'll see what we can figure out." We had all been given a short course in the system a few weeks ago, but I had the advantage of having worked with similar software when I wrote for *The Richmond Times-Dispatch*, my previous job. I had always owned a Macintosh, and knew a little about the thinking behind it.

I looked around the table. Handsome Randy Rivas, looking tan even in mid-March, had already let us know which local sporting events he planned to cover. Randy shot his own photos, but if he couldn't be two places at once, Becky took the photos while Mark or Cori wrote the copy.

Annie Gillespie, her curly red hair cascading down her shoulders, had outlined the schedule of town meetings and other local events that loomed on the Jasper County horizon. Which were pretty few; I mean, the biggest holiday of the year was something called the Plank Festival, and that was still months away. But Annie was almost the caricature of a reporter. Notebook in hand, spare pencil thrust securely in her hair, and an almost desperate desire to know *everything*, made her an important asset to a newsroom. Her only problem was that she was unlucky with men. Having followed her doctor husband to Jasper County when he was promoted to Head of Medical in one of the nearby correctional facilities, she had been left high and dry when he dumped her for a younger woman. And each of her attempts to begin the dating scene all over again had resulted in near-disaster.

Man trouble. I'm glad I didn't have to worry about that any more. I looked down the length of the table to the only empty chair. Ginette Cartwright had only been gone for a week, but I missed her. For a lot of reasons. She had put off returning to Pine Oak when her sister had showed up unexpectedly in Texas, where their father was recovering.

"Okay," I said. "Ginette will hopefully be back tomorrow, but the money needs to keep rolling in. Annie, will you check with the Winn Dixie Manager in Forester sometime this morning?"

"Sure."

"And, um, Cori, if you have a minute, will you check with Gibby's Flowers over on Boardwalk? They're having some kind of special."

"I don't see how there can be so many flower shops in one dinky lil town," she answered. "I mean, seems like nobody dies anymore—everybody's livin to a hundred. And there are a lot more divorces than marriages, seem like."

"That sounds like two good reasons to celebrate, to me," Annie commented wryly.

"I know that's right," smiled Cori, who seemed to have her own share of man trouble.

"Speak for yourself," spoke up Mark Patterson. In his mid-twenties, he was about Cori's age and probably had the hots for her. But then, in his mid-twenties, Mark had the hots for everybody.

I reached into my pocket and took out half a dozen brightly colored packets and scattered them across the table. Anybody know what these are?" I asked. Everyone reached for one and studied it.

"You're giving us bath salts?" asked Betty Dickson, sounding confused. "Are you trying to say—"

A giggle from the other side of the table cut her short. Rebecca Colley, our intern photographer, was shaking her packet of Blue Ice like it was a maracas. "I don't think you're really supposed to put these in your bath," she said. I had first met Becky when I was investigating a case of animal killings in which she was a more-or-less passive participant. One of her punky, black-clad friends, Pauly Hughes, had later been killed by a horse and Becky had repudiated her wayward ways. The fact that she was guided into photography by my ex-boyfriend was ironic, but lucky for her. Jack was the best teacher she could have. As it was, she was still more goth than not; her nose ring, flouncy skirt, and red low-topped sneakers cried out against her small-town upbringing.

"Pauley used to huff this stuff," she said casually, throwing the packet back on the table. "It's bad news."

"You mean it's a drug?" asked Randy

Becky just nodded.

"Did you ever try it?" I asked.

"The only thing I stick in my nose is my ring," she said decidedly. "I was over at Pauley's house once when he was doing the stuff. After a few minutes he started running around and screaming that he was being chased by electricity. Maybe that's one of the things that sent him over the edge."

"It'd send *me* over the edge," Cori said.

"Where did you get this stuff?" asked Annie, looking over each packet carefully.

"Arnie's Truck Stop in Hansen's Quarry, the Traveler outside Forester, and the Stop & Go right here in town. And they're not cheap, either. Everyone behind those counters knows that kids use this stuff to get high, and the higher the demand, the higher the price."

"What can we do about it?" asked Mark.

"Glad you asked, Mark," I told him. It was no secret that Mark liked a good time and spent many of his free hours drinking and trying to pick up women. I had a feeling he would put the Stop & Go on his list of things to do on his way home that evening. "Why don't you take some of these packets home and try them. You know, just to see what it's like." I was deadpan serious. "Then write an ongoing series of columns describing your moods and your visions. Kind of like Coleridge did. Or Timothy Leary."

"Really?" he asked, only slightly dubious.

"No, you fool," came a voice from the doorway of the conference room. "Can't you tell yet when Sue-Ann is pullin your leg? Ah swear, someday she'll pull it raht off and you'll wonder whah you ain't gettin noplace."

I spun halfway around in my seat. "Gina!" I cried happily. Then, more soberly, "I, um, I didn't expect you until tomorrow. I mean—"

"Ah caught an earlier flaht," she said, sweeping into the room. "Figured if ah didn't, ah maht be out of a job, what with no revenue comin in."

"I'll have you know that our advertising revenue hasn't dropped but about three dollars and twenty-five cents since you've been gone."

"Ah'm just kiddin," she said. "Ah know you've all been pitchin in to do mah job and ah'm grateful."

Ginette Cartwright was my age to within a couple of months. But while I'm pretty dark and of average size, Gina is blonde and tall. I dress casually while Gina dresses with professional precision. Rivals in high school, we had grown close since I had returned to Pine Oak after quitting my high-profile job in Virginia. In fact, in a weird twist of fate that neither of us had anticipated, Gina had become my girlfriend. Or I had become hers. Both. You probably already guessed that, but no one at *The Courier* office suspected it. We didn't like to have to keep it secret, but that's the way it had to be.

"Whoa," she said, looking at the colorful packets of bath salts on the table. "Looks lahk somebody's givin out condoms. Where's mahn?" She set her purse near the foot of the chair across from me at the table, and sat down. Betty frowned, Annie smiled, Becky giggled, and Mark looked interested as all get-out.

Cori passed a couple of the packets to Gina's end of the table, and explained. "These are bath salts."

"Oh, raht," Gina said. "Sue-Ann told me somethin about this when ah called in. But when did bath salts start comin in condom wrappers?" she added with a smile.

"The thing is, y'all," I said seriously, "They're *not* bath salts. This is a new, high-tech designer drug that's being sold under the radar. I've done a little research on line, and Becky is right on: these drugs are bad news." I then proceeded to tell them about the young man, Carlos

Murillo, that Clarence and I had discovered in the woods two days before.

When I had finished, everyone was silent except Gina. "Now let me get this straight, Sue-Ann," she burst out. "Ah leave town for a week and you go out in the woods and almost get yourself shot? And whah am ah not surprahsed? Is the boy all raht?"

"I don't know," I answered. "Joey Bickley found out he had escaped from the Hardy Juvenile Center and was salivating to take him back. When I went to the hospital yesterday to check on him, he was gone."

"Umm," mused Annie Gillespie. "Why is the boy at Hardy, do you know?"

"Not yet, but maybe together we can find out. Listen. I know that we go from month to month trying not to fall asleep until we scratch up enough fifty-year wedding anniversaries and flower-shop ads and hunting mishap stories to fill our pages. But every once in a while, a story comes along that makes all that worth it. What was that boy doing out in my woods? Where did he get the money to buy the drugs? How did he escape from the Hardy Center? Where are his parents? The bath salts angle is the most important, so come up with some ways to let our readers know to stay clear. Annie, I need you to call the Poison Control Center in Jacksonville and find out what they know about the ingredients. Mark, you do the same with the FDA. Find out about any other reported cases. If any of you have friends that are doctors, ask them, too. Cori, I want to know every store in Jasper County that sells bath salts and I want to know as many brand names as you can find as well as the different containers they come in. You don't have to buy anything, but take pictures with your cell phone. Randy, talk to the coaches and school principals in the area and see if they've heard anything. If not, fill them in. I'll try to get something on the boy."

I looked around the table again, where most everybody was writing on pads in front of them. "Okay, if nobody has any other business, that's it."

"Um, one more thing, Sue-Ann," said Randy Rivas, looking up from his yellow pad. "Betty had a good idea I wanted to bring up."

"Go ahead."

"She—well, she and I—think it would be a good idea to have a *Courier* bowling team."

"You mean with those jazzy bowlin shirts and red shoes?" asked Gina. "Sounds lahk fun. Sue-Ann was on the bowlin team in hah school."

"Really?" Randy said.

"Didn't ya know?" said Gina.

"It's just one night a week. Five people on a team. Men or women or mixed, doesn't matter."

"I thought you already had a team," I told him. I had once gone to Hi-Score Lanes and watched a few games, but I hadn't actually bowled in years. There were only four people on the team at that time: Randy, Betty, Betty's friend Krissy, and a man named Barney, who worked for Krissy.

"Yeah, well, Barney's ex-wife started hounding him so much that he moved to Panama City. Krissy's still going to bowl, though. Come on, Sue-Ann, we need two more people."

"What about you, Mark, you're a he-man," I said.

"Never bowled a game in my life," he said.

"Cori?"

"Not me. I got kids to look after."

"It's settled, then," Gina said with a smile. "Me an Sue-Ann'll bowl. Won't we, Sue-Ann?"

I figuratively threw up my hands. "Just as long as it doesn't interfere with work," I said.

"We'll see you there tomorrow night at seven sharp," Randy said.

"If not before," I suggested. "We've got a paper to put out."

"Oh, yeah. Right."

Chapter Four: Night Visitors

After work, there was just enough light for Gina and I to take our horses for a little trail ride. I was up on my chestnut Oldenburg mare, Alikki, while Gina was astride her gray mare Hurricane Irene. Irene was a big horse, but without the thick barrel you see on a lot of draft crosses, having inherited her Andalusian sire's bone structure and much of his conformation. She wasn't much on jumping, but her Clydesdale mother's power, combined with her father's agility and suppleness, gave her the potential to be a good dressage horse. And as for Alikki . . . well, let's just say that 500 years of superb German breeding had done her no harm.

Our trail took us through the pasture and near the place where Clarence and I had found Carlos Murillo. We halted for a few minutes while I filled her in on what I hadn't told her on the phone.

"So Clarence took the gun?" Gina asked.

"I'm pretty sure he gave it to The Creeper," I told her. "Gamma went on a musical gun rampage this morning."

"Want to go out there now?" she asked.

"We probably should, but I'm putting it off as long as I can. Right now I just want to spend some time with you."

Back in November, Gina had quit her job at *The Courier* and left town, telling no one—even me—where she was headed. The situation between us—as well as the fact that she was also dating the former editor, who was prodding her to marry him—had become unbearable. So

she simply changed her life. She ended up in Myrtle
Beach, South Carolina teaching part time at the Meher
Baba Spiritual Center and playing music at night. In the
month it had taken me to run her down—and the next
few weeks she had spent winding up her affairs there—
she had made great strides in both her guitar playing and
her performance. In fact, she had become such a local
favorite that I often wondered why she consented to
return to Pine Oak, even considering the fact that the
former editor had taken a job in another state. But she
had only just settled back into her routine as *The Courier*'s
office manager when her father suffered a heart attack
and she had to fly to Texas to be with him. I had begun
to cherish my alone time with her more and more. The
Creeper could wait.

We rode through the woods until we came to a large
stand of pines. Had we gone right, we would eventually
have run into the fenced compound that was Torrington,
with its mid-19th Century mansion, various outbuildings,
radio tower, and gardens. I turned in the opposite
direction, guiding Alikki onto a path through the thick
pines with their overhanging branches making an
effective ceiling and putting us in semi-darkness. It was
cooling off, but the exercise was invigorating. It was
mostly a silent ride, Gina and I just enjoying being
together with our animals, hearing the muted clopping of
unshod hooves over the layers of pine needles.

Halfway through the tunnel of pines, Gina half
turned in her saddle and said, "Ah've made a decision."

The seriousness in her tone put me on my guard.
"What kind of decision?" I asked cautiously.

"Well, you know that ah hadn't seen mah sister in a
lotta years. Almost never seen her kids." She stopped,
then began again. "Ah had a chance to be around em for
the first tahm really. An ah lahked em. Ah—"

"You finally decided you wanted to have some of your own," I guessed. She had wavered about having children since we had become a couple.

"Don't take the words outta mah mouth, Sue-Ann," she admonished. "Ah lahked Laurel's kids, ah did, but ah decided they're all ah need. All the family needs. Maybe sometahm when they're older we can invite em down here to visit and teach em to rahd."

"Sure, that would be great," I said, still cautiously. "So that's what your decision is? Not to have children?"

"Just wait for it, Sue-Ann." Gina made Irene halt, then made a half turn so that she came up alongside me, but facing in the opposite direction. I halted Alikki and we just stood there, our boots brushing together in their stirrups. "Couple days before ah went off to Texas, ah found a note stuck under mah door at home. It was from one of mah neighbors. It said that he wanted to bah mah place if ah'd sell. His daughter's gettin married to some deadbeat and he figured that if he bought them a house right close to his, he could keep an eye on em."

I just looked at her, waiting for it.

"On the plane home, ah desahded to say yes. Ah'm gonna sell it to him. And ah'm gonna move in with you." She paused. "If you'll have me."

There were tears in my eyes as I leaned from my saddle, took her in my arms, and kissed her fiercely. Both horses stood still for us. Good girls.

Gina broke the kiss and smiled. "Does that mean yes?" she asked.

I just nodded dumbly.

"But ah've got some other plans, too," she said. "Wanna hear em?"

I nodded dumbly again.

She turned Irene back around and began a brisk walk. I asked Alikki to catch up, which she did with a couple of long-legged trot strides. "Ah want you to sell me a couple acres of your property just to the south of your house."

"That's just woods," I said.

"Raht. It is now, but ah'm gonna use some of the money ah get from mah old house to build a new little house just off the road that ah can use for mah legal address. It'll really be a music studio with a room or two for visitors to stay if we ever have any. Our two houses will be separated by about fifty yards of woods and we can make a little trail behind so we can go back and forth."

I was disappointed, but knew that she was right. We just couldn't live openly as a couple in Pine Oak. Even being so close to each other might set off a bell or a whistle to anyone who cared to listen, like Joey Bickley, for instance, who already had his suspicions. I knew, too, and for the same reason, that it was a good idea for me to actually sell her the acreage that she wanted. A simple business transaction, although the money would go into our household expenses. But my disappointment was nothing compared to the elation I felt from Gina's finally making the commitment to be with me.

"Ah don't plan to actually sleep in the new place, but it'll give me somewhere to go if ah need to. An as far as the buildin goes, ah've got everythin planned out on paper—ah made some sketches on the plane. We'll go over em when we get back home, all raht? Raht, then."

And Gina went on talking for the rest of our ride about her plans for us, her studio, her music, our riding, and even our old age. I was mostly silent, enjoying everything. When I finally spoke, it was just a simple, short sentence.

"I love you."

Back at the barn, I said it again as we were unsaddling the horses. "I love you." And again as we were rinsing them off in the wash rack and using the squeegee to sluice off the water. I was splashing more water on myself than the ground because I was looking at Gina instead of Alikki.

I was in love with a woman. I had gone through this in my mind countless times but I had finally come to terms with it. Me, Sue-Ann McKeown, who had slept with as many men as she had fingers and toes. And as far as I knew, Gina had kept up with me. She was tall, blonde, beautiful, strong, and—surprise surprise—smarter and more mature than I was in so many ways. Yet she seemed to be as attached to me as I was to her. It was totally incomprehensible, but it was true.

I dropped the hose and stepped over to where she was rubbing Irene's face with a damp towel. Soaking wet, I put my hands behind her head and kissed her with every ounce of feeling I had. Her lips were so soft that I gasped. Then I pulled back a little way, without removing my hands, and said, "I love you, I love you, I love you."

"You been sayin that for a whahl now, Sue-Ann," she said. "Let's let these hosses loose and maybe you can show me what you mean."

I pried myself loose from her and picked up the hose. Then I aimed it at her, laughing while she shrieked. Before she could reach the hose in my hand and turn it on me, she was soaked to the skin and my hands were unbuttoning her shirt, tugging at her breeches, loosening her sports bra, and touching every square, bare inch of her.

"Damn it, Sue-Ann, you're lucky ah'm not wearin my expensive dressage boots," she panted as I kneeled in front of her and began washing her with my tongue.

Okay, I've always hated the phrase "making love." For one thing, it used to mean the simple act of flirting. Keep that in mind if you ever read a William Dean Howells novel—like I had to in college—it's not nearly as interesting as you might have thought. "Having sex" is a little better; I think that the word "sex" is sexier than "love" (although not nearly as romantic), but the term is still just a safe euphemism for "fucking," which at times can be sexy as hell.

There were times, though—and these were becoming more and more frequent for Gina and me—when it was just super-accurate to call it making love. They were times when the physical pleasure we received was equaled by the mental pleasure we obtained just from being in the same room together. Or in the same world together. Both were overpoweringly sexy and frighteningly romantic.

By the time we actually reached our bedroom—with lengthy stops in the barn and the floor of the living room, we were both so exhausted that all we could do was plop down on the bed, breathe hard, and try to recover.

"I love you," I told her.

"And I love you, Sue-Ann," she replied. "More than you can know."

We cuddled a little, and kissed each other lightly. I was slowly getting turned on for the third time in a couple of hours when the fucking doorbell rang.

"Oh, hell," I whispered.

"Don't answer it," Gina whispered back. I could feel her body tense and I knew mine was, too. The truth was that I almost never had visitors; even Clarence Meekins had only been there a handful of times. But Sgt. Joey Bickley knew my address and I wouldn't put it past him to spy on me—or even peek through my bedroom window. Although we couldn't be seen from the front door, the lights in the kitchen, living room, and bedroom were all burning brightly. Gina gently disentangled herself from me and padded silently into the bathroom. The fact was that if anyone—other than a few people at

Torrington—knew that Gina and I were a couple, our lives could be ruined.

The doorbell rang again, several times. I slipped out of bed and hurriedly threw on a robe. The bell rang again, and this time it was followed by a voice. "Ms. McKeown, are you in there? Ms. McKeown, I need to talk to you."

The voice was husky but definitely female. And as far as I knew, it was one I had never heard before. I took a quick look in the mirror. Yikes, I had lipstick marks all over my face. I hurriedly tried to rub them off, then I tried to slick back my still-wet hair with my hand.

"Ms. McKeown. I'm comin in. I need to—"

But by that time I was walking out of the bedroom. The woman had already opened the front door and taken several steps into the room. I was so surprised that I just stood there, bedroom door open, and stared at the intruder. The woman was equally surprised and stood rooted to her spot on the carpet. She was about my age, but a little shorter and stockier. Very thick, dark hair fell to her shoulders and she looked at me with deep dark eyes. Her clothes were worn and fashionless, like Goodwill castoff clothing—stained khaki work pants, thick, knitted sweater, and lace-up boots that looked almost as old as she was. Her stooped posture let me know that not only was this woman probably not a rider, but that she was being pounded by life.

"Who are you?" I asked. "And how dare you break into my house?"

"I din break in," she said, but I could tell she was nervous. "The door was open. I just wanna talk."

"About what?" I asked sternly.

She looked me over dubiously and wrinkled her nose. "You Miz McKeown?"

"I asked you a question."

"I din mean to interrupt anythin," she said, glancing into the bedroom.

"Just tell me what you want," I said, hastily closing the bedroom door.

She straightened herself up a little and looked me in the face. "Miz McKeown, I don wan no handout. I just wan what's mine."

I looked closely at her again, especially her face and her boots. Without the care etched into her features, she could have been called pretty. Not beautiful, certainly, but I imagined that when she was a girl she would have been a real cutie. She was Latina: her skin color, eyes, and cheekbones were identical to those of the boy Clarence and I had found in the field.

It wasn't hard to figure out that she was probably the boy's mother. Her boots told me that she was probably ex-service. Marines, maybe. But that didn't tell me if she was dangerous or not. I noticed that she was staring at my feet the way the woman in the elevator had stared at Seymour Glass's in "A Perfect Day for Bananafish." I glanced down as well and noticed a faint lipstick mark around my big toe. Yikes.

"Sit down," I said, "and let me get some clothes on."

I hurriedly gathered up the trail of clothing Gina and I had left on the floor and walked into the bedroom, pulling the door shut behind me. I threw on some jeans, a garnet FSU sweatshirt, and some slippers, then went into the bathroom and whispered a few words to Gina. When I came back out to the living room, my visitor, or intruder, was sitting upright, fidgeting, on the couch. I sat down in the chair to her right and took the initiative.

"Who was the boy I found in the woods?" I asked. "Your son?"

The woman just nodded.

"Okay, then tell me how your son got hold of your handgun and what the hell he was doing on my property."

"I—"

"But first tell me your name."

"Sandra. Sandra Murillo."

"Evidently your son is in serious trouble. I need to know about it."

"Why I should tell you?" She was still nervous, but wary, like a mouse looking for cheese in a house with cats.

"Because getting caught with a gun like that is a felony and your son might go to prison—which will be a hell of a lot worse than a juvenile home for a good-looking boy."

She nodded like she understood. "You know what I wan, then?"

"Your M-9."

"Yeah, thas right. You got it?"

"It's in a safe place."

"The police don have it?"

"No."

"Why you din give it to them?"

Instead of answering, I decided to be the asker. "Where were you stationed and when did you get out?"

"I guess you pretty smart, huh?"

"I'm a reporter. I notice things."

"You gonna write about me?"

"Not if you don't want me to," I said.

"Okay, then. Okay. I was in Fallujah in 2005— Second Marine Division."

"Umm. I was there in 2008," I said. "Baghdad, mostly."

"You was in the service?" she asked dubiously.

"I was a reporter with *The Richmond Times-Dispatch*."

"Yeah?"

"Yeah," I said. "And I only lasted six months. It almost killed me."

"Yeah, well," she said. "I din like it either, but it was my job. An I was older than a lotta of the women in my unit. I hada join cause I couldn get no other job. I had my boy to look after and he din have no father to speak of—he ran out on me when Carlito was only a baby. The bastard. But when I went to Iraq I had to leave Carlito with my mama, and she let him go wild. It was my fault; I shoulda been there for him but I wasn."

"But then you got out."

"Couple years ago, yeah. But then my mama got sick and died and all my military money was gone for her medicine and funeral and stuff. I had no house to live in, no job, nothin. Carlos and I, we just traveled around from one place to another. Sometimes we got work picking tomatoes and stuff, but some a the people we had to work with were inta drugs, and got Carlos hooked. Then he got busted. Shit, I din have no money for a lawyer, so they put him away in that juvie place. Wouldn give him to me cause I din have no home to speak of. But that place is shit. They talk about "rehabilitation," but all they really do there is fine differen ways to beat on people. I think some boys mighta really got killed there, so when Carlos escaped, he came to where I was stayin. That was okay with me; I din want him to be in that place no way. We were doin okay for a week or so—we got together with some Mexicans balin pine needles—I was born in Mexico, too, but I been a citizen since I was a teenager. Couple days ago I sent Carlo out to look for some more pine stands we could try gettin a contract for. What I din know was that when he went out, he took my gun and the little bit of cash I had."

"How did you know I found him?"

"I asked that doctor at the hospital. The young one with the mustache. Just tole him I wanted to thank the person who found him and made sure he got to the hospital."

"How did you know Carlos was at the hospital?" I asked.

"I got a cell phone. Carlos gave that doctor my number to call, but when I got there, Carlos was already gone."

"I guess the sergeant already took him back to Hardy," I said.

"No, that ain right. Carlos left."

"He what?"

"You think he was gonna stay around that place when he knew that they were gonna take him away again?"

"But where did he go?" I asked.

"He went to someplace safe," she said. "Like my M-9."

Just then Sandra tensed in her seat and turned toward the kitchen.

I looked, too, and almost jumped out of my slippers. A pair of tall soldiers, dressed completely in camo and carrying assault rifles, stood in the doorway. Their faces were streaked with blacking. An instant later, the front door opened and another soldier stormed into the living room, dressed like the two others, but female. The only reason I didn't scream was that I knew they were from Torrington. I had told Gina to call them when I went into the room to get dressed. One of the two soldiers that had come in the back door I recognized as Jeremy, a gung-ho Marine and gun nut struggling badly with Post-Traumatic Stress. The other was called Backpack, although he and I had never spoken. I had never seen the female soldier before.

Sandra Murillo stood up and looked around for a place to run. There was no place, not even a mousehole. "It's okay," I told her. "They're friends."

"I ain got no friends," she said.

Just then a man strolled casually through the front door dressed in street clothes. He was kind of short and thin, with a little gray beard on his chin to go with a gray mustache. Like the female marine, I had never set eyes on him before. "You do now, Corporal," he said with an educated voice.

Sandra Murillo and I stared at the man and said, almost in unison, "Who the hell are you?"

Chapter Five: Bonzos and Dykies

"My name is Frogmore," he said. "James Frogmore."

He was as unprepossessing a man as I had ever seen, looking like he could have been as easily at home in a dingy CPA office or on a covert spy mission. Although his clothes were nondescript, I will describe them anyway. Dark gray slacks of good quality, black, tie-up shoes of sturdy leather, and from what I could see beneath his London Fog overcoat, a starchy-collared business shirt like a Van Heusen. Something like my ex-boyfriend Jack—and millions of other men—wore. The disturbing thing was that he would have looked equally ordinary if he had been wearing overalls and a string tie. He made no attempt to close the door; just stood there and looked us over, as one Quarter horse might look at others over a fence. He gave us both a little smile.

"You can call me *Colonel* Frogmore," he said. "And this," he added, nodding at the woman in camo to his right, "Is my daughter, Lance Corporal Carol Frogmore, just back from her third deployment in Afghanistan."

I looked at Carol with as much suspicion as I felt for the colonel. She was tallish but mousy, with dishwater hair cascading from under her flak helmet and the kind of thin glasses you buy three for ten dollars in WalMart. She looked sort of pinchy, but at least she held her weapon with authority. No surprise, really; I had learned years before that the motto, "The Marine Corps builds men," no longer held true for just men.

The colonel—if he really was a colonel—paused for a few seconds, looked from Sandra to me, then said, "You must be Mrs. Cartwright."

I heard a snigger from behind me but when I looked, both Jeremy and Backpack were poker-faced.

"Did you find something amusing, Jeremy?" the colonel asked.

"No sir," answered Jeremy, rigid. "It's just that she ain't . . ." his voice trailed off.

"She isn't . . . what?" asked Frogmore patiently.

"That's Sue-Ann McKeown. Cartwright is a blonde. And she ain't no missus."

Frogmore took in this new information and spent some time processing it. "I see. Then where is—" That was as far as he got before Gina pulled open the bedroom door and strode out with blazing eyes.

"Listen, Mister Colonel. First of all, Jeremy and Backpack and Ms. Frogfa—Ms. Frogmore—need to stand down or git out. This poor woman is so scared she's about to piss herself. Shit, *ah'm* freakin out and ah'm the one who called you."

Sandra Murillo looked quickly at Gina, then at me, and hissed, "Just what I thought." Behind me, I heard Jeremy snicker again, but Sandra Murillo wasn't finished. "You bitches! Why you turned me in? What I did to you that you had to call these bonzos?" She looked like she might try to go for Gina, but before she could take a step, Carol Frogmore had stepped between them. I had never seen anyone move that quickly.

"Please sit down, Corporal," she told Sandra.

"I ain no corporal no more," Sandra said angrily, "An ain nobody in a uniform gonna boss me around." She sat down anyway.

Frogmore Sr. had not moved during this exchange, but after Sandra had seated herself again on the couch, he glanced over my shoulder and moved his head a few inches. When I followed his glance, I noticed Jeremy and Backpack slipping silently through the back door.

"My apologies to all of you," he said. "I have only been in Torrington a few weeks, and this is the first situation I've been asked to handle."

"What the fuck is Torrington?" asked Sandra Murillo.

When no one answered, Gina took control as she often did in tense situations. "Okay, raht," she said, sitting down on the arm of my chair. She had had time to put on a clean pair of jeans, running shoes, and a fluffy white sweater. She looked at Sandra Murillo and said, "Listen, hon, these people are here to trah and help you and Carlos."

"Don call me hon. I ain like you. All I want's my gun back."

"And we're thinking about giving it back to you, Corporal," said Frogmore. "But you'll have to let us take you to it."

"Why you din just bring it here?"

"You'll know that when we get where we're going."

"I ain goin nowhere," she stated flatly, and before even Carol Frogmore could react, Sandra had bounded up, deked the colonel to his right, then ran around his left side while he was leaning in the other direction, and through the open door. She would have made it to the street had she not crashed into someone just outside the door.

"Yow!" came a familiar voice. Clarence!

"Lemme up, you big bonzo!"

The rest of us in the room hustled outside. I was last, and I flicked on the porch light. What we saw was a tangle of bodies on the ground several yards from the door. Clarence was lying on his back like a long board, with his arms around a squirming Sandra Murillo, trying to hold her still while protecting his face from her fists.

He finally managed to get a big hand around both of her wrists and rolled her slightly over so that they were facing each other on the grass Then he had to place one of his legs over hers so that she would stop trying to kick him. "Hold on, now," he told her. "What's all the fuss?"

Sandra stopped struggling and looked at Clarence more closely in the glow provided by the porch light. Seeing no telltale military uniform, she whispered to him excitedly, "You gotta help me get away from these crazy people. They said they gon shoot me and bury me in the woods."

Clarence looked up and saw the four of us watching. "Well, I guess these folks are pretty dangerous, all right," he said seriously, 'but I know them and I'll make sure they don't shoot you. You'll have to be still and stand up, though. Is that all right?"

As Clarence relaxed his grip, Sandra nodded and stood up. Clarence rolled himself up after her.

"Okay," Sandra began, "But how you gonna protect me when—" But at this inopportune moment, Jeremy and Backpack dashed from behind the house, rifles leveled. "Aiiii!" she screamed, and clutched Clarence around the waist, hiding behind his big frame.

Slightly flustered, Clarence still managed to look at the two soldiers with disapproval. "You fellas plan to use those rifles on this little lady? If not, I suggest you put em down." He looked at me, Gina, and the Frogmores in turn. He looked back to me again. "God's balls, Sue-Ann!" he complained. "You sure are getting to be a magnet for trouble."

At Clarence's reference to God's nether regions, I heard another titter—this was the titteringest bunch I had ever seen. I glanced over and was surprised to see Carol Frogmore, staring raptly at Clarence. She saw me looking at her and she blushed—that is, if people can really do that, especially under streaks of black greasepaint.

"Tell me about it," I replied. "Clarence, this is Sandra. It was her son you and I found out in the woods."

He and Sandra Murillo looked at each other with interest.

"*You* foun Carlito?" she asked him.

"Me and Sue-Ann," he replied. "Why don't we go back in the house and talk."

"Place filled with dykies and bonzos," she explained.

Clarence frowned. "Let's go in anyway," he said. "And no running away this time, okay?" Sandra nodded and reluctantly let herself be guided by Clarence's hand on her shoulder. When she was inside, he stepped back and motioned Gina to follow her. Then he turned to Col. Frogmore. "I think I better handle this now," he said in a low voice.

"But we have to—"

"I know what to do. All of y'all need to go back to The Compound." Then he turned and walked into the house. I followed him and closed the door. That was that. The bonzos were gone and the house felt a lot more peaceful.

Clarence was seating himself beside Sandra on the couch and if the situation had not been so serious, I would have smiled at how Mutt and Jeff they looked. It was like a crane bending down to talk to a duck. Well, maybe I did smile a little.

"If we're going to talk," I said, "I have to have coffee." I walked toward the kitchen. There's rarely a time I don't have to have coffee.

"Ah'll help," said Gina.

From the kitchen, all we could hear were two voices talking softly. We didn't hear words, just emotions. Clarence's calm, Sandra's kind of frantic to begin with, then getting calmer. Gina and I put the coffee on, then we hugged each other, more from relief than anything else. Gina said softly in my ear. "Ah could hear what y'all were sayin from the bedroom," she said. "Ah kinda lahked it when Frogface called you Mrs. Cartwright."

I wrinkled my nose. "You think I smell like sex?" I asked.

She broke the embrace, gave me a peck on the lips, and opened the cupboard. "If you don't now, you will when ah get you back into that bed. Now let's tote these cups into the livin room before that woman runs off again."

But both Sandra and Clarence had settled more deeply into the couch. Whatever Clarence had been saying had the effect of not only calming down the Latina woman, but had brought tears to her eyes, which she wiped away hastily with the sleeve of her oversized sweater when she heard us coming back in.

"You two still here?" she asked with annoyance.

"We live here," I said.

"What have you all been talkin about?" asked Gina, handing one coffee cup to Sandra Murillo and another to Clarence.

"Just getting to know each other a little," Clarence said.

As if making up for letting us see her in tears, Sandra looked Gina and I over carefully. "You two really lesbos?" she asked.

"Dykies," I replied. "And it's not your business."

"You don look like lesbos,"

"Is that supposed to be a compliment?" Gina asked, standing over her.

"I donno, maybe," the woman replied.

"Well, you can shove your compliments where the sun don't shahn."

"Ha ha, you real funny." Sandra made a move to stand up but Clarence put out his arm as a barrier.

"Hold on now, you two," Clarence said. Gina moved back and sat on the arm of my chair again. Clarence looked at the Latina woman. "The world isn't a very good place right now," he began seriously. "There's wars everywhere you look, crooks in politics, and no money anywhere. No reason for it, maybe, but that's the way it is. It doesn't seem like there are very many people that are good, or who try to do right. But Sue-Ann and Gina are two that do. If I were in a tight spot, they're the two I would ask to help me. Not the police, not that bunch of commandos that was just here."

"Why should I care what you say?" Sandra asked. She stared into her coffee cup as if looking into the dregs of her life. "You prolly a bonzo just like them."

"I was in the military, if that's what you mean," said Clarence.

"M.P.?" she asked.

"That's right; how did you know?"

"Ha," she said, glancing at me. "That lady's not the only smart cookie in the jar."

In fact, I had not known that Clarence had been Military Police; he had never spoken to me about his time in the service. I could see, though, that at full height in uniform, he would have commanded a great deal of respect.

"We've got a problem, Clarence," I said. "Her son Carlos ran away from the hospital. Joey's probably got every warm body in the Sheriff's Department and the Highway Patrol looking for him." I briefly filled him in on what Sandra Murillo had told me before we had been interrupted by Col. Frogmore. From time to time I glanced at Sandra who listened and nodded from time to time. There were more tears, but not many.

Clarence listened in silence, then said, "What should we do, Sue-Ann?"

"I think the first thing we need to do is find Carlos."

"Then what?"

"Then we think of the second thing."

"Raht, then," spoke up Gina. "Are you hidin your son at your place?" she asked Sandra.

"Don have no place."

"You don't have a place to stay?"

"Here and there. Ri now I'm sleepin in an ol rusty bus near a cotton field. But Carlos, he's not there. He said he had some friends—I don know em."

Clarence sat up as tall as he could and I could see that he had made a decision. "Okay, Sandra. I'm going to take you someplace safe for a while."

"Yeah?"

"But it's a secret place. Nobody knows about it— not even the police."

"What kine of place is it?"

"It's a place where old soldiers can go if we have to go somewhere. People like you and me."

"And those other bonzos?"

"Yes. There's something a little wrong with all of them, but they don't hurt people and they don't snitch."

"An they got my gun?" she asked.

Clarence nodded.

"Okay, then les go."

"Where's your car?"

"What, you think I got a car?"

"But my truck is loaded down with watermelons. That's why I couldn't get here any faster."

"You can take mine," I said.

"And we'll follow in mahn," added Gina.

"Do they have to go, too?" asked Sandra Murillo.

"I think they should, yes," said Clarence. "But there's just one thing more."

"Whas that?"

"I'm gonna have to blindfold you."

"You mus be outta your coconut!" the woman exclaimed.

"The place we're going to is top secret," he told her. "There are only three people in this town that even know it exists, and that's the three of us here."

"You don trust me?" she asked.

"I don't have anything to do with it. It's the man in charge that makes the decisions, and I'm not the man in charge. You either get blindfolded or you don't get your gun. And we won't be able to help your boy."

"What, you're gonna help get him outta juvie?"

"If we can," he told her.

"Okay, then, but I don like it. We goin now?"

"Yes."

"Lemme wash my face and pee first, okay?"

Gina showed Sandra Murillo how to get to the guest bathroom; we didn't care to have her traipsing and nosing around our own room. When I heard the bathroom door close and saw Gina coming back, I said softly to Clarence, "Guess that's not the first woman you've had in tears, is it you big bonzo?" I quipped.

Clarence thought seriously about that for a few seconds, then said, "You know, I think it is."

Chapter Six: Fallujah

Walking into Ashley Torrington's sitting room can feel at first like walking into the office of a dungeon warden. The floors of the old, two-story mansion are creaky, the halls long, and Ashley's room so dimly lit that it is hard to make out much more than a figure in the far right corner of the room half sitting and half reclining in a very large and comfortable-looking armchair. In a few seconds, when your eyes grow accustomed to the dimness, you can make out a cold fireplace, a row of smaller armchairs, scads of framed photos on the walls, and a faded carpet. Most incongruously, the entire left side of the room is taken up with LPs, tapes, CDs, and various types of stereo equipment; Ashley Torrington's knowledge of contemporary music is exhaustive.

Ashley himself struggled to sit upright when Clarence entered the room with Sandra Murillo. This was made slightly difficult by the fact that Ashley had only one arm to straighten himself up with. As we continued into the room, it was obvious that the man had other defects as well. Much of his face and scalp had been horribly burned; between islands of scar tissue, tufts of hair occasionally sprouted up, grew, and cascaded down his shoulders. Although he sat in such a way to present his better side to anyone coming into the room, it was often hard to stifle a gasp when you first saw him.

Sandra, however, didn't bat an eye. "What is this place?" she asked.

"Well, my dear," Ashley answered. "It just might be home."

Because of his injuries, Ashley's voice was soft and more than a bit uncanny, as if his words were leaking out of some odd fissure in his skull instead of his mouth. It was almost hissy, kind of what I'd imagine a panther would sound like if it could talk.

"Yeah, and who you spose to be, my daddy?"

"My name is Ashley Torrington, although my grandchildren call me The Creeper—or worse."

"Yeah, I guess you kinda creepy, all right. What happened to you?" she asked. "You in a fire?"

"Please sit down, all of you. Move those chairs over here in front of me, Clarence. Sue-Ann, it's been too long since I've had the pleasure of your company. And Ms. Cartwright, my heart gives a little pit-a-pat whenever I see you. I'm so glad you decided to come back to Pine Oak."

Gina, who, before her sojourn in Myrtle Beach, had become even closer to Ashley than I had, smiled, glanced at me, and said, "Ah'm glad, too."

When he saw that we were all seated and facing him, he continued. "Now then, Ms. Murillo. I'll answer your question. I was napalmed in Vietnam."

"Yeah?" She thought about that for a few seconds. Then: "I thought only Americans used napalm."

"Um, yas. I got separated from my unit and was trying to help some civilians at the time. I lost an arm, as you see, and only barely saved my leg. Putting my eyes in bright light is like putting a live chicken in the oven. And, of course, most people—including myself—are disgusted by my disfigurement."

"I seen worse than you," she said, but then grudgingly added, "but they were dead."

"Yas," he hissed. "And maybe they were the lucky ones. All I can do any more is listen to music and ride my horses—yas, I can still ride with the best of them.

But I've also managed to find a purpose for my miserable old life."

"You mean you foun God or somethin?" she asked suspiciously.

"No, Ms. Murillo, I found Torrington. This place, this compound. It was built over a hundred and fifty years ago by my ancestor, who was the founder of Pine Oak. The town has long forgotten that this place ever existed. We use it for people like me and you—people who were hurt in some way by war."

"How do you know that I—"

"Although Torrington is secret from the town, Ms. Murillo, we still have ties to the branches of service. When Sue-Ann and Clarence found your son, they also found your service pistol. They both recognized that it *was* a service pistol and they were afraid that your son had stolen it from here. There are a lot of service pistols here, you see. And if the police found out about us and our weapons, Torrington would have been compromised."

"But he din steal—"

"Please, Ms. Murillo. One of us checked the serial number to find out who it was issued to. We can do that. We found out that it was issued to you. Another few calls and we found out many other things—when you enlisted, where you served, when you were discharged, the last time you contacted a VA hospital. Many things."

"You din have no right."

"No? Well, maybe not. But we have 37 ex-soldiers and their spouses on this compound right now. You met some of them this evening. We are people who would be uncomfortable in the outside world and very uneasy if we had prying eyes upon us."

"What about that fake colonel," she asked.

"Colonel Frogmore? Well, yas, I can see why you might think he was a fake, but he's really a colonel. A psychologist."

"Hah," Sandra snorted. "What's wrong with *him*? Too many patients?"

"Ummm, perhaps. But that's not the reason he's here. It's his daughter who is having trouble coping with reality."

"Yeah, well," she said. "I don like psychologists."

"Yas," Ashley said. "We know."

"Yeah? Well. Look, I din ask for any of that stuff. I din even want to be a Marine, but I had to, cause of Carlos. I din have no man, no good job, livin from place to place. I got a high school education, you know that too? So I joined up. It was easy. An I'd been workin in vegetable fields mosta my life, so I'm strong. Wasn't nothin for me to hump a few miles with a full pack. An I'm a good shot, too. Got Sharpshooting medals—both rifle and pistol. Just missed Expert by a couple points." Sandra gave a little smile, remembering. And just like that, she was off.

"Barracks? Hah. Camp Lejeune was like a hotel for me. Chow, too. An I liked most of the girls. We got close, you know, even though I was pretty much older than most of em cept the officers. We prolly had some dykies there, too, but I din ask, you know. And they din tell, hah hah."

"Hah hah," Gina mimicked sarcastically.

"If you don wanna listen, blondie, go fly a kite or somethin."

Gina just crossed her arms and sat back.

"Anyway, they din bother me. Only thing bothered me was some a the officers. Even the Latino officers. They treated us like *mierda* unless they were tryin to fuck us. But I din take up with no officer. I just did my job and tried to get through. Figured I could do my three years, then decide what to do next. Like reenlist, or maybe get trained for a good job outside. I signed up for transportation, thought maybe I could be a bus driver when I got out."

"But that din happen. What happened was we invaded Iraq and I got sent over there. Camp Fallujah, but some of us called it The MEK, which was the initials of some Arabic words I coun pronounce. Now I've been a lotta places in this country and in Mexico—and some of those places were pretty scary. I been in some fights and seen drunks and bonzos shootin their rifles. But in Iraq there was shootin twenty-four seven. Every night was another Fourth of July. Artillery looks like stars fallin up, or maybe scared pieces of the ground tryin to escape.

"Our post was outside the city of Fallujah—not too far, a fifteen-minute drive maybe—and all around us was desert. The roads leadin away from the post looked like roads goin into just more desert—roads goin nowhere at all. But eventually one of em led to the city. It was bigger than you'd think—paved four-lane highway with a median strip in the middle that had poles carryin electricity. Difference is that there wasn't much traffic on it; just a few cars every couple of miles or so. I spent some time in Fallujah in my off hours if I ever had any. Lots of mosques there and lots of jibber-jabber. Lots of rubble, too, but not everywhere. I even went into some shops, but I always had some of my unit with me. I din like the food so I din buy nothin much cept for some souvenirs I could send to Carlos back home. Mostly, I was savin my money. Din see too many Iraqi men, guess they were all out hidin or bombin people, but I saw a lotta women with these scarves over their faces, what they called *niqabs*. Some of those coverings were pretty an all, but I think that kind of thing is sick. I mean, my own culture is pretty macho, you know? I mean we invented the word, right? And sure, I been slapped around some by men, but I never liked it. Somebody tells me to wear a piece of cloth over my face so no other man can even look at me, I'd just tell em to fuck off, you know?"

"Ah'm startin to lahk this woman a little better," Gina broke in, but Sandra Murillo ignored her—was so engrossed in her memories she probably didn't even hear her.

"It was pretty dangerous in the city; you never knew if somebody was waitin for you behind a wall, or up in a tree, or aimin a rifle at your coconut from that building across the street. It was safe at the base, though. A lotta walls and sandbags and razor wire. You could see anybody comin for miles, and you could see dust even before that. And there was artillery firin all the time, loud. When I first got there I thought it was incoming and looked for a place to duck under like a duck. But it was just some a our guys bein bored. Sometimes they'd find an old vehicle somewhere and tow it out in the desert so they could have somethin to shoot at, but they really din need nothin, you know? They liked the sound and the feel of that big gun and they liked bein able to shoot farther than the next guy. But I think they liked best that they were wastin hundreds or thousands of dollars every time they fired the fuckin thing.

"There were some pretty big buildings in the camp, but most of em were for officers and admin. The rest of us lived in big tents. I heard that they started bringin in these little trailers with air conditioners, but that was after I left.

They put me to work in Supply. At first I was just carryin and stackin boxes in piles. Then they assigned me to one of the trucks, just drivin boxes from one place at the camp to another. They were pretty long days, I'll tell you, and hot. At the end of the day I'd rack out for a while, then head over to this place we called the Smoke

Pit and have a cigarette or two with some coffee. I've quit smokin now—can't afford it. I can afford a cell phone but not ciggies, hah hah. The Smoke Pit was a little cooler than some of the other places in The MEK. It had palm trees all around it and there were some lounge chairs there to relax in. Sometimes there was arty fire, like I said, but after a while I din pay no attention to it.

"We wore our camos and boots and green T's most of the time, and clothes had to be washed almost every day. I washed mine by hand and put them over something to dry. They dried fast, I'll tell you.

"One day my sergeant came up to me and said I'd been assigned to be on the Female Search Force. I said to him 'Whas that?' and he tole me that me and about a dozen other women would get training to search Iraqi women and children for contraband goin into the city. Well, I guessed it was better than stacking boxes and I figured maybe I could get a job as a prison guard when I got out.

"So I did that for a while. What happened, we'd go to these checkpoints right outside the city. Most of the time I was stationed at this one that used to be, I don know, maybe a church, but most of it was gone except for some walls with a lot of Iraqi graffiti on it. When people came up on the road wantin to go into the city, we'd separate the men and the women, then we'd take the women behind one of the walls and pat em down for contraband. And it wasn't no light patty-cake shit neither. I din much like feelin up all these women's titties and coochies, but I din want to get blown up either. Don know that it mattered much; I mean, who knows what they had stuffed up inside? I even heard that some Iraqi doctors started puttin explosives in women's breast implants, but I never felt any. Found some other stuff, though. One woman had a new rifle scope tucked away in her baby's teddy bear. Copper wires, nails, and some other stuff that could be used to make IEDs. Some a the stuff I din know what it was so I just turned it over. One day the girl I took over for said she was pattin down this woman in the crotch area and felt a penis, and it was hard, too. Turned out it was a man, hah hah, tryin to smuggle some rounds inta the city. He got turned in, too, and quick. Don't know what happened to him, but I don think it was good.

"Some of the women, specially the older ones, din like being frisked and who would, but some others took it pretty well. We saw em about every day so we got to know some of em a little. They joked with us sometimes and I learned a few words of Arabic. I guess we looked kinda weird to them—dressed in combat armor with helmets, flak jackets, and these protective scarves that covered our necks. Some of the girls had goggles that made em look like bugs, but I never liked em cause I never wanted to look like no bug. Plus we all had to carry our M249s at all times, along with extra rounds, and that stuff weighed a ton. I hated those SAWs. Not only were they too heavy, but they jammed all the time cause there was so much sand and dust around. I always carried my M9 on my belt, and I cleaned it every day, sometimes more than once.

"And a lotta time passed that way. It was almost into July and the heat was as bad as anything I'd ever seen in the watermelon fields back home. Over a hundred easy, and sometimes we were on duty for twelve hours at a stretch. I was feelin itchy—not on my skin so much, but in my head. My time was almost up and I got word that Carlos was gettin into trouble at home. I put in some requests to be reassigned back in the states, but nothing came of it. I learned to get through every day without thinkin too much—not that I'm such a deep thinker anyway, hah hah. Every day got to be the same.

We left the post at seven a.m. in an armored truck and drove to the checkpoints, then came back about twelve hours later. Everything was the same, all the time. I felt like I was doin everything in my sleep, but after a while, the dreams started to get bad. The other girls musta been having the same dream, cause we all wanted out. You know sandpaper, right? I saw a lot of it when I was in Supply. They have these different grades—sixty grit for heavy sanding, and say, 800 for real fine. Well, to me, the air in Fallujah was like the tiniest grit in the world, and it was wearin me down to a frazzle.

"One day it got up to somethin like a hundred and twenty degrees. Maybe that's why everything was so quiet around the checkpoints and why nobody seemed to be movin around the city. There were less Iraqi women comin in that day, and none of em cracked a smile, even the ones with kids. I was workin with a petty officer from the Navy that day—she was in the mess hall when she wasn't on frisk duty—and she just shook her head. It got worse when I caught this old *mujer* tryin to sneak in about a dozen fake IDs between her saggy old titties. When I told her to get them out she started screamin and trying to grab my rifle. I had to put that old bat in an armbar and call for backup. Crud, what a day.

"We were all glad when our transport truck showed up with our escorts. Actually it was two trucks—one for the men and one for the women. Sometimes some of the men and women rode together, but this time all the women were on the first truck. It was just an old seven-ton cargo truck that had some metal plates fitted on the sides for armor, but it had always gotten us where we wanted to go. And so we started back to camp. There was one Humvee in front of us, then the convoy with the men, then another Humvee a couple hundred yards back. We usually had a three-Humvee escort, but that day one of em had been pulled off to help guard some visitin general. Din make much difference to us; we were off duty and that stretch of highway had been pretty quiet over the last few months.

"I was in the back, sittin next to the petty officer. We were just shootin the shit bout home and stuff. She was even older than me, on her second tour of duty, and she wanted to get back to her two girls in Kansas or somewhere. Everybody—I guess there was a dozen of us—were pretty low key on that trip. And for the first couple of miles we only saw one car ahead of us. The stretch of road we were on used to have some stores and other businesses set off from the pavement, but they were all closed now and a lot of em had been destroyed by artillery. There were a few trees, too, but they din look like they belonged there. Or maybe they looked like they should have been there at another time. Not then. As we started gettin close to the car ahead of us, the guys in the lead Humvee made it move to the side of the road so we could pass.

"The lead Humvee passed, then our truck, and I looked over the armor at the car, wondering about the passengers and what jobs they had in Fallujah and how they must have felt at gettin told to move over for intruders. There was only the driver. From what I could see of him, he was a mild-mannered guy in his thirties, kind of short, black hair, black mustache. He looked calm. Maybe he was. But the next thing I knew, his foot was on the gas and he was burning rubber toward our truck. I yelled and hit the floor, and that's what saved me.

"The car hit us just behind the cab on the passenger side and exploded. The truck lifted up in the air like a bouncy-ball. I felt heat and there was a whoosh of flames all around, and girls screamin. I was screamin, too. The truck bounced a couple more times, went off the road, and turned over, throwin most of us out, which was lucky, because when I got my breath back and looked up, the truck was a mess of orange flames and black, black smoke. My ears were ringin from the blast and there was dust everywhere. I saw a couple of girls on fire and one that was pinned under the truck. Some guys were runnin down the road from the other truck, but then the sniper fire started. I looked around for my rifle, but it was long gone. I still had my pistol, though. I looked across the road and saw a few Arabs with rifles; they all had rags on their faces like bandits, but different. I started firin and yellin at the girls who could walk to run to the nearest building and get cover. I saw one of the guys from the men's convoy take a round in the side and go down.

"There was a girl tryin to crawl toward the building. She had lost her helmet and I saw that most of her hair had been burned off and her hands were a red mess. I ran over to help her but just before I got her to cover, I felt a bad sting and a jolt in my left thigh like bein stabbed by some drunk bonzo and I went down again, hard. At first I din know what happened. There wasn't no pain, but I coun get to my feet. It was only when I reached back to touch my leg that my hand came back all red and bloody.

"By then the first Humvee had turned back around and the snipers were hoofin it back out of there. I never found out if we got any of em, cept of course the driver of the car. Before I knew it, there was a medic trying to look after all the wounded, and we were all a mess. I managed to get up on my knees, but by then the shock had worn off and my leg hurt like holy hell. My pistol was still in my hand like it had been soldered there, although the clip was empty. I looked back toward the truck and coun really believe it. Just billowin smoke like the biggest cloud I ever saw, but black instead of white. Debris all over the road, and a few bodies, or parts of bodies.

"The driver's side soldier and the gunner on the roof of our truck were killed in a second—just blown apart. Three of the girls had been killed outright, too, including the one that had got pinned under the truck. The flames of the suicide bomb had come over the top of those welded-on panels and burned most of the other girls on the face and hands—wherever they weren't covered by our protective gear. I din get burned much because I had hit the deck, but then I caught that round in the leg. It din hit a bone or a ligament or nothin, but it was still the end of the war for me.

"The men helped us get in the second transport truck and we managed to get back to The MEK, where there was a kind of infirmary. It was good enough to get the bullet out of my leg, but they had to send most of the other women to a burn hospital somewhere in Texas. Never saw any of em again. They flew me back to Camp Lejeune, where I first trained. I spent some time in the Naval Hospital there, then served out the rest of my time in an office. Got a purple heart; do you know that? Wish I knew where it was now so I could maybe sell it, hah hah. You know, most of the time I was in Iraq I din like it much. The rest of the time I hated it, but now I'm not in it any more, I know that I'm glad I got to be part of it. It's history, you know. Maybe bad history, who knows, but history. Only thing I have left from that war is my M9. I like to think that I took out a couple of those towel-heads with that pistol and saved us all. Maybe I did, hah hah. Thas why I want it back."

Sandra Murillo stopped talking and looked around her, as if surprised to be wherever she was and with strange people. But she didn't seem to be a person who could be surprised by much for very long, so she just shrugged and pointed her chin at me. "I already tole this one bout how my *madre* got the Big C and how I had to use all my money for her medicine, and how my boy

Carlos kinda got away from me while I was gone. I don
blame him much, though. A kid should have his mama
around when he's growin up, right? A papa, too maybe,
but I ain't had much luck with men.''

After a few seconds of silence, Ashley angled his
head toward a small table to his left. "Clarence," he said.

Clarence, who seemed to be in the kind of stupor
that one gets in a movie theater, stumbled to his feet and
hurried over to the table. He opened the drawer and
took out a shiny holster. He handed it to the Latina
woman and sat back down while she undid the snap and
took out what looked to be the same pistol Clarence and
I had found in the woods.

"We took the liberty of cleaning it and giving you
something to carry it in. We also removed the
ammunition from the clip and suggest you hide this from
your boy in the future. In the condition he was in when
Sue-Ann and Clarence found him, he could easily have
shot both of them.''

"Yeah, but I din . . ." she began, then stopped.
"Yeah, okay, I know. I'm pretty stupid. When Carlos
called me from the hospital he musta been still fucked up
on somethin, cause he said that this one almost shot him
with a bow and arrow.''

"If Sue-Ann had wanted to shoot him he'd a had a
hole in him," Gina told her matter-of-factly.

Sandra frowned and looked from Gina to me to
Clarence and finally to Ashley. "Yas," he said. "Ms
Cartwright is correct. Sue-Ann was national champion
archer some years back. She can shoot more accurately
with a bow than most of the soldiers here can shoot with
a pistol.''

"Yeah?" said Sandra dubiously, but the doubt was
tinged with respect. I suddenly remembered a student I
had known in college who had called himself a poet,
although I don't know if he ever wrote anything. Most

people just ignored him, but the few who didn't seemed to find him mysterious and fascinating. Well, that wasn't a bad thing to be.

"But look, you people," she continued, lovingly stroking the gun metal, "Where I'm gonna put this where Carlito don get it? I mean, I'm livin in a old school bus right now, but tomorrow it might be in a big refrigerator box. Can't afford no bank vault. I got a cell phone, but not a bank vault, hah hah."

And at that very moment, the cell phone in question buzzed in the pocket of her oversized sweater. She fumbled it out, and answered, "Ello?" She listened for a second, then put her hand over the mouthpiece and looked at Ashley.

"It's Carlito," she whispered. "He's in trouble."

Chapter Seven: Red Rivers

Sandra Murillo got up from her chair and drifted to the far end of the room as she spoke to her son. Her back was to us so that we were able to hear only a smattering of urgent Spanglish. After a few seconds, though, her voice rose and we heard "Carlos, Carlito!" Then her cell snapped shut and she turned back around. We were all looking at her, concerned. Clarence stood up and approached her. "What's happened?" he asked.

"Aii, who knows?" she said with exasperation. "He was hidin out with some people we work with balin pine needles. Mexicans. He got in some kind of argument bout some money he borrowed. Or maybe he stole it, I don know. So he's runnin. He called me from a phone outside some open-all-night gas station, but woun tell me where he was goin."

"Uh-oh." It came out of my mouth before I knew it.

"What you uh-oh-in about?" Sandra demanded as Clarence led her back toward her chair. He didn't know what I meant either, but Gina did, and she spoke first.

"Those all-naht stations are where kids get those new kahnd of drugs," she said.

Sandra furled her eyebrows. "Doctor at the hospital said something about that. Some kinda fakey bath soap."

"Bath salts," I said. "But they make you high."

"Zat what Carlos was on?" Sandra asked.

"Yeah," I said.

"Don't you think we better try to find him?" Clarence asked.

"Where would we look?" I asked.

Sandra looked from one of us to the next. "I think I know a place," she said. "But I don think it's a *good* place. Ever heard of The Red River Saloon?"

The look on Gina's face told me that she hadn't; Clarence looked blank, too.

"I have," I said. But the memory I had of the place wasn't a happy one.

~ ~ ~

In the summer of 2008, things were falling apart for me. I was burned out from a six-month posting in Iraq, I had decided to break up with my long-time boyfriend, and I was suffering from a fairly rare glandular disease that was slowly but surely killing me. Then my mother died in a riding accident and by the time I was able to catch a flight out of Jordan, her funeral was over.

I spent the first day back home just wandering around the barn and the house I had not really lived in for fifteen years. My bedroom was the same as it was in high school, comfortably sparse. Bed, nightstand, vanity table, overhead fan. That's it; no posters of Kurt Cobain or boy bands on the walls, not even a bookshelf. I watched my mother's three horses grazing, but didn't feel like trying to ride. In the house I mechanically fielded condolence calls and responded to sympathy cards. I was in such a daze that most of the time I wasn't aware who I was speaking or writing to, and my father was no help. In fact, he seemed close to a breakdown himself.

My parents had been married for over 35 years. Cindy, my mother, was the dominant partner, but it was the kind of benign dominance seen in bands of horses whose leader was acknowledged naturally, without any kicking or biting. To my knowledge, Mike had never questioned any of her decisions. He was, in my mind, the quintessential mild-mannered high school art teacher. Neither a bad nor a particularly good role model. But now his wishy-washiness was more pronounced. He wandered from one room to the other, muttering to himself things like, "What will I do now?" and "Where will I go?" I assumed it was the shock of losing her—and remember, I had been around death-shocked soldiers for the last half year.

But late that night, tired from trying to cope and jet-lagged all to hell, my fitful sleep had been broken by the jangle of a phone that I always kept way too close to my bed. I hoped my father would answer it on the other extension, but when it continued I picked up the receiver and managed a faint "Hello?"

"Hey! You Mike McKeown's daughter?" The voice was loud, gruff, and very southern, but was almost drowned out by the noise of voices chattering under loud music.

"Um, yeah, why?"

"Because he's over here, drunk out of his fuckin mind. Fucker started to run out on a big tab, but that's not the way we work it around here. He doesn't pay up, I bust his fuckin ass."

"You've got to have the wrong number," I said, waking up quickly. My father, drunk? I had never known him to even go into a bar.

"Got the bastard's wallet right here. And he gave me this phone number before he passed out. You need to come pick him up."

"Wh-where are you?" I asked.

"The Red River Saloon," he said. When I didn't respond, he added "Waxahatchee. Know where that is?"

"I know where Waxahatchee is," I managed, "but not the bar."

"Better get somethin to write with, then."

I fumbled for the light switch. As a reporter I always had a pad and pencil on my nightstand, even when I felt like death itself was creeping up on me. "And hey," the voice continued. "Better bring your fuckin checkbook to pay for some of this shit your daddy smashed up."

The first thing I did was check my father's bedroom and, sure enough, he was gone. His Lexus was gone, too. Without even bothering to shower off my sleep, I threw on some clothes and found the keys to my mother's old Toyota Tacoma pickup, which had carried many a load of feed and hay. Then I made my way to the nearby town of Waxahatchee, famous for its mental hospital and nothing else. The Red River Saloon turned out to be within a mile or two of that facility.

Waxahatchee's small downtown area consisted of a couple of blocks of mostly brick offices and shops, with a restaurant or two thrown in for good measure. It was sleepy and slow—even on a weekend, and especially so after midnight. Just outside town, almost within gurgling distance of the Okachokeme River, I fumbled through a couple of wrong turns before I came to a block filled with rusty and tilting mobile homes. Junk stood in front of each one and an occasional dog on a chain stood up and barked as I passed. When the row of trailers came to an end, I slowly passed a welding shop, its massive wooden sliding doors shut tight for the night. Next to that was the local trash collection business, and I could smell the wet residue from garbage trucks parked in its front lot. After that, and set back from the road about forty yards, I found The Red River Saloon. It was a simple cinder-block building that looked like it had once been a warehouse. Pickups littered the parking lot and a tattered sign hung from chains on a pole. A larger building stood nearby looking like an old tobacco barn but littered in front with all manner of junk, none of which I could make out in the darkness. The bar, though, sounded loud and lively through the open window of the Toyota. Near the door, three men, two black and one white, were smoking cigarettes and holding bottles of beer. All three were dressed in stained trousers and old work shirts that looked heavily used.

I found a place to park, but as I made my way toward the door, the three men moved apart and surrounded me. They didn't say anything, but I could feel them inspecting every part of me, from my thinning hair to the bags under my eyes to my ill-fitting clothes. Maybe I should have been glad that some men still found me attractive, but all I could think of was that I had finally escaped from Iraq only to fall victim to a bunch of drunken crazies from near my own home town. I heard them muttering, "Ummm, yeah, fahn piece a tail, pretty honey, mmm-waaa!" but when I didn't answer and continued to walk past them, one of the men deliberately threw his half-filled beer bottle toward the ground. It smashed and splashed beer and glass all over my legs and shoes. He laughed loudly and lewdly. The other two laughed as well.

Then they stopped.

I had halted in midstep; I was still frightened, but fuming. I looked down at my shoes and the cuffs of my jeans. It was too much. "You fucking assholes!" I shouted. I opened my mouth to scream out a few more choice curse words but they lay dormant in my throat. The men were no longer ogling me; in fact, they were backing away from me, looking shamefaced. Then I saw that another man had appeared in the doorway—six-two, maybe, with a large frame and huge belly. Red complexion and a long red ponytail. At the moment, his eyes looked red, too. He glanced from me to the men, then to the broken glass in the parking lot.

"Pick it up," he said to the men. His voice was as hard as a stone.

"Aw, come on, Red," said one of the men.

"Yeah, Red, we—"

The red eyes caught fire. "What did you just call me?" he roared.

"Mistah Rivers," one of the black men said quickly.

"Sorry, Mistah Rivers," said the white man. "It was an accident."

The third man started bowing and scraping like he was an extra in *Gone with the Wind*.

"Won't be an accident when I cram that broken bottle up your ass," said Mr. Rivers. Then he laughed and turned to me. "Wouldn't be the first time either," he told me. "Thompson likes stuff like that, don't you, Thompson?"

"Yas suh, Mistah Rivers. I mean, no suh, Mistah Rivers."

Rivers stood there and stared at the three men until they got down on their knees and began to gather up the broken glass into their bare hands. "Fuckin convicts," he muttered, more to himself than to me or the men.

Then he turned his gaze toward me again and smiled, showing tobacco-stained teeth. "Either you're Miz McKeown or you're lost, haw haw." His laugh was like what I would guess it would sound like if someone could crush rocks in their bare hands.

I just stood there without anything to say. On one side of me were three morons and on the other someone who looked like he could apply for a job as tribal warlord in Afghanistan and dictate his salary.

"My name's Sam Rivers," he said loudly. "But *you* can call me Red."

I pretended I didn't see the paw he held out and quickly asked, "Where's my father?"

He lowered the paw, without losing the smile. "Come on in to my humble establishment," he said, "and I'll show you."

I stamped both my feet to loosen any drops of beer or slivers of glass, then followed him through the door.

It was dim inside, with only a few fluorescent lights nailed to the rafters and one behind the bar. Everything—the bar, the tables, and even a makeshift stage seemed to have been cobbled together from old two by fours, and they were smooth from long and continuous use. But despite their inelegance, the tables, the rectangular bar, the chairs, and even the floor seemed carved or shaped or stained in such a way as to look authentic in an ancient sort of way. Kind of like my idea of what a 12th Century Scandinavian alehouse might have looked like.

The patrons were rough, too, and of all races, as if there were ships in the dock. They were obviously all working men—men who toiled long hours at sweltering jobs—but there were women there, as well. They, too, wore clothes that had seen many hours in the sun or behind a hot counter somewhere. They glanced at me briefly, then turned away, not interested in Red Rivers' latest floozy or the latest dreg to turn up off the street.

Rivers led me toward a makeshift stage to the left of the bar. I could see a three-drum kit along with a couple of electric guitars on stands, but their owners had blended in with the drinking, smoking patrons. Just to the right of the stage sat a man with his head buried in his hands. My father. I hurried over and bent down. But when I touched his shoulder, he started up violently. "Daddy," I said. "It's me."

He tried to focus his gaze. "Suzie?"

"Yes. Can you get up? I'm taking you home."

"Want . . . want to stay here."

"Gotta have money to stay here, bub," spoke up Red Rivers over my shoulder. "Fact of the matter is, you got to have money to leave here, too."

I stood back up and faced the owner. "What do you mean?"

Red Rivers pursed his lips. "I told you on the phone, Missy. Your dad here got a little wild and started bustin up things. Glasses, chairs, a TV. Lucky he didn't get near those instruments. Ran up a little tab, too, before the bartender got wise."

I looked around in the dim light. Sure, a few chairs looked ragged and I spotted a 20-year-old television behind the bar. I doubted if it worked, but it didn't look smashed. And the idea of anyone actually running a tab in a place like that was ludicrous. I faced Red Rivers and I felt my mouth tighten up. "You know my father didn't do any of those things," I said tersely.

"Bout a dozen of these folks here will tell you you're wrong." I looked at the nearest table, where four half-tipsy patrons were paying close attention and nodding.

One of them, a small man in a John Deere cap, leaned forward and shouted out, "That's right, Mistuh Rivers, he shore tore the place up, ha ha."

"Lucky you didn't call the po-leece!," screeched out a toothless woman from the next table.

I looked around the room to see that almost everyone in the bar was now staring our way. I had been set up and everyone was in on it. In Florida less than 24 hours, I had no friends and was in no condition to fight. I closed my eyes. I didn't need this. I needed to get my father out of that place as quick as I could. "All right," I said. "How much?"

"Oh, couple hundred should cover it," he said. "Make it three. Maybe we can get one of those fancy new flat-screens. Might bring in a better class of customer, haw haw."

"That TV couldn't have cost more than—" I began.

"Hey. That TV was a collector's antique."

"And those chairs—"

"Handcrafted by local artists." I heard snickering from the nearby table.

I forced myself to close my mouth and pulled a checkbook out of my back pocket. "Just make it out to Samuel Rivers," he told me. "And don't forget that writing a bad check is a crime punishable by law."

"Don't worry," I said thinly. I never wanted to see this guy again, in court or out.

I thrust out the check and he pocketed it without a glance. He stood with his arms over his chest and watched as one of his roustabouts helped get my father into the Toyota. How I was going to get his Lexus back home was a question I didn't want to think about right then. I just made sure it was locked and that the keys were in my father's pocket.

He was contrite on the way home. The clichéd kind of contrite; how he'd never done anything like that before, didn't know what had come over him, Cindy's death, and so on. I wasn't judging; after all, I had spent the better part of the last six months drunk and crazy too.

Oddly enough, when we went back the next day to get the car, not only were the tires still on it and the windows intact, but it had been washed and stood there alone in the parking lot, gleaming in the morning sunlight.

So yeah, I had heard of the place. That bastard Sam Rivers had robbed me of $300, in addition to whatever my father had spent there that night. I hoped some drunk would smash his new flat-screen TV.

~ ~ ~

"That place is bad news," I told the assembled gathering, then I gave them the two-minute version of my own experience at The Red River. Ashley Torrington, of course, was still sitting in his comfortable armchair, but Sandra Murillo and Clarence were standing. I turned to Sandra. "What do you know about it?" I asked her.

"I donno, not much," she answered. "Mr. Rivers has a lotta odd jobs cleaning up in his bar or moving some of his junk."

"What kahnd of junk?" asked Gina.

"He's got a junk store right next to that bar," Sandra Murillo said. "Calls it Red Rivers' Bargains. You oughta see all the crapola he has there—furniture, TVs, books, bicycles . . . I saw a whole pallet of computer monitors there last time I wen. Sometimes he hires people like me and Carlos or some of the illegals to tote stuff for him. He hires prisoners, too, that are just out of jail. Gives them a place to stay and makes them do all his work for him. He's a bonzo and prolly a criminal, but I just donno where else Carlos might've gone."

"Do you know anything else about him?" asked Ashley Torrington.

"Says he used to be a po-leeze-man, or maybe a prison guard."

"Is Carlos in any danger if he goes there?" I asked.

"I donno; maybe not. Nobody be there now anyway. He'll just hide somewhere till morning."

"What do you think, Ashley?" I asked.

"Umm. Well, I don't think he's going to stick around whatever gas station he called from, even if we could find it—and there's quite a few around here. If Ms. Murillo thinks that her son is headed for that bar, then he probably is. So I think someone should pay Mr. Rivers a visit. If he's a threat to your boy, Ms. Murillo, we need to get him out of there."

"It might not be the best place for a boy," said Sandra, "But it's lots better than that juvie home."

"And let's not forget that Joey Bickley is looking for him," I said.

"Why don't we just let it be for tonight, then," said Ashley, "and hope that he already learned his lesson about those bath salts. Tomorrow I can send someone

over there to look the place over and see if they can spot
Carlos. Maybe Clarence can go, or Jeremy or Smokey."

Unexpectedly, Gina got up from her seat. "Clarence
has a business to run," she said, "and Jeremy would
probably shoot the place up. As for that grandson of
yours, he'd probably just get eaten up lahk a fly in a nest
of frogs. Ah'll do it," she said.

"You?" It's possible that the rest of us asked that
question in unison.

"Yeah, me. But raht now ah'm goin home and get
some sleep. Ashley, don't do nothin til you hear from
me."

"What are you going to do?" I asked.

"Ah've got a plan. Don't you trust me?"

"Of course, but . . ."

"Then let's git on home, lover girl." She winked at
Sandra and walked through the door. I followed.

Chapter Eight: Gigged

The next day was a busy one. Annie Gillespie had emailed me what she had found out so far about the bath salts that Carlos Murillo had ingested. In sifting through reports from officials at the Department of Health, the Drug Enforcement Agency, and poison control centers around the state I found out that this new generation of cheap designer drug was more prevalent than I had feared. Bath salts, along with something called synthetic marijuana, were beginning to cause problems across the country. The "salts" came in powder or crystals and they could be snorted or eaten. They were well known to have caused not only the types of violent behavior Clarence and I had witnessed, but almost across-the-board weirdness, like Becky Colley's friend running from imagined electricity. But there were instances of physical symptoms as well, such as kidney failure or temporary paralysis. Imagine the teenage girl who had taken a sniff or two and gone catatonic, who could hear her friends talking about her, discussing how they would dispose of her body if she died. It was frightening.

Annie had called a couple of state legislators to find out their take on these new designer drugs, but was still waiting for a reply to her messages. When I got to a stopping point, I checked in with Ashley Torrington and asked how Sandra Murillo was doing. He told me that he had provided her a room for the night and that her son had called her earlier that morning from a borrowed cell phone. He seemed to be all right, but when she tried calling the number back, she didn't get an answer.

Meanwhile, Gina had disappeared. We had driven to the office separately, as always—not only to keep our relationship a secret, but because we both made frequent use of our cars during the workday. Gina, who was in charge of wrangling advertising contracts from the rapidly shrinking business community, was often out most of the day. I was worried about her visiting The Red River Saloon by herself, but I kept reminding myself that she was a grown woman—one who had seen at least as much of life as I had and who knew how to take care of herself. As always, she had come in to the office that morning dressed to the nines. She spent an hour on the phone confirming appointments, then left the building. I relied on her—*The Courier* relied on her—to keep at least some revenue flowing in, but clients had dried up like the Okachokeme River in the heavy drought of summer. It was only a matter of time before *The Courier*'s owner would expect a return on his new high-tech equipment investment.

But in spite of Gina's persuasive talents, the economic realities in our town were beginning to look as dire as those of the big world. The major banks had fucked everyone royally, from Europe to the U.S. Greece was bankrupt and it looked like Ireland and Portugal were next. Major automobile manufacturers and financial institutions were being bailed out to the tune of billions of dollars. Some of the largest American cities were near default, so it's not hard to get the picture. But if you can't beat em, at least you can write a story about em. I called Mark Patterson into my office.

"What's up, Chief," he said as he plopped himself down in the visitor's chair.

Mark was a handsome young man, although not square-jawed and Latin like Randy Rivas. Mark's was more a casual, windblown handsomeness. I knew that he was from somewhere in south Florida and that he had left the University of Florida School of Journalism before actually graduating—a fact that he left out of his job application. I was not sure what had prompted him to apply for an entry-level job in Pine Oak and, although I do like to pry, I hadn't. Yet. All I was worried about was that he came to work on time (which he did, sometimes) and that his stories were well researched and well written (which they were, mostly).

"I've got something for you," I said.

"Give."

"Okay, I just got the latest figures from the legislative budget negotiations. They're planning on privatizing most of the prisons in the state and laying off a couple of hundred people at the mental hospital in Waxahatchee."

"What, *more* people?" He wasn't too surprised; our present governor's austerity was legendary, as were his ties to private service providers.

"Yup. So let's do a story about how the economy—including all these layoffs and projected layoffs—are affecting us here in Jasper County."

"Probably half the people that work at Wacko live in Jasper County."

"Right. And work up a list of small businesses that have gone under in the last year or so. Get with some of the bigger stores, too, like Piggly Wiggly and WalMart, and ask if they've had to reduce the number of their employees. The managers at WalMart probably won't talk to you, but get to know some of the employees. You're good at that."

"Thanks," he said dubiously. Mark's penchant for talking people up—especially young women in bars—was well known. As were his one-night stands. But I wasn't finished. "And see if you can get an update from the city manager about that ethanol company he's trying to lure to Pine Oak."

"Hokey Dokey," he said, and stood up.

"Okay, good," I said. "When you go out, tell Cori I want to talk to her."

In the few weeks she had been at *The Courier*, Corinthia Glenn had impressed me with her promptness, her attention to detail, and her neat, pert appearance, yet she continued to be somewhat of a mystery to me. I knew she had two sons, aged four and five, who were kept by one of Cori's relatives during the day. And as far as I knew, she was not married. I knew nothing else about her personal life.

She appeared in the doorway of my office dressed in a neat brown pantsuit. Her hair was freshly permed and her face carefully made up. Her only digression from magazine correctness was the fact that, instead of wearing an earring on the lobe of each ear, two were pierced into the side of her right ear, while the other was bare. It is little things like that that make someone stand out from the amorphous crowd and, who knows, it may be why I had hired her instead of many more qualified applicants.

"You want to see me?" she said.

"Yes, come in and sit down."

After she was seated across the desk from me, she asked, "You have a job for me?"

I smiled inwardly but not outwardly. "You *have* a job," I told her. "Several of them."

"Yeah, okay," she replied. "But it's kinda boring writing about nothing but marriages and deaths and these little piddling social events."

"So let me get this straight," I told her, leaning forward. "You want to be a 'real' reporter, right?"

"Um, yeah. Sure."

I leaned back in my chair and put both hands behind my head. "The worst thing about journalism school is what they don't tell you."

"What do you mean, what they don't tell you?"

"They don't tell you that what you're doing here now is "real" reporting. It's reporting about everyday people in everyday situations. Some of our subscribers— most of them, probably—just scan the front headline and skip the story. But they actually *read* about who in their community gets married or divorced or who gets born or dies. And they absolutely *love* finding out who gets arrested. They are more interested in that stuff than anything that has ever happened in Iraq, Afghanistan, and Tallahassee combined."

"Yeah, well, I guess if you put it that way . . ."

"I *do* put it that way. But having said that, I have a *different* assignment for you today."

She looked at me eagerly, "Yeah?"

"Have you ever heard of the H. A. Hardy Juvenile Center?" I asked.

Cori's face hardened like dark cement and she opened her mouth to speak but didn't. I saw her eyebrows descend, her mouth tighten. Then she shrugged as if she were shaking off a phantom and said, "I mighta heard of it," she said. "What about it?"

"That boy I found that had the bath salts. He was sent to Hardy a couple of months ago, but he escaped. The folks there are after him and so is the Sheriff's office. His mother is a woman I know—an ex-Marine that was in Iraq. I'd like to know how that boy escaped. And why. Question the warden or whoever runs the place about their security system. Ask him how they punish kids that break the rules. In other words, I want you to get into this man's head. You'll have the advantage because as far as I can find out, only the sheriff is supposed to know that Carlos escaped."

"The element of surprise?"

"Exactly. He might blurt out something he'd think better of if he knew what was coming."

"When do you want me to do it?" she asked.

"As soon as you're ready."

"I'll be ready in an hour or so—just as soon as I get the last few things ready for the Social Calendar."

It was a good answer.

~ ~ ~

Sometimes—although I didn't tell Cori Glenn this—working on a newspaper can be incredibly depressing. Stories about a bad economy, drugs, city managers on the take, boys in prison. Yeah. And by four-thirty, there was still no sign of Gina. I tried calling her cell but got shunted to voice mail immediately. I know I shouldn't have been worried, but . . . The world was way too much with me, so I decided to do what I usually did on similar occasions, when just giving up and falling on my sword became more and more the only option: walk next door to Benny's Bookstore and grab up some fat fantasy novel that I could get lost in for about a week. It was a habit I had picked up from an ex-boyfriend, who devoured the things ravenously.

The rest of the staff had gone home, leaving me to lock up, but just as I was about to turn out the lights in my office, I looked out the window and saw Gina's silver PT Cruiser glide into the parking lot. She parked, and hopped out, looking as fresh as she had when she went out that morning. As for me, I felt like a dish rag even though I hadn't left the office the entire day. She came through the door and greeted me with a "Hah, Sue-Ann."

But I was having none of that. "I've been worried sick about you," I began, exaggerating only a little.

"About me?" she said. She looked at the empty offices, then gave me a quick peck on the lips. "Wah?"

"You know why. Tell me what you've been doing all day."

"Well," she said, putting her purse down beside the chair and sitting down. "Ah got a couple of new accounts. One of em's just the other side of Forester. Restaurant called The Out of Towner, although that seems lahk a kinda strange name. They made me a good salad, though, with cucumbers and the kahnd of black olives that you don't see much in—"

"Gina!"

"Huh?" she said innocently.

"That's all very nice," I said impatiently, "but I want to know about that bar in Waxahatchee."

"Oh, raht. Well, ah got a new account there, too."

"What?" I was totally unprepared for this. "I thought you were just going to drive out there and look around or something?"

"Well, Sue-Ann darlin, just how was ah goin to fahnd out anything without goin in, and how could ah go in without some kahnd of a cover story?"

"I . . . I don't know. But it might have been dangerous."

"Wasn't, though. When ah got there, the bar was closed for business, but the front door was open. Ah walked in an saw a couple of gahs insahd sweepin and moppin and generally gettin the place in shape. Ah asked one of em for Mr. Rivers, and he told me he was next door at the junk store. Then ah saw the stage. Sue-Ann, you didn't tell me they played lahv music there. There were a couple of guitars on stands and ah was itchin to get up there and play one of em."

"But you didn't, right?" I said.

"Couldn't. They were all strung for a raht-handed player. Ah mean, there're some players—lahk Elizabeth Cotton—who just play with upsahd-down strings, but ah—"

"Gina!"

"Okay, raht. So ah didn't play any of the guitars, but ah didn't see that woman's son anywhere either so ah desahded to go next door."

"To that junk store?"

"Raht. The Red River Bargain Barn its called. So ah walked over there and went in. Mah goodness, Sue-Ann, that place makes Clarence's market look lahk an advertahsment for Spic and Span. Old chairs and desks stacked on top of each other, clothes, tools, ah even saw a pallet stacked with molds you use for making things with clay. Nobody was in the front but ah heard voices outsahd in the back, so ah squeezed through some of the stuff til I got to the back door.

"There was a horse trailer outsahd there, but instead of horses, it was packed with more junk. Ah recognized Mr. Rivers from your description—he still has that red ponytail. He was just standin there and telling some gahs what to do with the stuff they were bringing out. There were four helpers; three of em were tough-lookin hombres with tattoos. The other was Carlos."

"You found him!" I exclaimed.

"Raht."

"So what did you do?"

"Well, darlin, ah just kept cool. And it was kahnd of hard because that Rivers gah has about the dirtiest mouth ah ever heard. He was callin those helpers 'fuckin convicts and perverts and lazy bastards.' But they didn't look lahk it. They were workin pretty hard. Carlos was too—and he had to be if he was goin to keep up with those other men.

"An when Mr. Rivers saw me, he bout had a fit. Couldn't get over to me fast enough, askin if he could help me fahnd anything, because, you know, he had everything. Didn't take him long till he told me about this big selection of sausages he had and would ah lahk one?"

"Sausages?" I broke in.

"Ah presume he was talking about the one he had in his pants," said Gina. "Lahk ah said, he was real foul-mouthed. But there was somethin about that that was strange. Ah just don't know what it was. It was lahk he was all talk, but *not* all talk, you know what ah mean?"

"No."

"Well, ah don't neither. But you know me, ah can charm the honey out of bees and it wasn't long before ah had signed him up for some ads. Two contracts—one for the bar and the other for the bargain store. Gave me cash from his pocket, too." She looked across the desk at me triumphantly.

"But what about Carlos?" I asked.

"Ah left him there."

"But Gina—"

"Ah don't know, Sue-Ann. Ah didn't want to set anything off and for some reason, ah think he's safe there for a wahl."

I opened my mouth, but didn't say anything. Then Gina said what I was probably thinking. "It's pretty bad when it seems to be safer to leave a kid with some roughneck than with a sheriff's officer lahk Joey Bickley, but there you have it." Then she smiled and added, "An, hey, I got a gig."

I perked up. "Really? Where?"

"The Red River Saloon. Whatcha think we been talking about this last half hour?"

"But you . . ."

"He didn't even want an audition."

"But you can't . . ."

"Only thing is, ah have to wear a bikini."

"What!"

"He was only kidding. Ah think. Ah start on Frahday.

"Shit. I need a book."

"Yeah, you look lahk it. Goin next door? Ah'll come with."

When we walked in the bookstore, Benny was bent over his new tablet computer at the card table he used for a makeshift desk. He didn't look up, even though the bell attached to the front door had chimed merrily.

"Getting the hang of it yet?" I asked.

He looked up, startled, then smiled when he saw me. Then he cut his eyes to Gina. "Hey hey hey," he said. "The Glimmer Twins."

"Hmm?"

"Eh?" Benny hummed a few bars of "Satisfaction," by the Rolling Stones. "Jagger and Richards, the Glimmer Twins, heh heh. That's the name they used to produce some of their records."

"You've been listening to too much pirate radio," I told him.

"Arghh," he said, then went into a panther-like hiss. *"Yas, but I'm really The Creeper don't you know."*

Gina and I both knew he wasn't but I was glad that he was at least a listener of the weird radio station that Ashley Torrington funded.

I pointed down at the table. "Figured out the icons yet?" I asked, realizing an instant too late that every time I asked Benny a question I regretted it.

"Hmm? Oh, yah. One or two. Me niece started a blog for me, heh heh heh."

"A blog?"

"I'm callin it, um, "Amigos in Paradise.""

"What's it about?" I asked.

"Well, um, hmm, remember that play I showed you last year?"

"Of course." I remembered it only too well—a bizarre amalgam of Celtic folklore and the homoerotic imaginations of a dirty old man. As much as I liked

Benny, I had not been able to get through even a third of it.

"I'm making a novel out of it," he said, grinning. "But I've changed the names of the characters and put them in different settings. Some of them look different, too, and they've got different jobs."

"Sounds like it's something completely new, then," I told him.

"Yeah, well. Um. Except that the conversations are all the same, um hm."

"That's way too deep for me, Benny, but good luck to you. Or it."

"Maybe you can be a follower," he suggested before I had a chance to move away.

"Sure, just send me the link," I said, then looked around for Gina, who had wandered off into the spiritual section. I left Benny to his blog and started picking through the thickest fantasy paperbacks I could find, trying to figure out which I had read and which not. Deposed kings, warriors, princesses, mages, dragons, and elves. Yum. For some reason they kept me amused. When I was reading one I felt like a contented Borden's dairy cow—if they really are. In fact, a few moments into my browse, I lost track of time.

"You about ready?" Gina's voice was near my ear. "We probably need to go home and change."

"Change for what?" I asked.

"Tonaht's our bowling naht," she said.

"God, already?"

"We're gonna whup ourselves some ass," she said.

I ended up buying two books instead of one.

Chapter Nine: Hi-Score

When I pushed through the glass doors of the bowling alley, I found myself in another world. It was as if I had walked through a portal and into a Pandora's Box of unique sensations that could be found nowhere else: the thud, followed by the dull rolling of heavy spheres on wooden lanes; the click and clatter of pins clashing into each other; the shouts of the bowlers as pins disappeared beneath pin avalanches. Odors of beer and fried foods mingled with the oil of the lanes and bowling shoe disinfectant. And although smoking had been banned in bowling alleys for a few years, I could still imagine the haze of smoke wafting over the tables. If it sounds cacophonous, it was, but no real bowlers ever get it out of their system, and I found myself grinning.

I had missed it.

"Sue-Ann, over here!" came at me over the din. I looked straight ahead and saw Gina standing on Lane 5, waving at me with one hand while holding a yellow bowling ball in the other. I waved back and moved in her direction. The place was packed. By bowling alley standards, it was a small house; only 12 lanes, but I had bowled in smaller. Larger, too, but don't get the idea that I was much good. Although I had started bowling when Hi-Score Lanes had first come to Forester when I was 12, the only real coach I ever had was Jerry Highsmith, the former owner, and Jerry had died long ago, leaving the business to his varied family, and my bowling to my own devices. I had competed on my high school team and did okay against light competition, but after I left

Pine Oak for college, I had bowled only sporadically and mostly by myself.

I lugged my bowling bag over to the bowling area and sat down to put on my shoes. In fact, finding my bowling stuff and sprucing it up a little had made me late. Hell, they were already practice bowling and I hadn't thrown a ball in years.

In our bowling circle I spotted dour Betty Dickson from the office and her pal Krissy going over the score sheet. Gina had just thrown her yellow ball and squealed like someone who had never thrown one before and I felt a bit guilty about not knowing whether or not this was true. Randy Rivas, our fifth team member, sat down beside me and spoke over the noise. "Okay, Sue-Ann, we had the organizational meeting and got everyone signed up. Tonight we bowl for average. There's only a few more minutes of warm-up, so try to throw a few balls."

"What about you?" I asked. "You don't even have your shoes on yet."

"Bad luck about that," he told me. "I sprained one of my bowling fingers playing basketball this afternoon." He held up a thickly-bandaged hand. "Don't worry, though. I got us a replacement. He's in the bathroom."

I looked around toward the bathrooms and almost ducked out of sight when I saw Joey Bickley come clomping out in an oversized pair of red and white house shoes. "No way, Randy," I said. "If that guy is on our team, I'm out of here."

"No, no. Bickley's on another team. I got Bobby to bowl with us."

"Who's Bobby?" I asked.

"Our, um, receptionist," he said. "Bobby DuPre. Here he comes."

"Oh." I said. I had looked forward to bowling with Randy Rivas. I had watched his old team bowl a couple of times earlier in the year and had found him to be a decent bowler. Big Krissy was almost as good, but Betty probably only averaged in the 120s. That left me, who was rusty as nails in the rain, and Gina, who would be lucky to break 100. Bobby DuPre was in his sixties. He was a big man—although not nearly as tall and bulky as Joey Bickley—and could probably get the ball down the alley okay, but whether he could actually help the team win was questionable.

"Hey, Ms. McKeown," he said, and sat down by Randy. It was only then I saw he had walked out of the bathroom in his socks. His shoes were on the bench beside him.

"Sue-Ann," I responded automatically. "Oooo, Dexters," I enthused, staring at his bowling shoes.

"Yeah," he said. "They're pretty old, but still good. But you're wearing Dexters too."

"Not ones with replaceable sliding pads."

"Well," he smiled. "Sometimes they come in handy. It depends on how well the approaches are buffed."

An enormous thud followed by a burst of laughter caused me to look to my left, where I saw Joey Bickley sprawled almost on his face, half of his huge body over the foul line and the other half not.

I finished our conversation in my mind: no real bowler wears bowling shoes into the bathroom, where the porous leather soles might pick up splashes of water from the sink or worse. With wet shoes, Joey's slide to the approach must have ended in an abrupt halt, his momentum sending him toppling forward. I couldn't help smiling, and of course, when Joey picked himself up, I was the one he glared at. Well, too bad; it wasn't me that had fallen on my face.

The finishing slide, of course, was almost as important as the ball release, so when I got to the approach, I took a few practice slides before I was ready to actually throw a ball. My first shot clunked down and almost went in the gutter, but it had nothing to do with my shoes; it was my body telling me it hadn't performed this particular dance in way too long. The second throw was better, although I didn't make the spare. In fact, in practice bowling you don't care about hitting the pins at all. It's more important to find the correct rhythm and the right guide arrow on the lane for your ball's particular spin. It is easier to hit a mark 15 feet in front of you than a headpin at 60 feet.

I managed to get another couple of throws in before time was called. I threw my last ball at a full rack, aiming at only the ten pin, which was usually my nemesis. I ended up hitting it as well as the 6 and 9, and I was satisfied. I had taken off enough spin to keep it on the right side of the lane without it going in the gutter. Then the pin deck went dark to signify the end of practice bowling.

Gina looked at me in a commiserating way when I sat down beside her in the waiting area. "You'll get em all next tahm," she said.

"You and I have to talk," I told her.

It was only then, while we were waiting for the pins to be reracked and the score sheets put up on the screens over the scoring tables, that I had a chance to look around. Joey Bickley's team was on lanes 1 and 2. It was—no surprise here—all male. The other four men on his team were in their thirties or forties, but I didn't recognize any of them. Oddly, the team they were playing consisted of all women. They wore matching blue shirts that said "Willow's Florist" on the back. They also matched in that they all were in their mid to late fifties. It might have appeared to be an unfair match, but in a handicap league, everything tends to even out over the course of the season.

Our own opponents were probably the strangest people I had ever seen. They looked to be two sets of twins, but they could have easily been quadruplets. Two men and two women—thin as taffy and just as slight—all with thick, wiry red hair. I looked up at the score sheet. Rosie led off, followed by Sherry. Then came Biff and Baff. The anchor's name seemed to be Mama, who I spotted sitting on the bench by herself. She could have been any age over fifty, but if she was the mother of this family, she didn't look it. She was portly with thinning salt-and-pepper hair.

I glanced at our own score sheet, wondering who Krissy had chosen as our anchor, and wasn't surprised to see that she had chosen herself. She was a big woman—close to six feet, with lots of bone and frizzy hair tied back into a thick ponytail—and she threw the ball hard. Trouble was, she threw a very light ball and didn't get much action. I had seen her shoot a 200 game once, but I had also seen her shoot a 110. Gina was leadoff, then Betty, then me, Bobby, and Krissy. But as I studied the lineup, I saw Randy Rivas—who had volunteered to be Captain—saying a few words to Krissy, who seemed annoyed, but shrugged at whatever he had suggested. Then Randy took our lineup sheet to the front desk, where he had a few words with the young female Highsmith—I think her name was Jennifer—behind it. She nodded and bent over a keyboard as a middle-aged male Highsmith (Judd?) took up a microphone and gave us the usual last-minute instructions.

"Hey, everybody," the man began. "Looks like we have a full league this season. Wonderful! I see a lot of familiar faces, pretty and not so pretty—I'm talking about you, Fred, ha ha—and some new ones, too. So welcome everyone. The pins are set to go and the foul lights are on, so have fun and I want to see some high scores."

And so we began. Gina led off, a left-handed bowler just as she was a left-handed archer and guitarist. She threw a first ball gutter, but managed to coax five pins to tumble with her second. Betty had a very deliberate and very boring style—slow walk to the foul line, low bend, short follow through, and little spin. She was fairly accurate, but didn't get much action on her hits. Still, she managed an eight and a spare in the first frame. I managed a light pocket hit, leaving the 5 pin, which I barely managed to graze for a spare. Then I looked for Bobby to bowl. I hadn't seen him throw a ball yet; evidently he had finished his practice bowling before I arrived. Instead, Krissy went to the line. I started to tell her she was going out of turn, but glanced up to see that she was now listed as the fourth bowler and that Bobby had been changed to anchor. Interesting. In the previous incarnation of the team, Krissy had been anchor— usually the bowler with the highest average and the one you can count on to deliver a mark when it is needed. The fact that Randy had moved her to fourth seemed to rankle her. She was what I call a jerky bowler; her approach to the foul line came in fits and starts, and when she arrived, she bent like a feeding crane in a mudflat, swinging her bowling arm back over her head, and letting it fly in the direction of the pins as she jerked her body back up. She only managed to hit three on the left side of the rack on her first ball, then three on the right with her second.

Then it was Bobby's turn. Polishing his ball with a small towel, he waited until the bowler on his left had left the approach before he stepped to the line. He studied the pins, then took three short steps and a long slide, releasing his ball well behind the foul line as his right leg finished up behind him. The ball skidded toward the 9-board, where it caught some friction a few boards before it would have gone into the gutter. Then the spin cut in and carried it out of the danger zone and into the back end, where it hooked nicely into the pocket. Perfect strike. Nice.

To a bowler such as myself, everything that goes on in a league is interesting; you can learn something from watching almost every ball and every pin, every interaction between the players, every bit of body language. And body language in a bowling alley is more visible than anywhere else except maybe the end zone in a Super Bowl.

When Bobby came back to the bench after his strike, I put my hand out, palm upwards, and he slapped it lightly with his own. Call it what you want: the mild equivalent of a high five, a variation of a fist bump (which, in bowling, actually means "tough luck, but you'll get it next time"), a handshake without a grip. I call it a dap, and it's an art. And as the games progressed, I noticed that a number of players had their own personal daps. Krissy and Betty, for instance—when Krissy finally loosened up and started having fun—had several. Their normal dap—after one of them had made a spare—was for one of them to hold both hands out, palms upward, while the other slapped downward with her two. After a strike, they did the same thing, then reversed their palms and did it again. Once, when Krissy got her first turkey, they slapped each other's palms in turn, then Krissy jumped around and put her palms out in back of her, where Betty slapped them again. On the alley to our right, a woman and her teenage daughter dapped in what looked to be the style of a little girl's hand-clapping game, like "Miss Susie." Infinite variations.

Two alleys to our left, Joey Bickley threw a ball so hard that one of the pins caromed back out of the pit and slid halfway back down the lane. His dap came from above his head like a slam dunk, causing the dappee to yelp as if his hand was broken. It was silly, I know, but I appreciated the camaraderie that went with it. The effortless way that the mother and daughter executed their handslaps made it obvious that they practiced it at home. Betty and Krissy, too, for I remembered that they lived together. And not for the first time I wondered if they, like Gina and me, were a secret couple. Certainly they showed no outward sign of affection unless maybe you studied their eyes, which softened at times when they looked at each other. I knew that Gina was going to want us to develop our own signature dap, and I was okay with that. It would be fun. But I was also trying to figure out how to teach her not to throw the ball off the wrong foot without making her feel bad.

As the game went on, I had a chance to look at some of the other bowlers, and I recognized many of them. The team on Lane 8 consisted entirely of other members of the Highsmith family, at least two of whom looked good enough to turn professional. The team they were playing against was anchored by a man I had never seen before, but whose name came up in the office regularly: Cobra Conlon. He owned and ran the county's only other newspaper, a very right-wing weekly. He was also the moving force of the fledgling Tea Party in Jasper County. From his form, I gathered his status as anchor was due to the fact that it was his team: his bowling shirt read "North Florida American: For America." Cobra's team looked like they were getting their asses kicked royally, but as I said earlier, it was hard to tell.

In one way, the first week in a new handicap league is always the least exciting because you can't know which team wins until all three games are complete, when averages are computed and handicaps for each bowler assigned. These extra pins are then added to each bowler's score to arrive at the total. The Hoke family— Rosie, Sherry, Biff, Baff, and Mama— all bowled within a few pins of each other, none of them having games higher than 170 or lower than 130 the entire night. They would all have decent handicaps. On our team, Gina was going to have a lot of pins to add. Betty would have about what the average Hoke had, while Krissy, and me would have less. Bobby, surprisingly, would have almost none at all.

But it was hard to concentrate on the score because of the personalities. Both Biff and Baff carried small notepads in their back pockets on which they kept their own scores. Baff, who turned out to be six years younger than his twin brother, told me he had been keeping his scores in this way most of his life, although he didn't look like the type to be running computer programs that analyzed data, pointed out trends, or tried to devise ways of improvement. Instead, he seemed to see something mystical in his handscrawls and, in a rural accent that could have come right out of *Deliverance*, tried to let me in on it. All I could focus on, though, were his teeth, which were snagglier than any teeth I had ever seen except Biff's. Snaggly and brown, which I thought was weird because his mama's teeth looked perfect, as did his sister Rosie's. Sherry kept her mouth closed throughout the first game. After she made her first strike, though, she smiled at her mama, who burst out loudly, "Sherry-Beth, where's yore teeth?"

"Sorry, Mama," I forgot em," she said. The family was evidently a prosthodontist's dream. As someone who was thinking about getting into the horse-breeding business someday, the Hoke family gave me food for thought. As my mother used to say, there's no point to breeding to a mare that's not correct.

I rebounded from a poor first game (139) to score a lucky 201 in the second by striking out in the tenth. My team applauded and one of the current Highsmith owners announced it over the PA system, along with Bobby's 220. I decided to celebrate by having a beer and an order of onion rings. I was paying my bill at the snack bar when I felt rather than saw, a huge shadow fall over me, then heard Joey Bickley's version of a hiss near my ear.

"Think you're hot shit, don't you McKeown," he spat.

"Leave me alone, Joey," I said, not bothering to look around.

"You come back to town as a 'great' reporter and a 'great' shot with a bow an arrow. Now you think you're a 'great' bowler, too. You needed to fuckin stay where you were. Because of you, that goddamed teenager got away."

I had finally had enough, and I turned to face him. "I'm the one who reported him, remember?" I said.

"And then helped him get away."

"And why would I do that?" I asked. The thought came to me that Joey might have been right this time, although for the wrong reason. On the way to the bowling alley, I had called Clarence and told him that Gina had seen Carlos at Red Rivers' place. For all I knew, he and his mother could be in the next state by now.

"Maybe because he's a witness?" he said sarcastically.

I was on that like red on blood. "Witness?" I asked. "Witness to what, Joey?"

Joey's face changed from bullish to sheepish, and I knew that he had said something that he shouldn't have. "Never mind. All I know is that you told that doctor to let the boy go. If I find out that you know where he is, or that you're hiding him, I'll—"

I never found out what my punishment would be because just then, Gina came to my rescue. "Wah Joey Bickley, what a nahce surprahs. You and Sue-Ann catchin up on old tahms?"

Joey was caught off balance, but managed to sputter, "No surprise to see you here, Ginette. And no surprise to see what team you're bowlin on."

"Wah's that, Joey?" she asked blandly.

"With those dykes."

"Krissy and Betty? Lesbians? Mah mah. How do you know?"

"I just know, that's all. I can spot one a mile away."

"Well, ah sure hope ah don't catch nothin from those two."

"Don't make me laugh, Cartwright. I've got you figured out, too. You and McKeown here."

"Me and Sue-Ann? Wah what a nahce thought. Want to go to a movie or somethin sometahm, Sue-Ann? Maybe you'd lahk to watch, Joey?"

"Just fuck the both of you!"

"Listen, Joey," Gina continued more seriously. "Everybody that desahds not to go out with you—lahk Sue-Ann and me—doesn't have to be gay, don't you know? They just have to be *alive*."

"You've always been a bitch, you know that, Cartwright?" Joey said as he turned away and walked back to his lane.

"Woof woof," Gina called after him. Then, softly, to me, she said, "Come on, baby. Forget about that asshole. And can ah have some of them onion rings?"

And yes, I did love her. More than ever.

But I was watching Joey Bickley as he returned to his own lane. Before he quite got there, Cobra Conlon stopped him for a few words. I couldn't hear what they were saying, of course, but I noticed that both of them glanced in our direction before separating again.

"Okay, Sue-Ann," Gina said. "Let's go back there and knock em down." I had to blink before I realized that she meant the pins and not the men. But Joey had a way of nailing himself into my skull and my third game slipped into the 150s. I started out not being able to hit the pocket for the life of me. To make it worse, I missed some easy spares. It was only when Gina told me to picture each pin as Joey's head that things got better.

Chapter Ten: Cobra

When I woke up the next morning, Gina's side of the bed was cold. Groggily, I remembered that she was meeting with a mortgage representative to arrange the sale of her house. She was really going to move in with me. Forever. Wow. It was one of those moments that come upon you suddenly, like deer leaping gracefully over a barbed-wire fence when you make that first turn down the dirt road towards home.

The radio alarm came on. It was the Beatles singing "I heard the news today, oh boy." I hummed along as I got out of bed and did a few minutes of Pilates, working out the kinks of the previous night's bowling.

I was about to go into the bathroom for my shower when the lyrics of the next song from the radio made me stop in my tracks, my bare toes digging into the softness of the shag carpet.

> *Who wants yesterday's papers?*
> *Who wants yesterday's girl?*
> *Who wants yesterday's papers?*
> *Nobody in the world.*

It wasn't the first time that The Creeper—through his minions Gamma and her brother Smokestack—had used Mick and Company to send me a message. I sat down on the bed and listened until the song was over, hoping I was wrong. I wasn't. The next song was by Tom Paxton, the same sixties folksinger The Creeper had used for his earlier message to me about guns.

> *News, news, ain't that news?*

Ain't that something to see?
News, news, talking bout the news

The fourth song—if the chorus was to be believed—was called "Back in Time." I had heard it before but I wasn't sure where. Possibly it had been a staple on AM radio when I lived in Richmond and had gotten subliminally stuck to an unused part of my brain like bubble gum under a desk. There were no evident references to the news, though, and it wasn't until I padded over to my laptop and Googled a few of the lyrics that I made the connection. The singer was a man named Huey Lewis; his band: The News. Oh, oh.

Then the music stopped and DJ Gamma began her usual squiggly, giggly colloquy. Gamma was, in real life, Krista Torrington, the granddaughter of Ashley Torrington. She and her older brother Smokey, both in their early twenties, were the primary DJs for the "pirate" radio station located in the Torrington compound. The giggly voice was partly an act, because Krista had a good—and pretty—head on her shoulders, but she definitely had her quirky side. In the last few months we had become good friends and she fed the horses when Gina and I were away from the farm overnight.

"Good morning Sue—I mean, good morning everybody. This is Gamma here on N-E-W-S, your pirate radio news station. I hope you have your tea ready because today's news is huge." I could almost picture her taking a deep breath before continuing. "The top story this morning has to do with my name, and what could be more important, hey? Oh, you all know by now that my first name is Gamma, but do you know my last name? No, I didn't think so. Well, it's Globulin. That's right Gamma Globulin, tee hee. I'm an anti-body; get it, a voice injected into your bedrooms and kitchens to get you back up off your asses and onto your horses. Well, back to the music, which this hour is going to be the entire soundtrack of that horrible movie, *Newsies*. I didn't want to play it, but that gigantic rodent we call The Creeper made me. She giggled again and Broadway music began orchestrating.

I had heard enough. I turned off the radio and rushed into the shower.

~ ~ ~

When I arrived at the office I was not surprised to see Gina and Annie huddled in Annie's office, trying to read the front page of a newspaper at the same time. Annie looked up as I walked in.

"Sue-Ann, have you seen this?" she asked.

"Seen what?" I asked. I went into my own office only long enough to stash my purse in my desk drawer. When I got back in Annie's office, she refolded the paper and handed it to me. I saw by its red-white-and-blue banner that it was the latest issue of *The North Florida American* ("Real News for Real Americans"), the right-leaning weekly owned and edited by Wiley "Cobra" Conlon, who also wrote most of its content. The headline was hard to miss, as it took up almost the entire width of the page.

DRUGGED OUT TEEN GOES BERSERK, ESCAPES FROM HARDY
By Wiley Conlon

Officer attacked

On the evening of Sunday, February 27, a fight broke out in the mess hall of the H. A. Hardy Juvenile Center. According to police reports, a boy identified as Carlos Murillo, 16, tried to choke his roommate to death with a belt. When an officer tried to intervene, the Murillo boy managed to grab the officer's container of Mace and spray him full in the eyes before escaping through a window. By the time the officer, who was not named, could wash the chemical out of his eyes and get to a phone, Murillo was gone.

Did he have an accomplice?

According to *The American's* source in the Jasper County Sheriff's office, "I don't see how the boy could have got away without help, like maybe someone waiting in a car outside."

Murillo disappeared completely for a week. Then, on Saturday, March 5, a 911 call for an ambulance was received from the residence of none other than Sue-Ann McKeown, editor of *The Pine Oak Courier*. When the EMTs arrived, they found the missing boy on Miss McKeown's property and rushed him to the hospital with drug-related symptoms. Somehow, though, Murillo mysteriously escaped from the hospital later in the day, shortly after Miss McKeown was seen talking to the boy's doctor. Miss McKeown, who had fifteen minutes of minor fame for going to Iraq, has not returned several phone calls from *The American*. And *The Courier* has been strangely silent on Murillo and his disappearance.

"Moody and uncommunicative"

Murillo, who is now guilty of aggravated assault on a corrections officer, had been confined to Hardy for a variety of drug-related offenses and truancy from the many schools he had been enrolled in. Polly Dunaway, 10th grade math teacher at Hanson's Quarry Middle School, describes Carlos Murillo as "moody" and "uncommunicative." His grades were only fair, and he generally chose not to participate in the school's extracurricular activities.

As of this writing, it is not known if the boy, who is of Mexican descent, is even a legal citizen of this country. His mother, according to the Sheriff's Dept. source, "has no fixed home address and his father is unknown.

Delinquent still at large

Since his disappearance from Jasper County Memorial Hospital, there has been no sign of Carlos Murillo. The public is warned that the boy, who is described as being about 5'8" tall with dark black wavy hair, is dangerous and may by now be armed. Anyone seeing him or knowing the whereabouts of his mother, Sandra Murillo, should immediately call the Sheriff's Office.

Because I was already familiar with Cobra's ultra-conservative flamethrowing, the story was only a bit more shocking than I would have supposed. In fact, the first thing out of my mouth was "I can't believe that Cobra printed Carlos' name."

"I don't know how he even found it out," chipped in Annie. "The boy's a juvenile—not even seventeen!"

But I understood all too well, remembering the smug-looking conversation between Cobra Conlon and Joey Bickley at the Hi-Score the night before. But it was Gina who spoke my words for me. "Joey Bickley," she said.

"That sergeant for the Sheriff's Office? You think the Sheriff authorized him to give out that information?

"I doubt it, but I don't know the sheriff as well as you do, Annie. What do you think?"

"He's the kind of sheriff who lets his men do the work while he makes phone calls, but he generally follows the rules. There are a lot of juveniles in this county. Their parents won't be happy with him if they think he's going to be running the names of their kids in the paper every time they get in trouble."

I looked at Gina, who also knew Sheriff Anderson slightly. She nodded. "Ah agree," she said.

Annie spoke up again. "Is that man actually implying that you were responsible for breaking that kid out of the juvenile center?" Annie asked.

"Seems like it," I replied. As I spoke, I was flipping through the rest of the paper, looking for Cobra's editorial, which he called "An American's Opinion."

I found it. I knew I wouldn't like it. I didn't. I set it flat on Annie's desk so that we could all read it together.

> The doings at the H. A. Hardy Juvenile Center (See *Front Page Story*) is just another reflection of our Muslim President's long-range goal of letting illegal immigrants have

a free ride on the tax money of hard-working Americans.

The escape of the juvenile Carlos Murillo should never have happened because illegal immigrants like him and his mother *should never have been let into this country in the first place*. And why place someone in a taxpayer supported halfway house when he could have been just sent back to his own country instead?

And what will be next? Legalized gay marriage? That's what will happen if Obama gets his way. It's already gotten to the point where real, God-approved marriages between a man and a woman are declining. Some of our unmarried women are choosing lifestyles that hurt America as a whole. Look no farther than *Pine Oak Courier* editor Sue-Ann McKeown, who may have been involved in the mysterious disappearance of the Mexican juvenile mentioned above. A single woman. And what about *The Courier's* "office manager" Ginette Cartwright? Another single woman.

It is up to all of us as Real Americans to stem this tide of promiscuousness and get back to the homey values we all prize so highly . . .

The editorial went on to talk about other anti-American concerns like health care and voter fraud, but I had read enough.

Evidently, Annie had too. "Does *anybody* understand what he's trying to say?" she asked, seemingly flummoxed. She looked at the paper again. "He's not an idiot . . . well, he *is* an idiot, but he's not a stupid one, but how does he get from . . . He seems to think that it's Obama's fault that the boy escaped from Hardy. But what does that have to do with gay marriage? And why did he mention your name, Sue-Ann? And yours, too, Ginette? What does any of this have to do with you? I mean, I'm single, too. So is Betty, and we all work here." She looked helplessly from me to Gina. And then back again. And then back to Gina. Annie must have seen something that told a story to a good reporter—was it my expression? was it the way Gina was looking at me or the way our bodies seem to have of leaning toward each other?—because it caused the smile to drop from her face like a limb snapping off a pecan tree.

"Oh my GOD," she exclaimed.

Neither Gina nor I spoke.

"But you *can't* be," Annie almost wailed. "I mean, you were Mr. Dent's girlfriend," she said to Gina. "I heard the two of you were even thinking about getting married!"

"We didn't, though," said Gina softly.

"And you," Annie cried," turning her wide eyes in my direction. "You were—"

I cut her off. "Annie, none of that matters. What we did in the past is over."

"But the two of you don't even *like* each other!" she nearly screamed.

"That mighta been true once," Gina said. "But not any more."

Gina seemed to be taking Annie's discovery better than I was. I was so upset that I couldn't speak. Gina and I had been in love for almost a year now and, except for Joey Bickley's suspicions, had managed to keep that love a secret. Now the vituperous, small-minded editor of a dinky rag had seemingly brought everything down on top of us. Or had he?

"Annie," I began. "Gina and I are a couple. It's a fact. Is that going to . . . ?"

"Wow!" came a voice from the doorway, making the three of us jump. 'That is *so cool!*"

"Becky!" exclaimed Annie. I turned around and saw Becky Colley, dressed in who-knows-what with red, high-topped sneakers. She lounged in the doorway like she was born there.

"I mean," she continued, "it's kind of disgusting when you really think about it, but still cool."

"Fuck," I said. "Is there anybody else in here? Fox news, maybe?"

"Let's all sit down somewhere," Gina suggested. "Sue-Ann, your office is the biggest. Becky, get one of those chairs."

It was an intelligent suggestion. By going into my office, it put me behind the desk, reminding everyone that I was in charge. After Gina closed the door and the three women sat down, I looked straight at Annie, who seemed to have trouble meeting my gaze.

"Annie," I began. "And you too, Becky. We've just told you something about ourselves that almost no one else knows. We don't have the right to tell you to keep it a secret, but I'm going to ask you anyway. This is a small town, it's not a progressive town, and it's a town that can eat you. Cobra Conlon has absolutely nothing to go on. The only reason he printed that story was because Joey Bickley told him to."

"But if Bickley knows—" began Annie, but I cut her off again.

"Joey *doesn't* know," I told her firmly. "He only *suspects* because of something that someone told him."

"Cletus Donnelly saw us together once and told Joey," explained Gina.

"Cle—But he was a certified nut case," said Annie. "Nobody would have believed him even if he hadn't killed himself."

"Exactly. Joey just has it in for us for other reasons."

"So he would actually try to ruin your lives just because, what, you managed to capture Donnelly when he couldn't?"

"Something like that," I said. "But you made the point I was going to make. If people started believing that Gina and I are a couple, it might really ruin things for us. And for the paper. With some people's cockeyed ideas about sexuality, there would be a lot of people that wouldn't give us the stories we need, that wouldn't advertise, that wouldn't buy the paper."

Although I was looking at and talking to Annie, it was Becky that spoke up. "Can I at least tell Jack?" she said.

"No, Becky. Not even Jack." Jack Stafford was a photographer I met when I worked at *The Times-Dispatch* in Richmond. He had also been my live-in boyfriend for seven years. He had never understood our breakup, which had happened months before Gina and I had started seeing each other. On a failed relationship-mending expedition to Pine Oak the year before, he had met Becky and become her mentor in photography. He had also won her heart, although as in most things, Jack had no clue about this.

"You're right, though. Jack should know, but it should be me that tells him."

Becky pouted a little, but nodded.

I looked at my bureau chief. "Annie?"

"I promise," she said. "But what if people find out anyway?"

"We'll worry about that if it happens," I said

"We'll worry about it now," Gina spoke up. "Sue-Ann and ah both know that we'd have to quit. We'd probly have to move somewhere else. You'd be first in lahn get her job as editor. Ah think we need to get that out in the open."

Annie sat up straight in her chair. "But Ginette, you know I'd never . . . but maybe you don't. I applied for this job because I needed to get away from my divorce, that's true, but I had interviews in half a dozen places. The reason I chose *The Courier* was because I heard that Sue-Ann worked here. I read every one of her stories from Baghdad and wondered how someone could possibly do what she was doing. And every day that I work here I learn something new. Sure, I'd like to edit someday, what reporter wouldn't eventually, but not while I can still have Sue-Ann as a teacher."

It was a pretty long speech for Annie, and I was incredibly touched. I felt that my days in Baghdad had been worthlessly spent in drunken fear, but evidently I had managed to reach one or two people despite that.

"You're still on board then?" I asked.

"Of course."

"Becky?"

"Aye aye, Captain."

"But what are we going to do about *The American?*" Annie asked. "What kind of an editorial could we—"

"We're going to do absolutely nothing," I said.

"Nothing? But . . ."

Cobra is just testing out Joey's theory," I told him. "He actually hasn't done anything damaging, and he can't without proof. He has made some strong insinuations, true, but he's waiting for some kind of a response before he strikes again. And we're not gong to give it to him. You know what we're gong to do instead? We're going to get busy and write some good stories for *The Courier*—

including the story of Carlos Murillo. But it's going to be a lot different from what Cobra Conlon's conception of that story might be."

Just then there was a knock on my door, which opened just enough for Mark Patterson to shove his face inside. "Sorry, didn't know you were having a meeting. But have you seen this?" and he dangled a copy of *The North Florida American* out in front of him.

Annie got up from her chair and brushed past him, saying, "Don't pay any attention to that bullshit."

Becky got up, too, and tossed her purpled locks at him. "You actually *buy* that thing?" she asked.

"Um, no, but somebody—"

"Get a life, man," she told him.

Gina and I looked at each other and smiled.

Chapter Eleven: Warnings

It was mild enough that evening to sit out in the barnyard, and that was just what I was doing; lounging back with a fat fantasy novel, bending back the spine so I could read the words in the gutters and not caring that Benny would give me less in trade for it when I brought it back in. Gina was sitting nearby, but not with a book. Like a few other people I knew—including my former boyfriend Jack—she opened a book only rarely. Instead, she was making a rough sketch of the building she planned to construct on the acre of ground I was selling her—a combination music studio and lodge. She planned for it to be a place where she could play and record music and have a place to sleep and eat if the recording sessions went on into the wee hours, and, I silently worried, if she ever got tired of being with me. I didn't like that aspect of it much, but I was glad she was busy with a project.

Just behind the barn, I heard the shrill chatter of a woodpecker. Farther off, mourning doves called to each other plaintively. Early March is when the leaves of the live oaks begin to fall. In a day or so, I expected to see massive leaf storms raining down like oval confetti from a Fall parade. Fast forward a couple of weeks and the leaves would be joined by catkins, and visible pollen would fall like powder in the heavy breeze. The end of March would bring rainstorms whose rivulets would cut unwanted paths through the barnyard and encroach into the stalls where our three horses would stoically wait out the storm despite the puddles that would form under their hooves. Luckily, the temps would still be enough to keep away the flies and gnats that gathered around the urine and manure in warmer weather.

"Whah do you read those things, Sue-Ann?" Gina asked. I looked up from my book, where shimmering godlike beings cavorted with magic, and saw her peering at me over her sketch.

It was a tough question. I was the beneficiary of an excellent liberal arts education. I had studied Tolstoy and Proust and Austen and Wharton. I knew that the type of books I generally read were kind of crappy, but they kept me entertained. The fact that I had picked up the habit from another ex-boyfriend was something I wasn't keen to discuss with Gina. Still, Gina was my girlfriend and deserved an answer. But before I could think up a convincing response, she continued.

"Ah, mean, how does it happen that in every one of those books, the hero is a princess or a king that nobody knows about? And whoever it is, they always seem to have somethin to do with savin the entire world?"

I smiled. "How would you know?" I asked.

"Ah trah to be interested in things you're interested in," she answered. "So maybe ah skimmed through one or two when ah was in Texas."

I riffled through the pages, then lay the book down on the grass beside my chair. I picked up my glass of wine and took a sip. She was right. The books I read were rarely about what people saw through their back doors. They weren't content with their heroes helping their neighbors or making their communities a better place; they were about good and evil and about saving the entire world from immanent destruction.

"We all wish we had something we could do to save the world, Gina," I said. "But maybe you're right. Maybe we should check out something like Goodreads and get some recommendations. I don't know who's writing what these days."

"Maybe you can fahnd some good mysteries," she said.

Mysteries? I had read Tami Hoag's *Dark Horse* and kind of enjoyed it. Hoag was an accomplished equestrian and her portrait of the dressage world was off-puttingly realistic. But I had trouble with even that. "I didn't know you were interested in mysteries," I told her.

"Ah've read a few here and there," she said. "Mostly there."

"The thing about mysteries," I began, "is that somebody always gets murdered. You've been a lot of places. Do you know anyone who's ever been murdered?"

"No, but . . . well, what about the people in those mysteries *you've* had to clear up?"

"Pauley Hughes got kicked in the head by a horse," I said. "And Cletus Donnelly killed himself. There are no murderers skulking around and leaving clues for some idiot busybody detective. That's just not the way things are. Even when I lived in Richmond, the only people who got murdered were street-corner drug dealers. If everybody who gets killed in mysteries got killed in real life, there wouldn't be anyone left to read about them."

I didn't mention Iraq, where it seemed like everyone was a murderer. Even me. My ignorant insistence on covering a story within one of the hot zones of Baghdad had caused a young soldier to lose his life. I would never forget the boy they called Doof, who was a shy, happy-go-lucky private just trying to survive. His death while helping to defend my convoy from sniper fire was a rock in my gut that would remain there for the rest of my life. My interest in fantasy novels had started right after I got back from Iraq. Reading them kept me stupid and content—a redneck's version of an ideal woman. Yes, it was time to get on to something else. As I was refilling my wineglass, my cell phone buzzed.

"Miz McKeown," came a female voice that I didn't quite recognize. I heard rapid breathing, then "It's Cori Glenn. I . . . I think someone's trying to kill me!"

"Cori. What . . ." Gina was watching my conversation and her eyes widened when she heard my tone of voice.

"I need someone to come get me."

"I'll come," I said hurriedly. "Where are you? What happened? Are you hurt?"

"I'm at a place called Eat Now. It's—"

"I know where it is, Cori. Sit tight. I'll be there as fast as I can."

I snapped the phone shut. "Come on," I told Gina, getting up from my chair so quickly that I spilled the rest of my wine all over *Elantris*, by Brandon Sanderson. "Cori's in trouble."

"Ah heard, but what happened?"

"She wouldn't say. But we've got to go pick her up at Eat Now."

"Um, Sue-Ann," Gina began. She had stood up, but not yet gotten it in gear.

I stopped and looked at her, puzzled. "What?" Then I realized. "Oh. That's right. We're lovers, but it's a secret. God *damn* it!" But she was right. Working together was natural. Even being on the same bowling team wasn't scrutinized except by people like Joey Bickley. But spending time at each other's houses or showing up places together at strange times was different.

"I'll be back as soon as I can," I said.

"Ah'll feed the horses," she told me. "And call me if you need me."

"Okay." I gave her a hurried peck on the lips, and rushed inside for my purse and keys.

~ ~ ~

Eat Now: Home of Food wasn't the fanciest place in Forester, but the food was cheap and, for the most part, digestible. Beer and wine flowed copiously and the place was generally crowded with the under-40 set, of which I was soon to lose my standing. The place consisted of two rooms and an outside deck. The first room was both a bar and casual dining area, the second was reserved for diners who wanted a more quiet meal. The deck, made mostly of two-by-sixes, held another half dozen tables and was usually clouded by cigarette smoke.

I spotted Cori in the first room, sitting in a corner table looking haggard and disheveled, a lonely coffee cup in front of her. Oddly, she was sitting with Donny Brasswell, who happened to be one of my ex-boyfriends—the one that had turned me on to reading fantasy novels. I was so taken aback at seeing the two of them together that I stopped in my tracks. At that moment, Cori looked up and saw me. She sprang up and ran across the room to where I was standing. Her hair looked like she had been running a hand through it repeatedly, but it must have been her right hand because she held her left gingerly against her body. And even in the dim light I could see a bruise on her temple.

"Miz McKeown," she began, but that was all she could get out before bursting into tears. I put my arm around her and hugged her.

"Cori, what happened?" I asked, but all she could do was sob into my shoulder.

"Having a little lover's spat, *Miz* McKeown?" The voice was behind me, but I knew who it was before I even turned around. Sgt. Joey Bickley had chosen this moment to walk in the restaurant in a newly pressed white-and-tan uniform.

"Get out of here, Joey," I told him. "This is not the time."

"Fact is, I'm here on business," he said. "Someone called me about a hit and run and there's a car outside that looks like it might have been involved. You wouldn't know anything about that, would you?" Joey was deliberately ignoring Cori, who had unburied herself from my shoulder and was wiping her eyes.

"S-someone ran me off the road!" she began. "If I hadn't been wearing—"

"And just who are you?" Joey asked sourly. "The guy that reported the hit and run was a man."

"It was me, Joey," I looked around again and saw that Donny had gotten up from the table and joined us. "Didn't Tequesta tell you?" Donny was dressed in his Harrison Towing Company shirt and was, as usual, begrimed with the dusty and greasy reminders of a hard day's work. As boyfriend and girlfriend, we just didn't work the way we should have but had parted as amicably as is possible, I think, in a small town where everyone knows just about everything about everyone else and doesn't hesitate to gossip about it. He was now married to one of my high school classmates, who we called Linda C, and, rumor had it the two were fixing to become proud parents. It was good seeing him; in fact, I had never been happier to see him, especially when he took charge of the situation and led us all back to the table he and Cori had been sitting at when I arrived.

"Miz Glenn called me to come tow her in to the shop," Donnie was explaining. "When she told me what happened, I called Tequesta."

He courteously pulled out Cori's chair for her, then sat down beside her. I sat on her other side while Joey took the remaining chair across the table. To his credit, he didn't give me any more snide looks, just took out a notebook and ballpoint pen and looked up at her.

"All right," he began tonelessly. "Tell me what *did* happen."

Cori picked up her coffee cup with trembling hands, then put it down again, as if she didn't trust her nerves enough to get it all the way up to her mouth.

"I . . . I went out to that boys' detention home—"

"You were at Hardy?" Joey interrupted. "What were you doing there?" He shot an angry look at me, so I answered for her.

"She's the newest reporter at *The Courier*," I told him. "I assigned her the job of getting an interview with someone at Hardy."

"You what?" He put down his pen and his angry look turned into a glare.

"We're trying to find out more about the boy that disappeared," I told him.

"Didn't I fucking warn you to—"

"*Warn* me?" I asked hotly.

"Warn her about what, Joey?" asked Donny.

"You butt out of this Brasswell," Joey spat. "And my name is Sergeant Bickley. Everybody knows you used to play footsie with Miz Editor here."

Donny looked at him evenly. "Be careful, Sergeant," he said.

"Bullshit!" I said loudly. "I'm taking Cori to the hospital, then we'll call Sheriff Anderson and tell him in person."

"No, Miz McKeown. I'm all right. Just a couple of bruises."

Joey, too, seemed to realize that he had gone too far. He picked up his pen again, turned it around in his fingers a couple of times, then looked at Cori.

"Go ahead and tell me what happened," he said.

"Okay. Like I said, I went out to the detention center. When I knocked on the door, some officer-looking guy—one of the guys they call Watchers—

opened it and asked me what I wanted. I told him my name said I wanted to speak to the director. He said that the director was busy and I said I'd wait. He asked me what I wanted to see the director about and I told him I wanted to talk about the escape. But he told me that there hadn't been any escape and if there had been it was none of my fucking business and that I should leave."

Cori managed to pick up her coffee cup and take a sip. "Maybe I would have if he hadn't been such an asshole, but I didn't. I told him I was from *The Courier* and that I needed to ask the director some serious questions about how the boys were treated and what kind of punishments they got when they got out of hand. I said I'd wait all day if I had to and that it wouldn't look too good if I wrote something for the paper and had to say that the Hardy Center was uncooperative. The guy slammed the door in my face and I heard him stomping away in his thick boots. What he forgot was to lock the door, so I pushed it open a foot or so and looked inside. I saw the guy walk down a short hall, knock on a door, and speak to somebody inside. I couldn't hear what he said, but I heard the reply, because it was loud."

Cori looked up and caught my eye and held it. "The man inside shouted. 'All we need around here is another god damned reporter snooping around our business. It was bad enough the last time. Get rid of her." The officer said something else—maybe he was whispering, I don't know. Whatever it was caused the director to almost knock over the Watcher when he came out of that office and headed straight for the door like he was going to bulldoze right through it. I closed the door, but I don't think I was fast enough. He saw me looking. I stepped back a few steps before he opened the door and stood in the doorway like a gigantic prick. He was older than I thought he'd be—late sixties at least. He wore small round glasses and his beard looked like pubic hair.

Now Cori shifted her gaze to Joey, who was listening carefully—if grudgingly—and writing an occasional sentence in his notebook. "He just stood there, looking at me like I'd just thrown away his prize stack of porno magazines. Then he told me to get off the property before he called the sheriff. I tried to ask him a question, but he just slammed the door. I figured my visit was kind of a failure, so I walked back to my car, trying to figure out what I was going to tell Miz McKeown when I got back to the office."

She stopped and took a deep breath. Before she could continue, however, Joey burst in, "What does all that have to do with anything? Anyway, you were trespassing on private property and he had every right to tell you to leave."

"Yeah? Well maybe so, but when I was driving back home, I took a shortcut down 211. It would take me right into Forester where I had a straight shot back to Pine Oak. But 211 is kind of lonely and all of a sudden this car came up behind me and before I knew it, it was right beside me. Instead of just passing me, it started swerving toward me. I had to swerve too so I wouldn't get crashed into. I hit the brakes hoping that the other car would get in front of me. But my tires went off the road and I lost control. I spun out and hit a tree."

"Did he actually bump you?" I asked.

"I'm sure he did, Miz McKeown, and hard, too. But everything went so fast."

"Did you get the license number?" asked Joey Bickley blandly.

Cori shook her head. "I—I think I blacked out for a while. I hit my head against something—the window, I think. When I woke up, the other car was gone."

"Why didn't you call the sheriff right then?" Joey asked.

"I don't have a cell phone. I thought I'd be stranded out there all night, or that I'd have to hitchhike back, but my car started. It was rough going, but I managed to get into Forester and pull into this parking lot. I asked the lady at the counter to call a tow truck, but this guy was already here." She nodded at Donny "He's been taking care of me. He used his cell phone to call the sheriff and then let me borrow it to call Miz McKeown."

"That was sweet of him," said Joey, 'but let's get back to the accident. Do you remember the make or model of the vehicle that allegedly ran you off the road."

"Allegedly?" I burst out, but Joey interrupted as if I hadn't even been there.

"Ford F-150, Chevy Silverado, Toyota Tacoma, red, green, that type of thing."

Cori just shook her head. "It was light," she said. "And it wasn't a truck, it was a car."

"That narrows it down," said Joey sardonically. He wrote a few more words in his notebook, mumbling as he wrote. "Light color. Not a truck. Hmm."

"I noticed the driver, though," Cori told him.

"Yeah? Was it a man or a woman?"

"A man, I think."

"What do you mean you *think*?" Joey asked in exasperation. "You just said you saw the driver."

"Whoever it was was wearing a mask," she said.

Joey dropped his pen. "Are you sure?" he asked.

"He was right beside me. The only thing I saw when I looked over was his head; his eyes, really, because the mask was one of those handkerchiefs people wear around their necks. Like in the old west."

I saw Joey Bickley mumble the word "Shit" under his breath.

"It was the same kind of handkerchief that they make those boys out at the detention center wear," Cori continued. "I've been there before and I've seen em. They all supposed to look like boy scouts or somethin."

"Fuck," Joey mumbled.

I was just about to ask him if he was going to write those words down when his cell phone rang. He picked it up, grunted, and listened. Then he snapped it shut and banged his fist on the table so hard that Cori's empty coffee cup; turned over. Then he looked at me. "That was Officer Dollar," he told me. "Someone just drove past *The Courier* office and threw a brick through your window."

Chapter Twelve: The Morgue

I faked a trip to the Ladies' and called Gina on my cell. I briefly told her what had transpired and asked her to drive in to the office and see about the damage. Then I drove Cori to the hospital where a doctor I didn't know found that she had suffered a mild concussion and a sprained wrist.

Donny Brasswell towed Cori's car in to Harrison's and Joey Bickley drove back to his office, scowling. He had listened to the rest of Cori's story and was strangely perturbed—not at me, as would have been usual—but at the sequence of events. I tried to attribute that to the fact that he would have preferred not to have any real work to do, but that would not have been accurate. When Joey wasn't harassing women and making an ass of himself socially, he was a dedicated and effective police officer.

Cori sat silently in my cluttered passenger seat as I drove her home from the hospital. I could tell that she was mostly in shock—and pain, too, because once the adrenalin had worn off, she was feeling her injuries. But as I made the final turn onto the street where her mother lived—and where she kept Cori's children when Cori was at work—she turned in my direction and began to speak.

"I lied to you earlier, Miz McKeown," she said.

"I'm Sue-Ann," I told her.

"I still lied," she said, avoiding using my first name. "I pretended not to know nothing about Hardy. But I have a brother."

"A brother?" I waited for her response, but instead she just looked away again, as if she had said something she regretted.

"It ain't nothin."

When she didn't say anything else, I decided to gently prod her a little. "You don't have to tell me if you don't want to," I said. "But I'm very definitely interested."

She cradled her sprained wrist with her good hand, and her body straightened into a resolve. "Okay, then," she began, looking back at me. "I'm not ashamed of nothing. It was years ago. I was just starting college. Tywann was only about 15. He had stopped goin to school and was all the time hangin out in Forester. He got into this gang. They'd go to local football games and walk under the stands so they could steal wallets out of people's pants. Then they'd run. He thought it was a hoot. But, you know, how much money could they steal from high school kids, huh?" She answered her own question. "Not much."

She stopped and looked out the window and I could see that she was blinking back tears. I waited for her to continue.

"And one night they caught him. Of course, what did he spect? Only him, the youngest. The others ran and left him there, but he never ratted on them. He was too young to go to real prison, so they sent him to Hardy." She stopped and pointed to a weedy lot containing a mobile home and an ancient Ford truck. "Right there," she said. "That's where my mama lives."

I pulled into the yard and turned off the engine.

"So how was it for him at Hardy?" I asked.

"It was bad. Those kids in Hardy, some of em, they just no good. Sposed to be a school or something, but ain't no school there, just boys teachin other boys about how to make shanks or pick locks or score drugs or how to have, you know, boy sex. The bigger boys, they'd pick on Tywann, take the little goodies mama'd send him once in a blue moon. Tywann didn't like it there, wanted to come home, but my mama was dealin with her own shit; she had a crappy job in a laundry, bad luck with men, and my little sister was all the time giving her trouble. Wasn't nothin she could do for Tywann."

"So one night Tywann just has enough. He'd just got beat up again for nothin by two bullies and he knew that it was goin to happen again, over and over. So he waits until it's real late, then gets the lock off his locker and smashes those two hoods in the head with it while they're sleepin. After he got beat up again real good by the control freaks that run the place, he got tried as an adult and got 20 years in state prison for aggravated assault. He's there now."

"I'm sorry, Cori," I said gently. "I had no idea. I'll give somebody else the Hardy assignment."

Cori spun around in her seat, rustling several Styrofoam cups at her feet, and leaned toward me as much as she could with her seat belt on. "You can't!" she said with emotion. "If there's something to be found out about that awful place, then I want to be the one to find it."

I gave that some thought. "Do you think that director might have recognized you?"

"Naw. I only went there a couple times and I never saw that director. And me and my brother, we got different last names."

"Okay then," I said. Just then the door of the trailer was flung open and two small children came out a few steps and looked in the direction of the car. "Look, we'll talk about it on Monday."

"But tomorrow's—"

"Thursday staff meeting, right, but you've got to take it easy for a couple of days or you're not going to be any good to anybody. Don't worry; I won't decide anything until Monday. There's another staff meeting then."

By now, the two youngsters had recognized their mother in the passenger seat of the car and had come running up to her window. Cori smiled and waved at them. Then she reached over with her right hand and unfastened her seat belt, grimacing as she did so. Then she opened the door and gave me a last look. "Thanks, Miz McKeown,"

~ ~ ~

Back at *The Courier*, Gina, who had dressed hurriedly in jeans, sandals, and a t-shirt, was gingerly picking up glass shards from the carpet and putting them in a large trash receptacle. Sheriff's Deputy Bill Dollar was pulling out the remaining jagged edges from the window frame with a pair of pliers. Gina nodded at me when I walked in. "How's Cori?" she asked.

"Pretty banged up," I answered. "I told her to stay home until Monday." I looked at Officer Dollar—those of us who had gone to school with him sometimes called him Dilly—and said, "Thanks for staying with Gina. And it's nice to see you. You haven't been around for a while."

He smiled as he dropped the last of the shards from the frame into the trash can. "It's been pretty quiet around here lately," he said. "Until tonight."

"Who did it, do you know?" I asked, knowing that he didn't.

He walked over to the reception desk and picked up a brick and a piece of paper. He held out the paper. "This was tied to the brick," he said.

I took it from him and read the ragged scrawl. BACK OFF BITCH. The brick was just a common brick—the kind three fourths of the houses in Pine Oak were fronted with.

"Ah can't figure out who it's addressed to, me or you," quipped Gina. She had gotten up the last of the glass and was plugging in the vacuum cleaner to get any residue she couldn't see. When she was finished and Dilly was satisfied that the window frame was safe and ready to be reglazed, I asked them both to come in to my office.

I addressed Dilly first. "Listen, Billy," I began. "I know Sergeant Bickley outranks you, but you're our friend. I think we're going to need your help on this."

"You've never led me wrong before," he said. "But what's the sergeant have to do with anything?"

"It's just a hunch. Joey seems to be way too interested in our investigation of the Hardy Center. It's like we've stirred up some kind of hornet's nest. That's what newspapers are supposed to do, but this is kind of unexpected. All I was trying to do was discover a little more about the boy Clarence and I found out in my pasture. What we're finding out—"

"What *are* we fahndin out, Sue-Ann?" Gina interrupted.

"Right. Okay. There were a couple of things that Cori said that make me think there's more to this than just an escape from a detention center."

"Lahk what?"

"Cori heard the director say that they didn't need to be bothered *again*. That it was bad enough the *last time*. What's this about 'again'? What 'last time'?"

I looked at Gina for an answer. "Don't know," she said.

"I know we haven't done any stories about Hardy since I've been here," I continued. "So if something happened, it must have happened more than a couple of years ago." I looked at Dilly. He shrugged.

"I've been with the sheriff's department for ten years next week," said Dilly. "And I don't remember anything major."

I looked up. "Major?" I asked.

"You know, nothing except maybe a few complaints from parents about their boys not getting enough to eat, or maybe getting a little bruise or two. But Hardy's not the Ramada Inn, right? They do a lot of sports there—baseball, football, boxing. Every kid in the world gets scraped up some."

He was right, of course. But what if there was more to it? What if Hardy had a history of abusing the boys in its care? I looked at him seriously. "Do you think you could get me the names of a couple of the people that called in complaints? There's probably a log, right?

"Sure, but—"

"And Billy, you can't let Joey see what you're doing. Nothing is worth you getting into trouble over."

"I can take care of myself," he said stoutly. I wasn't so sure. Although Dilly had been with the Sheriff's Department longer than Joey had, he was still a deputy while Joey had made sergeant. There were probably a lot of reasons for that. Joey was very gung-ho for one thing, while Dilly put his family first and his job second. For another—

Gina broke into my thoughts. "You said there were a *couple* of things," she said. "What's the other?"

"Okay, number two. Joey didn't have any trouble believing that someone from Hardy had run Cori off the road. Why not? I mean, let's face it, it's pretty improbable that someone from a piss-ant correctional facility would try to kill someone just for showing up at their front door. Usually Joey would just assume that I—or anybody I was friends with—was either lying or crazy. But when Joey left Eat Now, he looked like he was going straight out and bite somebody's head off—and I don't mean figuratively. What's up with that?"

"He knows more than he's sayin," said Gina. "Do you think any of this has to do with that editorial in *The American*?"

"I don't know. Probably not, but we've got to consider it a possibility. Another possibility is that Hardy is in some way connected with getting those boys the bath salt drugs that Carlos Murillo was snorting."

"Ah don't lahk either one of those possibilities," Gina said.

"Neither do I."

"So what can we do?" Dilly asked.

"I think the first thing we need to do is check out the morgue," I said.

"The morgue?" Dilly asked. "What morgue? Who died?"

"No one," I answered. "At least not yet. And we need to keep it that way. I'm talking about *The Courier*'s morgue.

"Huh?"

"A morgue is a room where newspapers keep back issues and old files," I explained.

"Shoot, Sue-Ann," said Gina. "No one's been keeping up with all that since way before Cal left."

"I know," I said. Cal Dent, the former editor, had assigned Betty Dickson to be in charge of the morgue. She had never liked doing it, and since I had come on board she had let it go completely, giving me the excuse that she had too many other responsibilities with the new computer equipment. Giving the place a once-over had been on my back burner. Until now.

"Is there anything I can help with?" asked Dilly.

"Nothing right now, Billy," I told him. "Looking through that mess is going to take weeks. Thanks for helping with the glass, though."

"What about the window?" he asked. "Can we get somebody to put some plywood or something over it for the night?"

I had already thought of that. "I'm going to stay here tonight," I said. "I have a lot of work to catch up on. I'll call the glass company first thing in the morning."

"You sure?"

"Yeah." I saw the concern on his face and added, "Don't worry, I have a bow and some arrows in the truck."

"Better give me your keys and ah'll get em," Gina offered.

After the archery tackle had been stashed in my office and Dilly had gone, I opened the door of the morgue, turned on the lights, and let out a grunt that described what I saw more accurately than words could have.

The morgue is simply newspaper jargon for a place where old issues of a newspaper are stored. When I worked for *The Richmond Times-Dispatch*, I had a few dealings with the woman responsible for keeping these old files and knowing what was in them. It was her full-time job. At *The Courier*, I barely had the money to keep enough reporters; hiring someone to keep the morgue seemed like an idea whose day would never come. In fact, I was pretty sure I knew as much as anyone about our own morgue, which was a small, very dusty room with thick shelves holding decades of bound and unbound back issues of *The Courier*. A line of wide metal filing cabinets right out of the Fifties lined one wall. A long wooden table and two chairs accommodated anyone wanting to see the files. At some point a former editor had been fastidious about sending old issues of *The Courier* to the bindery, but that was way before my time. My predecessor had been too busy divorcing his wife and bedding Gina to show any personal interest in the morgue. Coupled with Betty's indifference, it had devolved into woeful chaos.

Interest in tracing one's family history had come late to white, middle-class Pine Oak, but in the last couple of years it had become quite the fad. All kinds of people— from spic-and-span offices to clay-dusty farms—had invaded the office asking to see that old picture of grandpa or to copy a wedding announcement from someone's 1980 nuptials. I had tried to dutifully dig out what they wanted, but often I had to just leave the seekers in the room with the shelves of material. Until recently, our copy machine had been ancient and not really up to the task. Lately, though, with the advent of smartphones and digital cameras, *Courier* visitors just snapped their own photos of the requested articles and emailed them home.

But with everything else I had to do, the morgue had become a jumble of paper waiting to be placed in some kind of order.

I stepped in the room and looked around. Gina came in behind me and began cleaning up what the last dozen or so family historians had left strewn around.

"How are we ever going to straighten this place out?" I asked hopelessly. Yet even as I spoke, I had visions of somehow putting all old issues of *The Courier* on microfiche or even scanning them in to searchable computer files.

"We're not," Gina said simply, lifting a huge stack of back issues from the table and setting them on the floor. When I looked a question at her, she continued, "Bobby will do it."

"Bobby?"

"Bobby DuPre."

"Right." When I had interviewed Bobby for the receptionist job, his intelligence, confidence, and well-spoken manner had pushed him to the top of the heap of applicants. I remembered now that in a former life he had worked in libraries and bookstores. Even around the office he was always looking for something to do. If I didn't assign him the morgue, I was afraid he would start writing stories or taking pictures.

"What ah need to know first, Sue-Ann, is what we're lookin for."

"A story about something that happened at Hardy," I responded. "Any kind of scandal or complaint. Letters to the editor. Police reports. But it'll take forever to sort this stuff out enough for us to even look through it in any kind of order."

"Maybe we don't need to," she said.

"What are you thinking?" I asked.

"Hold on a minute and ah'll tell you." She walked out of the room and came back with a roll of paper towels. She began wiping off the now-clear table. I sat down in one of the chairs waiting for her to finish.

"What were you going to tell me?" I asked.

She looked up at me as if she had just remembered I was there. Then she smiled a secret smile. "Ah've got the key," she said.

"What key?"

She reached into her jeans pocket and extracted a small key on a simple round ring. "This one," she said.

"Looks like a filing cabinet key."

"Raht. Cal gave me this way back when so that Mama and Papa Kinderhook didn't steal all our old photos and stuff."

I had seen the filing cabinets, of course, but never had any desire to go through what I imagined were years of old paperwork: invoices, correspondence, and what not. In fact, I had been relieved to find the cabinets locked and secure, not only from messy guests, but from me. Now I felt ashamed that I could have become editor-in-chief of a newspaper without having even glanced into the cabinets.

"What's in em?" I asked.

"Wait'll you see," she answered.

"Gimmie," I said.

"Not yet," she said, again with that secretive smile.

"What?" I said.

"Sue-Ann," she began. "Ah don't know if it's the adrenalin of all this danger we maht be in, or what." She pushed closed the door of the morgue and pulled me from the chair. "But ah'm as hot as a fire in a stove." She pushed me gently down onto the table, kissing me furiously as she fumbled with the buttons of my blouse.

I found that my own fire was burning kind of fiercely too, and in only a few minutes we were both panting and sated, half naked in the close room. It was the kind of love you make on the fly, like James Taylor and Carly Simon in the bathroom in the midst of a high-brow party.

But quickies are good, too, like small pieces of the finest chocolate. "Wow," I said, hunting for my bra amidst the newspapers and cardboard boxes. "I've never made love in a morgue before." I smiled and looked at Gina expectantly, but she pretended to be concentrating on stepping into her jeans. "Gina!" I cried. "You didn't!"

"Maybe yes and maybe no," she said, zipping up the jeans.

I thought I had gotten over my jealousy of Gina's relationship with Cal Dent, but guess what? Cal was gone now, had another girlfriend now, and Gina was living with me. Still, the idea of . . .

"C'mon," she said holding out the key. "Let's take a peek."

The key slid in, the lock popped out, and Gina pulled the first drawer open with a metallic creak. Inside were file folders, each labeled in thick, neat script, with a purple fountain pen: Abercrombie, Allen, Anderson, Arnold—and each folder contained browning and fading newspaper clippings about the person whose folder it was.

A second cabinet revealed a treasure trove of photographs and contact sheets.

"Looks lahk we hit the jackpot," Gina told me, smoothing a few strands of hair that had somehow gotten separated from her austere ponytail. "But what name are we looking for?"

"How about Hardy?" I suggested. "If anyone ever did a story about the place it would probably be filed there." I gave her hair a little muss up.

"Quit, Sue-Ann." Going back to the drawer of the first cabinet, she walked her fingers through the folders until she found what she was looking for and pulled it out. The name, in purple pen, was written simply as Hardy, H. A.

"You were raht, Sue-Ann," she said. "But it looks lahk somebody got here before us." She opened folder. "It's empty."

It was disappointing to the max. Everything was going so well, so smoothly, and now this. But how could anyone have gotten into filing cabinets that had been locked for years? I took the folder from her. "Wait a minute," I said. "Look at this." Below the word Hardy, visible only when the folder was open, were two more words, written in the same hand and with the same purple pen. It said, "Formerly Sadberry."

"Sadberry," she said softly, "What a name. But it seems lahk I've heard it somewhere before."

It did have a vaguely familiar ring to it, but if I had heard the name, it was many years before. I opened the next drawer of the filing cabinet and found what I was looking for right at the front. "Sadberry Orphanage." And it was by no means empty.

I took the folder to the table and opened the cover.

"You found it, Sue-Ann," Gina said excitedly over my shoulder. What looked like a front-page story stared back at us. It read, SUICIDE AT SADBERRY.

Chapter Thirteen: Eyewitness

Suicide at Sadberry
By Bill Rumsford
Editor in Chief

A grisly sight greeted Sheriff's Department deputies Saturday evening when they answered a frantic 911 call from Sadberry Orphanage in Forester.

Upon their arrival, they found Allen Tilley, 16, in the closet of his bedroom, one end of his Sadberry Orphanage tie fastened to the clothes rack, the other end around his neck.

Marcus Sadberry, director of the orphanage, told the deputies that the boy had been found by Lance Duggan—one of his assistants—during a routine bed check at 9:15 p.m. When Duggan saw that the boy's bed was empty, he glanced into the closet, which was standing open, and found the boy dead.

"We didn't cut him down because he was already dead," said Sadberry. "And we didn't want to move the body until investigators got here."

According to Sheriff O. M. Gill, orphanage officials, including Sadberry and Duggan, are cooperating fully with his department.

Although Mr. Sadberry has not returned phone calls from *The Courier* offices, he issued a short statement through the Sheriff's Department regretting the tragic incident. He further stated that Tilley's roommate, Joesph Krebs, had recently been placed with a foster couple and was not present on the night of the tragedy.

According to Sadberry, Allen Tilley had been depressed for several days—since the anniversary of his mother's death from cancer. The boy's father died in Vietnam and he had no known surviving relatives.

Although no foul play is suspected, this is not the first time Sadberry Orphanage has been the scene of violence.

In January of 1980, another boy who lived at the orphanage was found wandering down Highway 90 covered with bruises and rushed to the hospital. There, he told a Sheriff's deputy that he had been in a fight.

A year later the facility was briefly shut down for violating state codes pertaining to child-care facilities.

Various other reports of possible abuse have emanated from the Orphanage over the years, but no actual wrongdoing has ever been proven.

Sadberry's Orphanage was founded in 1970 by the current Sadberry's father, who died earlier this year in a rest home.

Other news stories, as well as some handwritten notes, were also in the file. Gina and I glanced through them, but we were too tired to really study them. They were short articles for the most part, giving details on some of the incidents referenced in the suicide article. It was mildly suspicious stuff, but as the article had said, nothing illegal had actually been proved against Marcus Sadberry and his staff.

Only one article was actually written *after* the suicide story. Stuffed almost willy nilly in the back of the folder was a story entitled, "Sadberry Closes." The date was written at the top of the article in the same purple ink that we had seen on the H. A. Hardy folder.

It was a small, single-column article written about two months after the death of Allen Tilley. Surprisingly, it gave no details about the orphanage's closing, only saying that Mr. Sadberry had decided to "pursue other interests." It made no reference to the suicide and said nothing about where the remaining children were to be placed. And tellingly, the piece did not have a byline, although I suspected it was not by Bill Rumsford.

I put everything back in the folder and looked at Gina. "There are a lot of unanswered questions here," I told her.

"Don't ah know it."

"And we're going to need help."

"Ah was afraid you were goin to say that," she said. "You're goin to call Cal?"

"I don't see how we can avoid it."

~ ~ ~

I know you probably don't think this is a very good time for an aside, but look: it was getting on to midnight in the tiny town of Pine Oak. Gina and I were stuck guarding the office because some nut had thrown a brick in the window and we couldn't get it fixed until the next morning. And unless suspicious people tried to break in during the wee hours and I had to put an arrow through them, there wasn't much excitement to look forward to. So this is as good a time as any.

Calvin Dent had been my predecessor as the editor of *The Pine Oak Courier* . He had hired me to work for him just after I came back from Iraq and quit my much-higher-profile job at *The Richmond Times-Dispatch*. At the time, he and Gina had been dating and had talked about marriage. When Gina suddenly and bewilderingly found herself in love with me, she had freaked out and left town without telling anyone—even me—where she was going.

Although Cal was puzzled and hurt by Gina's abandonment, he soon found solace in his next office manager, despite the fact that she was married to one of his golf buddies. Soon after this, he was offered the editorship of a larger newspaper in Louisiana, and took his new girlfriend with him.

I eventually located Gina and brought her back to Pine Oak and here we are.

I had talked to Cal only sporadically since I became editor. Although I mentioned to him that Gina had returned to her job at the newspaper, he had not asked about her reasons for having left and I had not volunteered anything. And of course, he had no idea that Gina and I were lovers. No one did except Clarence Meekins and a few people in Torrington. And, oh yeah, Annie Gillespie and Becky Colley. Hell.

Time passed pretty slowly that night, which turned out to be unexpectedly cool. I closed the door of my office and turned the heating system on. I actually managed to get a little work done on some articles I was researching. I also found the number of Johnson Glass Company in Forester and made some notes for the staff meeting at 9:00. Gina worked in her own office for a while before going back into the morgue to begin a Gina-like organization of the room and its files. I was napping at my desk when I felt a hand on my shoulder and jerked awake.

"It's just me, darlin."

"Oh, hey. I guess I nodded off."

"You needed to sleep a little," she told me.

"I looked out the window of my office and saw it was already light. "What time is it?"

"Getting on to seven," she said. "Ah'm goin back to the house and take a bath. I'll see to the horses."

"Okay, thanks, but if you want me to wake up you have to give me—"

"Coffee's brewin in my office. You goin to be all right here by yourself?"

"Sure. Go ahead."

"Bah the way, Benny from the bookstore came bah just before daylaht."

"Benny?" I asked. "What did he want? Why was he here so early?"

"Donno. And he usually doesn't make much sense, to me anyway. Ah told him you were asleep and he said he'd talk to you later."

"Umm."

"And Dilly Dollar's been drahvin bah most of the naht. He stopped in the parking lot bout six and ah went out to talk to him. No luck on fahndin out who threw the brick."

"We know who threw the brick, Gina," I said. "We just don't know why."

"But we're gonna fahnd out, raht?"

"Raht. Now git."

She got.

~ ~ ~

The staff meeting was a closed-door affair due to the fact that the front window was still glassless and it was cold in the main room. The glass people had been out, measured the frame, and gone off again to cut a piece to size.

As soon as everyone had taken their seat around the conference table, I filled them in on what had happened the night before: Cori's visit to the detention center and her cold reception, her accident, the brick, and the morgue. Everyone listened, incredulous. I looked around the table, but it took a few seconds after I finished before anyone spoke up.

"Do you think there's a connection?" Mark Patterson asked. For once, he didn't seem over-tired from woman-prowling the night before. He even looked spiffy in a new blue blazer, dark against the light blue of his shirt.

"What do you mean?" I asked.

"You know, between everything. Cori's visit, the crash, the brick . . ."

"We have to assume there is," I said.

"But Sue-Ann," protested Annie Gillespie. "This is Pine Oak. Stuff like that doesn't happen in a small town."

"What if it does, Annie?" Gina asked.

Annie thought about it for only a few seconds. "Then we have to be careful."

"That's raht."

"And if there *is* a connection," I added. "We have to make it. We have to tie all these things together."

"Well," piped up Betty Dickson. "What can we do?"

I looked down at the notes I had made during the night. "Here are your assignments. First of all, Bobby." I looked across the table at the big receptionist. "I want you to organize the morgue. Study the bound volumes and find a way to bind the loose issues. If there are issues missing, contact some of the local libraries and see if we can copy them."

I turned to Betty Dickson. "Betty, I think you were the last one to actually work with the morgue so I want you to help Bobby if he has any questions. Locate the bindery and bring him up to speed on what you know. Bobby, you can bring anything you need to work with up to your desk. If you need to be in the back for any length of time, whoever's still up front will handle the reception desk and the phone. This is important. Later on, when you have everything going the way you want it, I want you to begin updating our obituary files. I'll get Becky to help you."

"Got it," he said. "I'll start now. That way I can keep an eye on the office while you all are in here."

"Perfect."

I didn't have to refer to my notes for the next assignment. "Becky," I looked at the young woman sitting next to Mark. Today she was wearing a yellow scarf and red sweater and her hair was light blonde. "The morgue has tons of files of old photographs. I want you to organize them and eventually scan them into some kind of database. I want you to add your own pictures to the file as well. Randy, yours, too."

"What else do you want me to do," asked the wiry sports reporter.

"You're the wild card here, Randy," I told him. "Our eyes on the street. You're in contact with a lot of students and kids who used to be students. The next few games you cover, ask some easy questions about Hardy. I want facts, but rumors and gossip might be just as good. Did you get anywhere talking to the coaches about those bath salts?"

"A few maybes, but I could see lights blinking in some heads."

"Okay, follow up on those. A lot of the teachers attend their high-school games as well as the coaches, right? Pick their brains if the opportunity comes up. Write everything down and you can coordinate a sports and drugs story with Annie's larger one."

I looked back at Mark, who was sitting to Randy's right. "Mark, I want you to get on your computer and write a story about how a brick was tossed through the plate glass window of *The Pine Oak Courier*. I want it lurid and exciting, got it?"

Mark grinned. "Got it, chief," he said. "Can I mention Hardy?"

I thought about that for a minute. "Yes," I decided. "Mention that a *Courier* reporter was forced off the road after a visit to Hardy, and that the Sheriff's Department is looking for a link between the accident and the vandalism. Don't use Cori's name, though."

"Got it. Can I start now?"

"If you can stand the cold in your cubicle," I said.

"Nothing to it," he said. "Later, all." He got up and went to his computer as revved up as I'd ever seen him—at least for a story.

"Next," I said, looking around the table for anyone I'd missed. Annie Gillespie was looking at me expectantly. "Annie," I began. "How's your piece on the bath salt drugs coming?"

"Mostly done, I think," she answered. "I'm just waiting for a couple of callbacks and a couple of figures. Do you want me to take up where Cori left off?" she asked. "Maybe I can—"

"I want you to back her up," I told her. When Annie looked disappointed, I continued, "Look, Annie. You're my bureau chief. Cori is technically under your supervision. You know that you can't just step in and take over someone else's investigation. Just provide a little guidance, a little of your experience—and make sure she doesn't get killed. The story is still Cori's. I think she deserves it. Something she did touched a wound and I'm going to leave her to her own devices to prod that wound a little. When she comes in on Monday, call her into your office and ask her how she's doing. If you have any ideas, let her have them. And if she asks for help, give it to her."

"Gotcha. But . . ."

"But you want something real to do," I guessed.

"I just hate sitting here while everybody else is out doing stuff."

"Okay, then. Do something."

"But do what?"

"You're a good reporter; figure it out. Find something I haven't thought of yet and go for it. Just don't step on Cori's toes."

"Okay, I'll try."

The meeting was over and as everyone left my office the glass company truck arrived with *The Courier*'s new window lashed to its side. I went out and talked to the driver, who handed me an itemized bill and told me I could mail in the payment.

When I got back inside, Betty and Bobby were going through one of the bound issues of *The Courier* while Mark typed away on his story and Randy sat back in his chair perusing what looked to be the sports pages of *The Tallahassee Democrat*. Annie was in her office, scrutinizing the brick and the note that had been lashed to it. She also had the Hardy and Sadberry files I had taken from the morgue. Gina had gone out canvassing for ads, so it seemed to be a good time to call Cal Dent. I closed the door to my office, took a deep breath, and dialed his cell. He answered on the second ring. "*Shreveport Times*, this is Cal—oh, hi, Sue-Ann."

"Cal," I replied. "How's it going?"

"Busy busy," he replied. "This on-line business is kind of new for an old street reporter, but I can't complain. I heard you were planning to do an on-line version of *The Courier*. How's that coming?"

"Planning stages, still," I answered.

"Good luck with it. To what do I owe the pleasure of this call?"

"Well, believe it or not, we may have a situation here." And with that I briefed him on Cori's visit to Hardy, the accident, the brick with its warning, and the morgue files.

"Wow, Sue-Ann," he said after I had finished. "It looks like you might have something dangerous going on there. But how can I help you? I'm just an office jockey now. Sorry about that morgue, though. I always meant to bring it up to date but never seemed to have the time. I assigned Betty to it after a while, but, well, you know Betty. I doubt if I even went back there half a dozen times."

I wondered with a pang of jealousy how many of those times had been with Gina, but I kept my trap shut. Instead, I asked the question I had called about. "Listen, Cal. What do you know about Bill Rumsford?"

"Not much, really. He was *The Courier*'s editor for a long time, but that was almost two decades before I got there. From what I heard he was either a real crusader or a scandalmonger. Take your pick."

"What would *you* have picked?" I asked.

"Crusader, I think. I read some of his editorials and talked to a lot of people that respected him."

"What happened to him?" I asked.

"I'm not sure, Sue-Ann. I guess he just got old and retired. I'm pretty sure that he's been dead for years."

"I'm sorry. I would have liked to interview him about Hardy. He really seemed to have a thing about it. Was he married do you know?"

"No, no idea."

I drummed my fingers on my desk as I asked the next question. "Who replaced him as editor?" I asked.

"I guess you haven't spent much time in the morgue either, Sue-Ann," he laughed. "The next editor's name was Scarborough. People called him Flattop.

"Flattop?" I asked.

"He wore his hair like a marine in the 50s. There used to be a picture of him hanging in the office."

"What was he like, do you know?" I asked.

"Well, I guess you'd say he was more of a politician than an editor. More like that guy, what's his name, Cobra Conlin from that idiotic rag in Forester. It's like Rumsford went out looking for news while Flattop let it come to him. He ran the paper down so bad that the owners had to sell it for almost nothing to the people who own it now."

"Is that when they hired you?"

"Oh no, there were five or six editors between me and Flattop. Just barely managed to keep it going. Finally the owners fired the entire staff and hired me to kind of revitalize it."

"You did a good job, Cal," I told him with sincerity.

"Well, I might have gotten it on the right track again. I'm glad I got you aboard."

"Thanks, Cal. But what happened to Flat—Scarborough?"

"Oh, he's still around. He moved out to a small farm in Forester, I think. The first couple of months I was in Pine Oak, he would come in and want to, you know, 'help.' I tried to be polite, but I finally had to tell him that I had it under control. He got the message, but he didn't look happy about it."

"Did you ever hear about any abuse at Hardy? Or any drugs?"

"Just a few rumors. Remember, Sue-Ann, that Jasper County has a couple of state prisons and is within throwing distance of a mental hospital. Hardy's not much more than a halfway house and nobody pays much attention to it." He stopped, and I could imagine him thinking for a couple of seconds before he said, "But maybe somebody should."

"Somebody is, Cal," I assured him.

"Everything else going okay?" he asked, and I knew he wanted me to talk about Gina, but I wouldn't.

"Everything's copacetic," I said. "You?" I wanted to hear a little about his relationship with Linsey Colley, who had moved to Louisiana with him, but I really didn't need to. Her daughter Becky was in close touch and enjoyed gossiping. So it wasn't much of a disappointment when Cal (in my mind I saw him shrug) just tossed off a quick answer.

"Same here."

"Okay then. I guess I'll let you go. Thanks for talking."

"Call me anytime."

I decided to go home for lunch, take a hot shower, and think about everything that had happened. I was opening the door to my Toyota when I saw a movement down the row of storefronts. The door of the bookstore was open halfway and Benny Benedict's head was peering out. I was surprised to see him; his old red Jeep, usually parked right in front of his store, was nowhere to be seen.

"Afternoon, Benny," I called out.

"Hey-ya," he replied, and stepped outside. Although it was still in the fifties, he wore his old khaki-colored shorts and rubber flip-flops.

I didn't have time to deal with Benny's quirks and foibles right then, but I took an inward breath and walked over and met him halfway between our offices. "Gina told me you came over earlier," I said. "What's up? New invention?"

He looked surprised. "Huh? Yowser, well, only the magnetic tweezers, heh heh."

"The what?" My mind said be silent, but my mouth made the sounds anyway. I hit myself in the head mentally a dozen times. When would I learn not to ask Benny questions?

"Magnetic tweezers," he grinned. "Remember the last time you hit your thumb with a hammer?"

There was nothing I could do but answer and try to find out where he was going. "Um, not really, no."

"But it hurt, right?" he asked eagerly. "Yow?"

"Yes it did. Yow."

"Well, um, hmm, what if you used tweezers to hold the nail while you hammered it? No more black thumbs, heh heh."

"And it's magnetic so you wouldn't drop the nail," I said wonderingly. "And some of those little nails are too small to hold . . . It's brilliant, Benny."

"Yuk yuk. But what's wrong with it?"

"Hmm?" Then I realized that I always had a way of telling him how his inventions were either flawed or silly, or already existed in a simpler form. But every once in a while his ideas were uniquely creative and even useful. "Not a thing, Benny," I told him sincerely. "When you get some, I want to buy one."

"Okay, sure. I'll, um, put one aside. Maybe open a hardware store, heh heh."

"I'm not sure you need to go that far, Benny."

"Well, um, hm, you never know."

"I know that's right, but where's your Jeep?'

"Let me niece borrow it. Wanted to go home for the sister's birthday. The old bat. Whoops, did I say that?"

"So how were you supposed to get home?" I asked.

"Home? Hmm. Never thought of that. So I just camped out here last night. Worked on the novel."

"Wait a minute. You were here all night?"

"Yep. Workaholic, that's me."

"Listen," I began excitedly, "you didn't happen to see someone drive by here last night and throw a brick through the window of *The Courier*, did you?"

"Arghh. Sure. I came over earlier to see if you were all right, but the police were there. Don't like the police much, um um. Boyfriend trouble again? Little spat, maybe?"

"What do you mean boyfriend trouble?" I asked, taken aback more than a little by that simple question.

"You know, that guy you're dating. The guy that drives the tow truck."

"Donny? Donny Brasswell?"

"Yup, that's the name. Reads the same kind of books you do."

"You saw Donny throw a brick through my window?" I asked incredulously. Although Donny and I had once been close—and although he had once shot up my mailbox after a lover's quarrel—I thought that we both had moved on. He was married to Linda C and I was . . .You saw his tow truck?"

"Naw," Benny answered. "Wasn't driving his tow truck. He was driving his car. That old white Camaro.

And as far as I knew, there was only one old white Camaro in Jasper County.

Now a real mystery novel would have ended the chapter there. Yikes, it was her ex all along. WTF?

But I knew something that Benny didn't know. "Benny," I began. "Did you actually see Donny's face?"

"Naw, too dark and too far away, but who else would drive that car?"

That would be the person that Donny had sold the Camaro to a couple of weeks before we had broken up.

"Thanks, Benny." I smiled. "You're a peach. I hope you never get your Jeep back and you have to spend the rest of your life sleeping in the bookstore."

I was joking, of course, so I was kind of surprised when he looked at me with longing eyes and said, without any of his fake accents or exaggerated huffing or puffing, "Me, too, Sue-Ann."

Chapter Fourteen: Investigations

The next morning I was glancing through my on-line news services when I came on a story about a burglar who got the idea of using the light from his cell phone to get around in a strange house after dark. No more bulky flashlights. But before I could read to the end, my own cell phone rang. It was Donny.

"Donny," I said. "Thanks for calling me back."

"I had to tow some jerk in from East Jesus last night, Sue-Ann," he said. "Asshole was trying to stay awake playing a video game on his iPhone and went in a ditch. I didn't get your message until this morning. What's up?"

"Donny," I began. "I think it was your old Camaro that ran Cori off the road the other night."

"What?"

"Your Camaro. Bookstore Benny saw it in the newspaper's parking lot on Wednesday night. Whoever was driving it was the one who threw that brick through the front window."

"That's insane. Wait a minute, he *saw* this?"

"He was working late. I need to know who you sold that car to, Donny."

"Wait a minute, Sue-Ann. My Camaro isn't the only one in Jasper County."

"Yes it is, Donny. In fact, you used to brag about that. I'll concede that the car might have come from somewhere else, but what are the chances?"

"Yeah.

"Do you remember who you sold it to?"

"Some woman in Forester. I didn't know her."

"Some *woman?*"

"She said she was buying it for her son."

"Do you remember her name? Or her son's name?"

"Um. You know I'm not too good with names, Sue-Ann."

"You must have given her a receipt. Did you keep a copy for yourself?"

"I guess, but I don't know what I did with it."

This was frustrating. I was as close to an answer as I was to the chair in front of me, but it was just out of my reach. "Can you look around for it?" I asked.

"Sure, okay, I will."

"How's Cori's car?" I asked.

"Cori? Oh, yeah. I don't know. I guess it's getting some body work done. I know I saw it in the garage when I came back in. I just bring them in."

"Okay, Donny, thanks. And can you look for that receipt? It's important."

"Sure. I will. See ya."

I hung up the phone a little depressed, but still determined to get to the bottom of what was happening. But what *was* happening? How did one thing fit in with another, and what had set things in motion? And most important, how could I stop them?

Newspaper work—just like police work—can be a complex series of investigations. But these investigations are seldom glamorous. A lot of the work can be boring, repetitive, and time consuming. Phone calls often take the place of real interviews, and real leads are few and hard to come by. The phone call from Donny made that clear. I was stuck.

Then I had an idea. I picked up the receiver again and called the Sherriff's office. It was answered by a voice I didn't recognize. "Hi, this is Sue-Ann McKeown from *The Courier*," I said. "I'd like to speak to Sergeant

Bickley." Joey had been on my case ever since Carlos Murillo showed up on my property. Maybe if I threw him a bone, he would lighten up a bit, although I doubted it. But here was also a chance to have someone do my work for me. Donny was a good guy, but not an organized one. The chances that he still had a copy of that receipt were slim; the chances of him actually coming up with it nearly nil.

"Hold on," said the voice. Male, I think.

A few seconds later, Joey Bickley's unwelcome voice came on the line. "Bickley."

"Joey," I began. "This is Sue-Ann. Listen, remember that brick that somebody tossed through my window at work?" Too late, I realized that I had just opened a conversation the way Benny would have. And Joey wasted no time letting me know it.

"What do you think, McKeown?" he said testily, "That I forget things that happen after twenty-four hours?"

"No, sorry. It's just that I found an eyewitness."

"Somebody saw the thrower?" he said warily.

"He saw the car the person was driving."

"Yeah?"

"Yeah. It was an old white Camaro. Probably the same one that Donny Brasswell used to own."

"Who was the witness?"

"Benny Benedict. The owner of the bookstore a couple of doors down from *The Courier*."

"Weird little fucker. Is he a liar?"

"As far as I know, he's a very honest man."

"Did he get a license number?"

"No. It was dark."

"So what do you want me to do about it?" he said.

"Look, Joey. There's probably only one Camaro like that in Jasper County. If you want to find out who owns it, I'm sure you have the resources."

"Maybe I do, but why would I care who broke your window?" he said.

"You're not that stupid, Joey," I said, and hung up.

I hadn't expected much from that conversation except more of his usual bluff and abuse. But he had given me something else. Under normal circumstances I agreed that he would probably pin a medal on anyone harassing me, but for him to pretend not to make the connection between the brick and Cori's accident was just silly.

Joey knew something. And he didn't want anyone else to know that he knew it.

There seemed to be no end of little mysteries and I was determined to find the answer to as many of them as I could.

The story about the burglar with a cell phone was still on my screen, so I read on. Turns out that in fumbling around with the cell phone, he accidently hit the Record button on the phone's mini video camera. When he was arrested later, the police had the entire robbery documented on the man's own phone. Hoisted on his own petard, as it were. What kind of an idiot?—but before I could finish that thought, my phone rang again.

"Sue-Ann. It's Donny." He sounded excited, which was odd for Donny.

"Hey, Donny. Didn't I just talk to you?"

"Yeah, but I know who bought my old Camaro."

"Really?"

"Yeah, the guy's name is Neely Burks."

"I thought you said you sold it to a woman."

"Yeah, Neely's mother. But he has it now."

"I guess you found your receipt, then," I said.

"Nah. Who knows where that old thing is. Neely brought the car in to the garage just a few minutes ago."

"What?" That was unexpected.

"Yeah. And guess what?"

"Go ahead and tell me," I said.

"One of the front bumpers is banged in and there's traces of paint on the dented place. Looks like paint from Cori's car."

Bumpkins in small towns.

After I thanked Donny, I looked up, then dialed, the phone number of the Hardy Juvenile Center. A woman's voice picked up. "Hardy Center."

"Hello. My name is Sue-Ann McKeown. I'm the editor of *The Pine Oak Courier*. I'd like to speak to the Director."

"I'll see if he's in."

Almost a minute went by before she picked up again, and just before she spoke, I heard a click on the line, as if someone had picked up an extension. "I'm sorry, but Mr. Sadberry's not here right now."

"That's too bad," I said. "I wanted to ask him whether he knows anything about a brick that was thrown through the window of my office."

"I'm sure he—"

"Or if he wants to comment on the story coming out tomorrow about how one of *The Courier*'s reporters was sideswiped and run off the road just after she left Hardy yesterday."

Another few seconds of silence, then "I told you that Mr. Sadberry—"

"I'll call back," I said.

"He won't speak to you," she said.

"How do you know that?" I asked. "He's not listening in on another line, is he?"

"Of course not, I told you—"

"This was his only chance to respond," I said. "Bye."

Almost everything I had said was a bluff, but it had felt good. Now if only Joey could find out . . . But why wait for Joey? I took up the Jasper County Phone Directory again and looked for Burks. There were several, but none of them listed Neely as a first name.

I had done this more than once when I worked in Richmond and had found that the person you wanted was almost always at the bottom of the list. So I dialed the last number first: Wilton Burks.

After several rings, a man's voice picked up. "Lo?"

"Hi. Mr. Burks? Is Neely there?"

"Neely? Neely? That'd probably be Bertha's boy. Whychu try her?"

So much for large city knowhow. I should have realized that one Burks was probably kin to all Burks.

I dialed the number for Bertha. It took awhile but a woman's voice finally came on. It was the kind of voice that went with a woman who had just had to wipe flour off her hands before she picked up the phone. "Hello?"

"Miz Burks? Hi, I'm looking for Neely."

"He's at work raht now."

Jackpot.

"Oh, sorry. This is Harrison's Towing. He left his car here and Mr. Harrison has a question about it. Can you give me his work number?"

"Of course."

And she did. And it was the same one I had called earlier. So I dialed it again.

"Hardy Center."

"Hi. This is Sue-Ann McKeown from *The Courier* again. Can I speak to Neely Burks?"

The line went dead.

Ha.

I must have spoken that last syllable aloud, because when I looked up, Annie Gillespie was standing in my doorway and looking at me curiously.

"Everything all right, boss?" she asked.

"Sue-Ann," I corrected. Then I saw the pages in her hand. "Come in and sit. Is that the bath salts story?"

"Right. I got the last piece this morning." She put it on my desk and I glanced through it quickly. It looked well-researched, yet written at a low enough grade level for our audience.

"It looks good, Annie," I said. "I'll go over it more carefully later. Right now I'm trying to get to the bottom of this brick thing."

"Any progress?" she asked.

"It's early days yet, but it seems like everything might be coming together."

For the next few minutes I brought her up to speed on what I had learned in the last hour or so. Her eyebrows went up when I told her about the paint on the bumper of Neely Burks' Camaro, but she didn't say anything.

It would be tempting to say that Annie was the person on my staff that I knew least well, but that would not be the truth. I knew less about Randy Rivas and almost nothing about Bobby DuPre. Still, *The Courier* staff was a family that did not socialize after hours. I knew that Annie had a degree in Journalism from the University of Florida and that she was thirty-eight years old. That was an easy one to remember because she was almost exactly a month older than I was. I knew most of that from her application, which I kept in a file in my office. She didn't have the luxury of looking at mine, although I remembered with a little twist of unease that she knew about me and Gina. Odd that it was only a little twist.

"Is everything all right with you, Annie?" I asked.

"Oh sure," she said. She looked at a pencil she had been carrying and tried to stick it behind her ear. But in trying to negotiate her way through her tangle of red hair, she found that there was one already there. She ended up putting it on my desk. "Remember how you told me to look for something that no one had thought of yet?"

I nodded.

"Well, I took the brick to John's Paving, which is about the only place around here that makes them. The guy I talked to said it was hard to tell where it came from because it was old—probably came from some building that had been torn down. No way to trace it. I didn't get anywhere with the paper the note was written on, either. Or the handwriting. But then I thought of something else."

"Really?"

"Yes. Well, it was really you and Ginette that gave me the idea."

"What is it?" I asked, curious.

She smiled and gave her head a little shake. "It might turn out to be bullshit," she said. "But I'm meeting with someone tomorrow who might be able to answer some questions about Bill Rumsford. And about Sadberry."

I frowned. "That's great, Annie," I began. "But this is not one of those things where you say you'll tell me later and then get kidnapped or something, is it?"

She laughed, and I admired her two rows of perfect teeth. "No fear," she said. "You've been reading too many mystery novels."

"That's the reason I don't read *any*," I told her. "But tell me when you have something. Anything else going on? I mean on a personal level?"

"Umm. You know. Everything I do is pretty predictable. Remember that biomass story I wrote a couple of months ago."

"Of course. And the follow-ups you did."

"Yeah, right," she smiled. "Well, I met one of the executives from the company at a City Council meeting.

He'll probably end up moving here if his company gets that contract."

"Which seems iffy right now," I said.

"It does, yeah, unless the economy picks up. But Hal—his name is Hal Powers—flies up every couple of weeks or so for talks, and last week he asked me out."

"Really, for when?"

"For last weekend," she said, but her voice was rueful rather than exultant. "He took me to a seafood restaurant he'd heard about in Panama City."

"All that way? Sounds promising."

"That's what I thought. Candlelight dinner with a handsome, well-spoken, *successful* man, intimate conversation . . ."

"I remember," I told her."

"I mean, I didn't necessarily want to end up in a balmy seaside motel or anything, but . . .

"But?" I prodded.

"But, well, maybe I wouldn't have refused."

"So what happened?" I asked. My elbows were on the desk and I was cupping my face in my hands as I listened.

"Well," she said, brushing stray strands of hair out of her eyes, "seems like he had a wife."

"He's married?"

"I said *had* a wife. He's divorced. But she's all he could talk about the whole night—I mean the whole dinner and the whole drive back. Want to know about her? She's thirty-five, a Scorpio, has an MBA from Johns Hopkins, blonde, unresponsive in bed . . .

"He told you all that?"

"And more."

"Check one off the list, I guess, and move on."

"My list is getting pretty short," she said.

"What can I say, you know?" I began. "Tomorrow's another day, the best is yet to come, you're just waiting for Mr. Right . . . ?"

She laughed. "Here's my favorite," she said. "Everything happens for a reason."

We laughed together.

"Hey," she said. "I called Cori."

"Great. How's she doing?"

"Um, she wasn't there. Her mother said she was out working on a story."

"And let me guess. She didn't say where she was going."

"Right. You think she might be in danger?"

I looked at her seriously. "Annie, I think we all might be."

Chapter Fifteen: Gunshots

When I got home that evening, Gina was sitting on the couch, surrounded by sheets of music and holding the little Seagull parlor guitar she sometimes practiced on.

"You look like a paper factory," I told her.

"Hi, darlin," she said, looking up from a handwritten score on her lap.

I tiptoed through the mess and gave her a light kiss on the forehead.

"There's still a couple of hours of sunlight," I said. "Let's go for a trail ride."

"Ah'd lahk to, Sue-Ann. But ah have to get in a little practice for tomorrow."

"Tomorrow?"

"Ah'm playin that gig at the Red River Saloon tomorrow naht."

"You're not really going to do that, are you?" I asked.

She looked up in surprise. "Yeah, of course. It'll be the first tahm ah've played out in Florida."

"But that Rivers guy seems so slimy."

"Ah can handle him, Sue-Ann."

"You don't think I'm going to let you go by yourself, do you?" I smiled.

"Then *we* can handle him. Now git. Go rahd."

"You don't mind?"

"You haven't been on Alikki in a week," she said. "Go have fun."

So I put on my breeches, barn boots, and half chaps and brought in Alikki from the pasture. At 16.1 hands, Alikki wasn't the tallest horse in Jasper County, but she was no pony either. I petted her up, gave her a good currying, and picked out her feet. A little touch massage along her withers and spine soon had her licking and chewing, relaxed and content. I threw my Wintec Isabelle saddle over a clean blanket, girthed it up, and mounted.

As we approached the ring, she showed a little resistance, but once it was obvious that we were going around it—and that she wouldn't have to do any real work—she moved with more alacrity. We took the path that skirted the pasture where Emmy browsed with her aunt Irene, both of whom looked up only briefly as we passed before returning their muzzles earthward.

The pasture gave out into a narrow trail through a thick forest of oaks with an occasional pine and runty magnolia thrown in for good measure. A couple hundred yards further, the trail ran into the stand of tall pines that Gina and I had ridden through a couple of days earlier. Most pine groves in north Florida are planted by State Ag services and harvested after twenty years or so for the timber, which is then cut into two by fours or pulped to make paper or diapers and such. This particular stand, however—which defined my property line to the west— would never be cut down. Its main function was to serve as a barrier between Torrington and the rest of the world. And if you knew the right trail through the trees, it was also a pathway to it. But I had no intention of visiting Ashley this evening. I was reveling in the closeness I was feeling with Alikki and just wanted to ride out the remaining daylight. The sky overhead was clear—no clouds to keep in the heat—so it seemed that a coolness was descending from the treetops. Alikki was a bit frisky, so after a minute or so I steered her into a row between the pines and sent her off at a brisk trot. It was darker between the pines, the branches keeping out most of the remaining sunlight. It was cooler, too, but not uncomfortable. Once she settled down, I began putting her through a series of walk/trot transitions. When I was satisfied, I asked her to halt, then to walk backwards four steps. Then I petted her and rubbed her mane.

"Good girl," I told her. I knew that despite having to practice her gaits she was happy about being out in the cool woods with me. My companionship was one of her rewards, and hers was mine. We turned down another row and I put a stronger leg on her. "Go ahead and run," I murmured in her ear. Then, louder, "Canter on!"

No, she didn't run like the wind; that's not the way of dressage, but she attained a pretty good pace, her hooves almost quiet on the thick bedding of pine needles. It was her ears that told me something was wrong. They flashed in both directions, then she sidestepped into a low-hanging branch, almost unseating me. I pulled her to a halt as gently as I could, then I heard it, too. Music. Country music. Maybe a dozen rows down in the direction her ears were pointing I spotted a vehicle, deep in shadow. The music was coming from its radio. Two or three people were moving around under the trees.

Although I couldn't make out any faces, I realized that this was a group of immigrant workers—Mexicans probably—engaged in the task of baling pine needles. In fact, as I looked closer, I could make out a short, dark-haired woman raking the needles into piles. A large, red, cagelike box stood close by. Two other figures—males?—we're working a bit further out.

This was not good. I knew that many Mexicans came to North Florida to work the tomato, cotton, and watermelon fields found in such abundance here. In off seasons they sometimes contracted with local farmers or landowners to harvest the thick carpets of pine needles in their pine stands. The bales were then hauled away to be sold as mulch. But I had not given anyone permission to collect pine needles and I was certain that Ashley had not. It was far too close to Torrington for strangers.

Before I realized what I was doing, I asked Alikki to walk towards them. I had not brought a bow or arrows so I was pretty defenseless if these people turned out to be dangerous, but I had to tell them they were trespassing. We walked cautiously at first until a streak of light broke through the tops of the pines to reveal a surprise. One of the men was Clarence Meekins. Although he still had his back to me, there was no mistaking his gangly, six-foot-four frame or his trademark Oshkosh overalls. With relief, I moved Alikki into a soft trot.

As we got nearer, I recognized the other man as Jeremy, and I thought I knew who the woman was, too.

Our approach was masked by the loud music and by the work they were doing so that no one noticed us until we were almost upon them. I watched the woman lifted up a long pole set into the top of the baler—the weird-looking cage-contraption I'd noticed earlier—then reach down and heave out a heavy rectangle of baled pine straw. Clarence turned around and said to her, "Here, let me have that. Oh, hey, Sue-Ann."

The woman—Sandra Murillo—turned around quickly, but by that time I had halted only a foot or two away, and Alikki's head filled most of her vision.

"Yiii," she cried, and hopped away a few steps, eyeing us both warily. "You again," she said with some distaste.

"Yep. Whatcha all doing?" My own voice was pleasant, but loud over the radio and I was glad to see Clarence reach into his truck and turn it down.

Sandra ignored my question. "Din know you were a horsey-girl."

"Yep."

"Your friend a horsey-girl too?"

"We're both horsey-girls."

"I don like horsies, I don think."

"Why not?"

"I think they might bite."

"Sometimes they do bite."

"That one bite?" She was looking steadily at Alikki as if she had never seen a horse before up close, and maybe she hadn't.

"No. Mares usually don't bite. Do you want to pet her?" I dismounted and pulled the reins over Alikki's head.

"Maybe." Sandra edged closer and looked up into Alikki's eyes. She put out a tentative hand, then stopped, unsure where to place it.

"Here," I told her, touching the mare's neck just below her withers.

Sandra reached out again and stroked Alikki's neck gently. She looked at me questioningly. "She likes it?"

"Very much. You've made a friend." And indeed, I was kind of surprised—but proud—that Alikki was not fussing or pinning back her ears. Alikki had been badly mistreated by a local farmer and as a result, shied away from all males—even the docile Clarence. She seemed to have taken a shine to the Mexican woman, though. "But what are you all doing out here?" I asked again.

"We baling pine straw; what's it look like?"

"Clarence?"

"She's really good at it," Clarence enthused. "She convinced Ashley that we should harvest all these needles." He motioned toward a half dozen piles of pine straw that had been raked near the baler. "We can get a little extra money."

"Yeah?"

"Sure. She's showing me and Jeremy how to bale. Later we can bring out a bigger crew from Torrington. There's enough straw in this stand to fill a boxcar."

"You think?"

"You watch," Sandra Murillo said. Giving Alikki a final pat, she strode over to the baler. Up close, it still looked like an upended cage, but heavier and sturdier. It was painted red, with the back and two sides solid metal. The front resembled nothing so much as the door of a heavily guarded dungeon cell, with two bars running from top to bottom near the middle. I could almost picture a haggard and pale inmate gripping these bars and looking out. It was, in fact, a door and it was standing open on its hinges. On top of the box, the pole-like lever was connected at the end with a rectangular metal plate, which revealed that the top of the box was open. On the left side were attached what looked like a hundred lengths of orange baling twine—the same kind that bound the bales of hay I fed my horses. Sandra Murillo took two of these strings and attached them to hooks at the top of the baler. The lengths were long enough to reach the ground with a foot or more to spare. She arranged these to suit her, then shut the door with a clank. "Here, you," she shouted to Jeremy, who had heretofore been lounging under a tree, against which stood both a rake and an assault rifle. "You fill it up."

"Me?"

"I'll help," offered Clarence.

Both men took up their rakes and stuffed armfuls of the pine straw into the baler. Sandra stood nearby watching. When it was full, she reached in and pushed the needles deeper. She also took out a couple of sticks and stray oak leaves. "We don wan no sticks," she said. "Okay, one more."

Clarence piled another giant heap of pine needles into the box.

"That's enough," Sandra said. She took hold of the lever and brought it down towards her. The plate at the end then acted as a plunger, pressing the needles down into a compact rectangle. She locked the lever down, then, in a feat of legerdemain I couldn't begin to follow, she pulled the ends of both strings together and knotted them firmly. She then pushed the lever back up, unlatched the door of the baler, and tipped out a perfect bale of pine straw, hard and tight.

"Ha," she said, as if to say, you have your horsie, but I have my baler.

"Cool," I told her.

I wanted to try it, too, but I didn't trust anyone else to hold Alikki, even Clarence, and she pinned her ears back even looking at Jeremy. Although Jeremy hadn't said anything since I arrived, something in his face let me know that he was watching me a little too closely. I had nearly skewered him with an arrow on my first visit to Torrington; maybe he was looking for revenge. I considered him a certifiable psycho.

"I guess I'll let you get to it," I told them. "But wait a minute, Where's Carlos? Did you go to Waxahatchee and pick him up?"

She frowned. "No. He called again and said he din wanna leave that place."

"And you let him stay?" I asked, trying not to let my incredulity show.

"I don like my boy to be roun convicts much, but he said he was safe there."

I turned to Clarence. "Do you know that guy Rivers?" I asked him.

"Never met him. Heard a few things, though."

"Like what?" I asked.

"He used to work at the prison but for some reason he quit. Or was fired. My mother knows someone who told her about it once."

"Carlos said he's makin a little money now and that he'd call in a few days. I think he'll be okay. He's a tough cookie."

I rode home slowly in the last light of evening. It was starting to get very cold. I hoped that Sandra was right about her son. For some reason I began imagining Carlos somewhere on the road, prey to every type of predator. I visualized him getting cold, going into a truck stop to get some food and get warm. Seeing the bath salts over the counter . . .

Then Alikki pinned her ears back again and stopped cold in the middle of a pine row. I followed the direction of her gaze and saw someone walking stealthily through the trees. He saw me and for an instant our eyes met.

Joey Bickley. And he was carrying a rifle.

The first thing I thought was that he was off duty and out hunting. The fact that it wasn't hunting season made little difference to Jasper County bonzos (gawd, did I really say that?). Then I got scared when I realized that he was heading toward Torrington. Was *that* what he was hunting? I had known for months that he suspected that *something* was out there.

I had to warn Clarence, but I knew I couldn't just turn around and ride straight back, so I turned Alikki in the general direction of my house, intending to circle back around when I was out of sight. But I had gone only a couple of steps when his voice shouted out, "McKeown!" and I sent Alikki into a fast canter. We were running like the wind when a shot rang out.

The shot scared Alikki as much as it did me, and she wheeled and took off back the way we'd come.

"Stop!" I heard Joey shout, then he squeezed off another shot that echoed in the trees like an angry whisper.

Alikki had no intention of stopping. There were a couple of tense moments as she came dangerously close to the trunks of a few pines, giving me a face full of pine needles, but luckily I didn't come off. For one reason or another I hadn't put on my riding helmet, and now I was regretting it. When we were out of Joey's range—and sight—I managed to slow Alikki down, although she continued blowing and snorting and twitching her ears every which way.

Joey in the woods was a bad thing, like maybe a copperhead in your mailbox. If he kept his direction, he would run into Clarence—along with Sandra and Jeremy, two people who definitely did not want the pleasure. Farther on, he would run into the Torrington Compound. I had to warn Clarence.

Fortunately, Alikki had bolted in the right direction, or a reasonable facsimile of it at least. I let her walk for a minute and was about to ask for a brisk trot when I spotted Clarence running towards us, followed closely by Jeremy. I stopped and dismounted.

"God's banana, Sue-Ann!" he said excitedly. "What happened? We heard shots."

I hastily described seeing Joey Bickley in the woods, our eye contact, his shout, then the rifle reports. "What can we do?" I asked, dismounting and stroking Alikki's mane to reassure her. "It looks like he was headed this way."

I heard a chuckle from Jeremy and noticed without surprise that he was carrying his assault rifle, which he used kind of like Linus used a security blanket. He raised it level and checked the rounds. "Let him come," he said.

"Damn it, Jeremy," said Clarence. "What did Colonel Frogmore say about that?"

"But he's trespassing," said Jeremy. "The law says—"

"I don't give a gee-whiz about the law. What you have to do is—"

"But Jeremy's right about trespassing, Clarence," I broke in. "Even a law enforcement officer can't go wherever he pleases."

"So I can shoot him?" Jeremy asked eagerly.

"No, Jeremy," said Clarence. "We're just going to ask him to leave."

"We are?"

"Not you, Jeremy. You don't exist, remember? You have to get back to the Compound. Go on foot and take Sandra with you; if Joey saw her he'd have a fit. Now go."

Jeremy turned and began walking slowly and disconsolately back to the truck. "On the double, damn it!" Clarence shouted. "And report this to the Colonel or Mr. Torrington."

This time Jeremy moved like the well-trained soldier he was and disappeared into the shadows of the trees—even darker now that night was falling. Then Clarence turned to me and said, "Point me in the right direction."

I pointed. "But he has a gun, Clarence." Again I regretted not bringing a bow and some arrows. No weapons, no helmet; what was I thinking?

"I'm hoping he won't shoot me," he answered.

"I'm coming with," I told him, and remounted my horse. But we had only gone a few rows into the trees when we heard Joey stumbling in our direction. When he saw us, he pulled up, breathing hard, and raised his rifle. Clarence moved toward him while I held Alikki back.

"If you point that rifle at me, Joey," Clarence said menacingly, "you'd better shoot me. Otherwise I'll take it from you and break it over your head. Did you just take a shot at Sue-Ann?"

"Hell no, Meekins. I shot up in the air to make her stop." Joey was blustering, but he lowered the arm that held the rifle.

I broke in: "Do you know what happens when you fire a shot close to a horse?" I asked angrily. "Mostly they just bolt, but sometimes they buck, too. If you shoot too close to someone on a horse, you might just as well shoot them in the head because they'll be just as dead." For some reason, the thought of my mother's own death came into my mind just then. She had not been wearing a helmet either.

"Yeah, well I'm sorry about that. I just wanted to talk and you're always running away."

"And now you know why," I spat.

Joey, unable to hold my gaze, turned to Clarence. "What the hell are *you* doing out here, Meekins?"

"I'm not sure it's your business, Sergeant," Clarence answered, "seeing as you're on private property. People went to a lot of trouble putting up those No Trespassing signs."

"I'm looking for that fugitive kid that escaped from Hardy," Joey said.

"I'll have to see your search warrant, then," said Clarence.

You know I don't have one, Meekins. Anyway, seems like you're trespassing, too. And so is McKeown there."

"I'm the legal caretaker," Clarence said calmly. "And I've given Sue-Ann permission to ride here whenever she wants."

"Legal caretaker for who?" Joey asked, ignoring the last part of Clarence's statement.

"The owners."

"And who are the owners?"

"The owners want to be anonymous."

"Yeah, well I've looked at the property records. What the hell is the Torrington Trust?"

"That's the owners."

"And they don't want anyone to know who they are?"

"That's right. But what's that to you? You said you were just out here looking for a runaway boy."

"Whether that boy is out here or not, I know that you or McKeown or somebody is hiding something out here, and I'm going to find out what it is."

"What could we be hiding?"

"You tell me," Joey replied. "For one thing, what are you doing out here? And don't make me laugh by telling me that this is just another one of your secret get-togethers."

"Want to see what I'm doing?" Clarence said. "Come on." And with that he turned his back and began walking towards the place where he had been baling.

It didn't take long before we saw the truck through the trees—his battered blue Chevy flatbed that had, over the years, carried tons and tons of vegetables, fruit, and other market supplies. Thankfully, there was no sign of Jeremy or Sandra. It was getting to be time for owl sounds, but Joey's gunshots had silenced them.

When we came within touching distance of the baler, Joey asked, "What's that thing?"

"It's a pine straw baler," Clarence said. "I sell pine straw at the market."

"How's it work?"

"I'll show you." And even though Clarence had probably only done it a time or two before, he ran through the process for Joey, packing in the needles, tamping it down with the plunger, and tying the twine to hold it together. He fumbled a little with the unfamiliar knots, but I don't think Joey noticed. He opened the door and tumbled the bale out next to the ones Sandra had done. It was kind of wonky, but acceptable.

"What do you need three rakes for?" Joey asked.

Clarence looked flustered—he hates to lie about anything—so I took over. "In case two of them break," I said.

"Funny, McKeown. I can see carrying a spare, but two just don't make much sense." Joey began walking around the area; in fact he looked like the snooper he was. He studied the ground for a while, but a pine needle carpet leaves no tracks. "When you gonna get a new truck, Meekins?" he asked, looking at the balding tires and rattling the wooden-gated sides. Then he looked inside and his face changed. "And what—he began, but cut himself short. He seemed to force himself away from the truck like a dieting glutton forces himself away from the table.

"Well, I'll . . . I'll just be getting back," he said. "Care to give me a ride?" His voice was snarky.

"I'll show you the way back," I said quickly. "Clarence is going to be here for a while."

"But—" Clarence began.

I gave Clarence a hard glance. "Come on, Joey," I said. "Let's go." I turned Alikki towards home and began a slow walk. I had passed the truck while Joey was talking and taken a glance inside. On the front seat was a scruffy denim purse. A hairbrush rife with longish, dark hair left little doubt that it did not belong to Clarence.

Chapter Sixteen: Green Baloney

The band's name was Roadkill, and they looked it. Five old men in Goodwill castoff clothing, holding or standing next to instruments that would have embarrassed most pawn shops. When Gina and I walked through the door of the Red River Saloon, four of the men, each of which was at least 50 years old, were sitting on a makeshift stage, smoking cigarettes and nursing cans of Pepsi. The fifth, a short, thin, white-haired man in his 70s, was energetically fingering his unplugged bass guitar and making faces.

"They look like shit, don't they?" came a gratingly loud voice from behind the bar—one I recognized even after a year and a half as belonging to the owner. I looked back and saw Sam Rivers approaching, giving us both up and down leers. "But they not all that bad. Specially when you know that they ain't nothin but convicts." He looked at Gina, who was dressed in faux-fur-topped boots, a thick white sweater, and designer jeans that had gold swirls on the back pockets. "Didn't think you'd show up, Missy," he told her.

"My aunt had a dog named Missy," Gina told him evenly. "An ah don't particularly lahk dogs. So ah'd appreciate it if you called me Ginette."

"Ginette it is, haw haw," Rivers responded with real mirth. "Whatcha goin to play for us tonight?" he asked.

"You'll have to wait and see," she said, looking around the room.

I looked, too, and found that the room was already half full. Several customers were sitting at the bar on the right side of the room while a dozen others were eating, drinking, and being merry at the rough wooden tables scattered about. "They won't throw nothin," he said, then reconsidered. "They won't throw *much*, I mean."

"Ah've got thick skin," she told him. Then she carried her guitar case toward the stage. The members of Roadkill all glanced at her, but they were stealthy looks, as if they weren't sure that admiring an attractive woman was allowed in their contract. It was more unnerving than the open leers of their boss, who Gina had left me alone with.

I had to look up at him, but not quite as much as when I looked up at Clarence. "Hello, Mr. Rivers," I began, holding out my hand. "I'm—"

"You that McKeown woman from the newspaper," he finished. "Seen your picture. Then I remembered that once upon a time you had to come out here and pick up your daddy, who was a mite under the weather."

"You have a remarkable memory, Mr. Rivers." I had to raise my voice to be heard over the diners and drinkers, but only a little. It wasn't that they were subdued—it was more like they were deliberately keeping their voices down, like students in a schoolroom.

"Call me Red," he said. "I might not be good for much, but I never forget a pretty woman. Or an ugly one, either, haw haw."

"Sue-Ann," I told him, shaking his meaty paw. The light in the saloon was brighter than I would have imagined, which is to say that it was only semi-gloomy. Light enough to see that Rivers was dressed in dungarees, a thick, checkered lumberjack shirt that buttoned up the front, and black, grimy looking lace-up shoes. He was a couple of inches over six feet tall, but somehow he looked more massive than that, as if he were made out of modeling clay. He had thick lips and a face marked with the kind of capillary damage you often see in the cheeks of heavy drinkers. His hair was the kind of dark red seen only in commercials, and I wondered if it was real. Although he was only in his fifties, he very well may have been covering up some gray. Odd, because he wasn't a man who I would have guessed had any vanity.

"So you read *The Courier*, um, Red?" I asked.

"Whenever I see it," he answered. "Picked up one this morning and read about those bath salt drugs. Hard to believe the things people stick up their noses."

I had been scanning the room as we spoke, looking for Carlos Murillo, but there was so sign of him. I wanted to prod Rivers about Carlos, but he changed the subject. "So you're Miz Cartwright's boss?" he asked.

"She's the office manager, I'm the editor."

"She any good?"

"She's the best office manager I've ever seen."

"At music, I mean."

"I think she's wonderful at that, too."

"Where'd you hear her?" he asked.

Well, obviously I couldn't tell him that I heard her in my living room every night, but I didn't lie either. "She used to play at a club in Myrtle Beach," I told him.

He blinked. "Hard to play in Carolina when you work in Florida, "he said.

"Long story," I told him, but two can play the game of changing the subject when conversations approach too closely to things you want to keep hidden. "I didn't know you served food here," I said.

"Hamburgs, hot dogs, a little fish. Lotsa beer, but no whiskey."

Now if ever I had been in a bar that looked like it served whiskey—rotgut whiskey at that—it was The Red River Saloon. I must have looked unconvinced, because Rivers went on, "Convicts don't need to be around much whiskey."

"What do you mean by convicts," I asked.

"Convicts," he said. "Prisoners. Jailbirds. Inmates. This is mostly an inmate bar. Some guys reach their EOS and got nowhere to go."

"EOS?" I asked, feeling stupid.

"End of sentence. Some of em's been in prison most of their lives, got no family, no home, no skills to speak of. So they come here. I hire some of em to do odd jobs, give em a place to live until they move on. That band up there: most of em convicts, but at least they got some musical skills. See that old man with the bass? That's Saul. He's seventy-two years old. Used to sit in with Danny and the Juniors back in the Fifties. The little black guy talking to your friend there? We just call him Smith. When he worked for me in prison I was always having to write him up for singing in the chow line. Now I pay him to sing."

"So you worked in the prison?" I asked. That jibed with the information I had already gotten from Clarence.

"I was a sergeant before I quit," Rivers said. "That was years ago, though. Got sick of it; too much corruption. Try and write a story about that sometime, though, and see how far you get."

My reporter's instincts were aroused. "What kind of corruption?" I asked.

"Drugs, business deals with inmates, sex, you name it. Know how much you can get for a cell phone in prison? A pack of cigarettes? Probably those bath salts for that matter. Female officers can get even more, depending on how they sneak em in." As he said this his eyes deliberately moved down to my crotch.

"I get the picture," I told him uneasily, and changed the subject again. "So you hire convicts to work for you?"

"Cooks, bartenders, whatever. Lotta my customers useta be inmates, too. Some guys get out and stay in the area. I can tell an inmate from a mile away. See that guy sitting at the bar?" He pointed an oversized, reddish finger toward a hard-looking black man having a beer with a hard-looking woman. Both of them were dressed kind of spiffy in clothes so colorful they almost lit up the dim room. "Watch this. Hollister!"

At Rivers' shout, the man almost stumbled getting off his stool and turning to face him. "Yassa, Sergeant," the man answered in a voice that was more humble than his appearance suggested.

Rivers walked closer and I followed. "You stayin out of trouble, Hollister?" he asked.

"Yassa, Mista Rivers. Doin' alright. Me and my wife, we out on the town. Heard Mr. Smith was singin in the band." He smiled but stopped, as if not sure whether to continue, but something in Rivers' relaxed attitude made him spit it out. "But we come *anyway.*" With that, his smile turned into a guffaw, which was joined by Rivers' own raucous laugh.

Rivers signaled the bartender. "Give Mr. Hollister a beer on the house. And one for his missus, too."

"Thank ya, Sergeant."

My original opinion of Red Rivers was changing. He was oafish, yes, and sexist, and vulgar, but he seemed to actually care about his ex-charges. I cut my eyes to the stage, where all five members of Roadkill were clustered around Gina, admiring her Gretsch sunburst. The man called Saul moved toward a junkyard of equipment and pulled out a pint-sized microphone stand while one of the others untangled a skein of cord.

"She doesn't have a pickup on that big thang?" Rivers asked me.

"She told me that if she wanted an electric guitar she'd bah one," I answered. "But she doesn't mind mic-ing up if she has to."

"She doesn't waste any time, does she?" he asked, as Gina positioned a larger mic stand for her voice, put the guitar strap over her shoulder, and played a few notes. She asked the keyboard player something and he went over to his instrument and sounded a note. She nodded, and proceeded to make sure her instrument was in tune. She thumped both microphones and satisfied they were on, looked over the room. More people were filing in, and they weren't all convicts either. I saw Annie Gillespie from the office come in and take a seat at a table by the door. She had come with Betty Dickson and Betty's friend Kristy Jablonski from the bowling team. They were curious, I suppose, about whether Gina had any talent as a musician. Betty, who had never gotten along with Gina, was probably hoping for the worst.

I was mentally giving Betty the finger when I saw Joe Rooney walk through the door, blinking. Joe was a lawyer that had once had the office next to *The Courier*. I was surprised to see him, but even more surprised to see who he was with. I hadn't set eyes on Monica Sorensen in several years. Monica was an attorney who had been a friend of my mother's—one that she sometimes had lunch with and who may even have visited the house once or twice. Although Monica specialized in criminal law, she was also able to explain aspects of civil law that Cindy needed in her work as a real estate agent. Was she dating Joe, I wondered. And what were the two of them doing in such a dive?

Before I could think about it, Gina was speaking through the mic, the head of her guitar drooping lazily down toward the audience.

"Good evenin," she said. "Ah'm Ginette, and ah'm gonna play a couple of tunes. Get y'all warmed up for the *real* band." She nodded her head toward the members of Roadkill while the patrons booed and cheered in equal numbers. She had their attention, anyway, and that was good. "So are y'all ready?" she shouted.

"Yeah."

"All right!"

"Get on with it, Barbi!"

"Strum that big twanger!"

"She can strum *my* big twanger, haw haw," Rivers shouted out, and the crowd guffawed. Gina let the voices die down a bit before she suddenly brought up the head of the Gretsch and launched into a rock-gospel song we had heard recently on the pirate radio station. The guitar immediately drowned out the laughter and clashed around the room like an admonishment.

> *Are you ready?* she sang.
> *To sit by His throne?*
> *Are you ready?*
> *Not to be alone?*
> *Someone's comin to take you home,*
> *And if you're ready He will carry you home.*

At the beginning she played heavy on the bass strings, then switched to a ska beat on the higher strings for the next verse. She was using a raucous voice—one I rarely heard—and almost growling out the lyrics.

Her audience was paying attention all right, but I wasn't sure whether it was because of her music or her appearance. Before the song was even halfway through, though, Saul jumped on the stage with her, grabbed up his bass, and began backing her with a series of notes that bopped over and under Gina's own playing.

The audience perked up.

"Tighten up, Saul," someone shouted.

"*Damn* it, man," yelled someone else.

From the first, it was obvious that this old trooper had been playing longer than Gina or I had been alive.

He was familiar with the song, had probably played it with numerous bands in his career. He knew just what to emphasize without being intrusive and how to back off when Gina was vocalizing. He just grinned and nodded to the hecklers, and in the end, the audience shouted for more.

And Gina (and Saul, who looked like a white-topped mop) gave it to them. When Gina went into her version of Brenda Lee's "I'm Sorry," it didn't take Saul more than half a dozen notes to figure out her key and join in. He knew this song, too. Hell, he may have even played with Lee for all I knew.

> *I'm sorry, so sorry,*
> *That I was such a fool.*

It was certainly a kinder and gentler Gina who sang the countrified lyrics in a soft, almost tearful voice. The diners didn't exactly go silent—it was a bar, after all—but they listened.

After that, Gina played two songs written by Maryanne Simmons, a songwriter I had done research on several months earlier and whose music Gina had taken a shine to. The first, "Pay the Moon," was another soft, sad, and melancholy tune with just a hint of madness. The second, "Ashley and Me," was an up-tempo song Maryanne had written about our friend The Creeper, Ashley Torrington, several decades earlier.

It was nearly impossible for Saul to have heard either of these songs, but he still kept up. So, too, on the last song of Gina's set, Nina Gordon's spritely "Now I Can Die," he just smiled, nodded and kept the beat.

> *He takes me everywhere he goes and he goes*
> *everywhere*
> *He likes to try on all my clothes but not my*
> *underwear.*

When Gina got to the last line of the song, "I understand everything and now I can die," she half turned to Saul and chopped off five quick strokes on the finishing chord, bringing the neck of the big Gretsch up, then down in a tomahawk motion and cutting off the sound by quickly placing her hand over the vibrating strings. It was musicians' code and Saul, the veteran, caught Gina's signal and stopped his own last note on a dime, as it were.

The silence of the cut-off notes was replaced by clapping and hooting from the tables and I was surprised when Gina lowered the neck of the guitar, walked back to Saul and shook his hand, then gave him a little shoulder hug before approaching the microphone again and telling the audience, 'That's it for tonaht, folks. Ah lahked bein here, but if y'all want to hear any more, you're goin to have to ask that big red man at the bar there to let me come back sometahm."

It had been a short set—far shorter than the ones I had seen her play in Myrtle Beach and I was surprised that Gina had ended it so soon. Yet the set had been complete, giving the audience a taste of several of Gina's strengths: the range of her vocals, her masculine chords, her musical preferences. It was like she was giving The Red River Saloon an appetizer as well as giving herself a taste of the atmosphere of the place.

While she packed up her guitar in its hard-shell case, Roadkill scrambled up on stage and began plugging in. I had grabbed a table in the middle of the room and was waiting for Gina to join me. Although Red Rivers didn't actually sit down beside me, he hovered over me like a bodyguard and when Gina approached he held out his hand. "That was real nice, Ms. Ginette," he said. "How'd you like to have a steady gig?"

"Ah have a job already, Mr. Rivers," she answered coolly.

"I mean playing here on weekends," he explained. "Every Saturday, maybe, or a couple Saturdays a month. Whatever suits you."

"Ah'll think about it, Mr. Rivers. But ah lahk this place. Ah lahk rough people who can appreciate what ah'm trahin to do up on that stage. Ah'm kinda rough mahself. Ah haven't got it all down yet, but maybe ah can learn somethin from your band."

"Ha," Rivers snorted. "Buncha old deadbeats, but couple of em might know a little music at that."

Any further conversation was interrupted by the first notes of Roadkill—a few preliminary bass notes, followed by the slow church-organy sound of the keyboard and a slow riff picked out clumsily on an old Gibson solidbody that had seen better days; better nights, too. The little man they called Smith stepped up to the microphone and started screeching James Brown, or at least, in a voice that sounded like James Brown. There were some hoots but there were also several people who were singing the words along with him."

Smith was a short, soulful man who looked like he would have been equally at home without backup musicians. Sometimes off key, sometimes out of rhythm with his backbeat, he seemed oblivious to everything, even his audience.

After their introductory offering, though, Roadkill settled into more blasé material—soft love songs and instrumentals in which Smith, when he wasn't singing, just swayed from foot to foot occasionally tapping on a tambourine that was missing some of its little cymbals. It was difficult to talk over the music, so Gina and I mostly just watched and listened. Rivers had drifted to another table, and I did a double take when I saw that it was the table where Joe Rooney and Monica Sorensen were sitting. He shook hands familiarly with both of them and sat down. What business could Rivers have with two lawyers, I wondered.

I went to the bar and ordered Gina and I fish sandwiches and draft beer. I gave a wave to Annie and Betty at their table. Annie smiled and gave a thumb's up sign while Betty scowled. On the other side of the room, Monica Sorensen caught my eye and waved tentatively at me. I waved back. I also nodded to Joe Rooney, who had once been not only a neighbor to *The Courier*, but one of Cal Dent's golf partners. When Cal left town, all his friends had disappeared too. I thought of County Commissioner Ray Colley, who also seemed to be lying low since his wife Linsey had run away with Cal to Louisiana. It was a strange world with a lot of changing partners. I glanced at Gina, who gave me a smile when she saw me staring, then went back to watching the band. She was a partner I never wanted to trade.

The latest in what seemed to be an interminable set of noodling ended and Saul stepped to the microphone. He spoke in a surprisingly low voice with what sounded like a New Joisey accent. "Hey!" he shouted gruffly. "Are you hungry out there?" There were a few boos and one man yelled out "*Hell*, no!"

Saul chuckled, then nodded to the guitar player, who strummed a single chord. This time it was Saul that went to the microphone—his first lead vocal of the night. And the song he sang was in a completely different vein than all of the previous ones. This is what he sang.

> *They issue me with baggy clothes;*
> *My shoes don't fit my feet.*
> *They put me in a work crew when*
> *I should be on the street*
> *I work so hard I'm hungry;*
> *Hey Sarge gimmie somethin to eat.*

I want some ham and rice
A steak'd be so nice
I want some cheese and macaroni
But all they had was
Green baloney.

My friends I know you all agree
That stuff is just a sin.
And workin hard without no food
Will make you pretty thin
I know I need a doctor;
Hey Sarge you gotta take me in.

The doctors made me worse;
I had an ugly nurse;
They gave me pills that looked so phony;
All made out of
Green baloney.

Green baloney: a disgrace
Green baloney, in my face . . .
Green baloney in my dreams,
Green baloney makes me scream
Oh, no, don't sentence me to
Green baloney.

I've done my time I'm getting out
My transport's in the zone.
My wife has married someone else,
My children are all grown.
I don't know who will give me work;
Hey Sarge wontcha give me loan?

I'll take a five or ten,
I'll buy a big fat hen,
I want some mony mony mony.

But all he had
Was green baloney.

Green baloney: a disgrace
Green baloney, in my face . . .
Green baloney in my dreams,
Green baloney makes me scream
Oh, no, don't sentence me to green baloney.
Don't punish me with green baloney
Don't torture me with green baloney.

Most of the audience, which by now was almost standing room, roared, clapped, hooted, stomped their feet, and exhibited just about every other type of approbation you can imagine. It was almost as if they had come to the Red River Saloon just to hear that song. Saul just smiled and nodded. When the noise died down a little, he swept the room with his eyes, then said in his growly voice, "*Yeaah*, green baloney. Most of youse remember that stuff. Naw, *I* never ate it, that stuff had toxic chemicals. One day one of the guys took his tray up to the sergeant and he said, 'Sarge, look at this baloney. It's green!' So Sarge went up the cook and said, 'You can't serve these men that baloney. It's green!' Then the cook looks back at Sarge and puts his hands on his hips like some old *yenta*, and says to the Sarge, 'Sergeant, that baloney's *sposed* to be green!' *Yeaaah*, that's the truth."

Through the laughter, several voices rang out. "And we ate it, too!" yelled the man called Hollister from his seat at the bar.

"Didn't have nothin else," said a second man.

"I know *that's* right," said a third, shaking his head.

"We'll be back out after a little break," announced Saul.

"You mean after your *nap!*"

"And don't forget to take your medicine!"

I took the opportunity of leaning closer to Gina and saying, loud enough for only her to hear, "You were great, baby."

She turned to me and smiled, but before she could reply, a voice behind me made her glance over my shoulder.

"I didn't expect to see you here, Sue-Ann"

I turned in my seat and saw Monica Sorensen. She was dressed in a long leather coat over a light-colored dress and half heels. Her hair was short, but nicely curled; it seemed that she had prepared carefully for her outing with Joe Rooney.

"Hey, Monica," I replied. Monica and my mother had become acquainted after I left Pine Oak for college, so I had only met her once or twice on holiday visits. Not enough to have formed any opinion of her. Gina nodded at her and stood up. "Ah'll see you in a bit, Sue-Ann," she said, and disappeared toward the bar, where Saul greeted her with a smile and a toasting gesture with a glass of water. Without an invitation, Monica sat down in Gina's chair.

"I heard you were back in town, Sue-Ann," she began, then she laughed. "Of course with you being the editor of *The Courier*, a body'd have to be deaf, dumb, and blind not to."

"The hazards of newspaper work," I replied. Close up, and even in the dim light, I noticed nuances in Monica's face that I never had the chance to see before. One of her front teeth was slightly crooked, for instance and her nose looked like it had been broken sometime deep in her past. She was somewhere in her late forties, but no gray showed in the dark curls that ringed her features. She spoke with the confidence that comes with long practice in front of a jury.

"Still, I should have called," she said. "I looked for you at Cindy's funeral."

"The hazards of being in Iraq without reliable transportation," I answered.

Her laugh was kind of self-conscious, not sure what my tone indicated. I wasn't either. I was upset that Gina had left so abruptly, but I understood the reason.

"Are, you dating Joe now?" I asked.

Joe?" she asked, bewildered. "Oh, *Joe.*" She glanced toward her table, where Joe Rooney was still in serious conversation with Red Rivers. "Joe's just a colleague," she said. "He's Mr. Rivers' lawyer, but he invited me to come out here with him tonight to talk about . . . well, I'm not sure what. I guess Mr. Rivers just wants a little legal advice."

Not surprising, I thought, considering the man's customers. I wondered why Joe decided to come out at night rather than asking Rivers to drive to his office during normal business hours. I had more than a slight suspicion that Carlos Murillo might be part of their discussion.

After a short hesitation, Monica continued, "I . . . I guess Joe thought maybe I might like the music, so we could kill two birds with one stone. The woman was good. Is she your friend?" Monica, having done her own version of changing the subject, glanced toward the bar, where Gina was drinking beer and chatting with several members of Roadkill at once. And I noticed that Annie Gillespie had joined them.

"She's the office manager at *The Courier*," I replied. I was dying to hear more about "the kid," but I knew enough about lawyers—and reporters—to respect confidentiality.

But Monica really didn't care what I was dying to hear, or about Gina, for that mater. She was looking across the room at the table where Joe Rooney was still talking with Red Rivers.

She looked away and laughed nervously when she caught me staring. She looked around for something to drink—something to do with her hands—but she had left her glass at her own table.

"I liked your mother a lot, you know," Monica said finally.

"I appreciate that," I said sincerely. "She was special."

"She was the only one I knew that could take me out of the courtroom atmosphere. I loved going out to her place, although I guess it's your place now. I never rode any of the horses, but I liked to be around them. Around their smell and their gentle noise."

The memory seemed to allow Monica to relax more deeply into the rough chair. "You know," she began again, "Cindy told me once that being a lawyer and training horses were similar. We both believed that things should be *correct*."

"That was her favorite word," I replied, smiling.

"Murdering somebody isn't correct," Monica went on. "Stealing, beating up on people, abusing children; none of that is correct either. But for Cindy, the word meant so much more."

"Yeah," I remembered. "If you wanted to be a good rider, you had to sit correctly in the saddle. If a horse acted up instead of moving with the aids, that horse wasn't being correct. Oh, here's another: if a mare, say, was built downhill—with its rump higher than its withers—it would be harder to bring her into an upright posture, which is what you need for dressage. That mare wouldn't be correct."

"That's way over my head, there, Sue-Ann. "But for me it was kind of a purity thing. So many lawyers take cases just for the money; no cash, no representation.

That didn't seem correct to me either. So I learned by it. Anyway, I guess that's what I came over here to tell you. That I still think of her."

"So do I, Monica; every day. I know she was grateful to have you as a friend. And grateful for the legal advice."

"I know enough real estate law to get by," she said, smiling. Then the smile faded as she remembered something. "Then the other thing came up and she just *insisted* that I represent her."

"What thing was that, Monica?" I asked.

"You know, her divorce."

My lungs seemed to stop in mid-breath. No, Monica, I thought. I very definitely did *not* know.

Chapter Seventeen: The Adventures of Robin Hood

It was after 11:00 when we finally got home, and although I had told Gina about my conversation with Monica Sorenson, there were parts of it that I didn't want to think about right then, and I was way too wired to sleep. So after undressing for bed, I searched Netflix for my favorite movie and cued it up on Instant Play. It was *Robin Hood*. Don't ask me which version—the Errol Flynn/Olivia DeHaviland version is the only one worth the name. I have watched it countless times—and for countless reasons—but for Gina, it was a first.

We were snuggled together in the big bed with its white comforter pulled to our chins. The room was a bit chilly, but warming up quickly. On the screen, Robin had just deposited a large buck on Prince John's banquet table.

Divorce was a word I had never associated with my parents. I mean, I know they never had very much in common, never did much as a team, but they had always seemed to manage. Monica had told me that they hadn't been getting along for years. Was this true? Were they just pretending whenever I would visit? But how many times was that; maybe once a year?

On the TV screen, Robin had just shot one of King John's guards in the chest with an arrow. "Did you see that?" I cried. "Do you know how they did that?"

Gina hit the Pause button and frowned at me. She hates it when I talk during movies, which is always. "Stop-action photography, ah guess," she said.

"No, no," I said excitedly. "The movie was made in the 30s—they didn't have all that stuff then. That guy really got shot in the chest. He was wearing a lot of padding."

"Errol Flynn shot him?"

"No. It was Howard Hill. One of greatest archers of all time. He was the archery consultant for the movie."

"What if he missed?" Gina asked.

"Howard Hill could shoot an aspirin out of the air at twenty yards. Anyway, the actors who got shot were paid a hundred and fifty dollars for each arrow."

Gina hit the Play button and we watched on for a while.

I suppose that my mother and father had been young once, and happy like Robin and Marian. I had seen pictures of their wedding, a very traditional one in a small church in Forester. Cindy had streaked Mike's nose with wedding cake icing and laughed. But Cindy liked to laugh. She was laughing in the pool at some motel near Weeki-Watchee Springs, where they had gone for their short wedding trip. Her and Mike's faces were sticking through oval cutouts in a poster of two mermaids. It was ridiculous, of course, but she loved it. Mike? Well, he was game anyway.

In the movie, a caravan led by Guy of Gisbourne, rode through the forest, escorting ill-gotten taxes—and Marian—to London.

"Nahce pally she's rahding," Gina said uncharacteristically.

"Stop the movie!" I cried.

"Hush, Sue-Ann. Ah'm trahin to watch."

"Stop it."

"Whah?" she asked, but she paused it.

"Know what that horse's name is?" I asked mischievously.

"Now how would ah know that?" she asked.

"It's name is Golden Cloud," I replied.

"You wanted me to stop the movie to tell me that?"

"Yeah. No. I mean that Golden Cloud is a golden palomino stallion. Right after this movie was shot, his owners rented him to a cowboy singer. The cowboy liked the horse so much he bought him and renamed him. Guess what the new name was??

"Ah'm not guessin, Sue-Ann."

"It was Trigger!" I said triumphantly.

"Come on now, Sue-Ann. Trigger's Ashley's horse. He would have to be eighty-some years old. Oh, wait, you mean the *original* Trigger?"

"Right as a rabbit and just as frisky," I told her. "It was Roy Rogers' horse."

And Gina really did think that was worth stopping the movie for—you probably do, too—and when she pressed the Play button again, she was watching more carefully.

And as we watched, I tried not to think any more about my parents. But it was hard. Especially since Mike had been so peremptory in getting rid of Cindy's things. When I finally got back to Pine Oak after breaking up with Jack in Richmond, even her computer was gone. Now why was that? Suddenly I could see him going through the house, searching through Cindy's belongings, seeing what he could sell before I got home. It's hard to sell a used computer, so he probably just dumped it in the trash. But why? Were there files on it that Mike didn't want me to see? A diary, maybe? Shit. If I hadn't been so fucked up when I came back from Iraq . . ."

Gina was enjoying the movie, as I hoped she would. I wanted to pause it again and talk about the origin of the color Lincoln green or the various saddles and bridles of Medieval horses, but I kept silent. I longed to tell her about the longbow that Robin used—how long it was, what wood it was made from—but whenever I opened my mouth, Gina would say "Shush."

I shushed.

But during the archery competition scene, I couldn't hold back any more. "Ooo, ooo," I squealed, and grabbed the remote. "That's him." I hit Pause just as a character dressed in a leather jerkin and green hat came into the center of the screen. I could make out his short goatee and mustache.

"Who?" she said with mild exasperation.

"Howard Hill. The archer. He plays the character of Owen the Welshman."

"That's nahce, Sue-Ann, and ah appreciate you wantin me to know all this stuff. But whah don't you just wait until after the movie's over?"

"I might forget later."

"You never forget nothin."

"Yeah, but, you know . . ." If people really blush, which I doubt, then I blushed. Certainly I felt something coursing through the veins of my face; it was coursing down the rest of my body, too. The fact was that Gina liked to have sex after watching a movie. Not every movie, but most movies. Another fact: I liked it and didn't want to interrupt it by talking about what we had just seen. Ergo . . .

Gina read my reaction correctly and huffed, "Ah'm not that kahnd of girl." But then she leaned over (she didn't' have to lean far) and gave me a peck on the cheek. She took that opportunity to steal back the remote and hit the play button.

We weren't married. Florida didn't allow same-sex marriages even if we were inclined in that direction. And reclining there in our large bed, propped up on half a dozen pillows and kept warm by a fluffy comforter, I realized that it was something I did want. At that moment—and at most other private moments—I felt as married to her as if we had gone through a legal ceremony.

And there would be no divorce. I knew right then that it was Gina and me forever. Don't ask me how I knew, but I did.

My eyes were glazed with tears as I stole a glance at her profile, and I sent a thought her way: *I want to be married to you for real*, I told her silently.

I think she heard me, because she glanced from the TV screen, gave me a fleeting smile, and turned back.

And after the movie was over and Robin got the girl and rode off; after Gina and I had kissed and touched and tongued each other to near-oblivion and lay facing each other, sweaty and happy on top of the mussed-up comforter; after the TV went black and the only sound came from Kitty Amin crunching niblets out of his bowl in the kitchen; only then did Gina ask curiously, "So Robin Hood split that other guy's arrow raht down the middle."

"Right," I answered. "And to this day splitting one arrow with another is called a Robin Hood."

"And when you do that, you win, huh?"

"Um, not exactly," I said. Damn. Gina had found the single flaw in my favorite movie. "I mean it would be a tie, wouldn't it? They got that part wrong."

"Wonder what Howard Hill thought of that?" she said.

"They either paid him to keep his mouth shut," I replied, "or he shot a couple of producers without waiting for them to put on any padding."

~ ~ ~

The next morning, I called Myra Van Hesse early enough to get her before she left for church. She answered perkily on the second ring.

"Hello?"

"Myra, this is Sue-Ann."

"Oh, hi, Sue-Ann. Good morning."

"Sorry for calling so early, but—"

"Just sitting here having my morning coffee," she answered. "Is something wrong? You sound kind of . . .

"Yeah. I guess I'm a little spacey this morning and I need to get away from everything for a bit. I know it's last minute, but do you think you could give me a lesson sometime today? I can come out there and ride Facilitator if he's sound."

"Oh, he's always sound, you know that. But, Sue-Ann, our church is trying to come up with an Easter program and I'm in charge of the choir music. I'll be busy all day. Maybe we could do it after work sometime this week. It's been too long since I've seen you."

"I agree, Myra. And I'll let you know about next week. I guess I'll just take Alikki for a trail ride and try to get my ya-yas out."

"I can't pretend to know what that means, Sue-Ann, but I don't think it's good. If you're goin to be ridin that young mare, make sure you wear your helmet. I can't help but think that if Cindy had been wearing hers, she might not have—"

"Wait a minute, Myra," I interrupted. "What do you mean Cindy wasn't wearing her helmet? She was a stickler for helmets—never let me on *any* horse without my helmet."

"My land, Sue-Ann, I know that's true. But still . . . Ever since Cindy died, it's been a thorn in my mind, just sitting there, making me uncomfortable without actually being able to reach in and pull it out. But for some reason she wasn't wearing her helmet that day."

"How do you know?"

"I was there that day, Sue-Ann. Not when she had the accident, but just after. We were planning to go out on the trail together on Facilitator and Trifecta. Then we were going to work Alikki some in the round pen. I hadn't heard about the accident, so I came over at the time we'd planned on, but nobody answered the front door. I walked around to the barn, but everything was organized as usual. The saddles were all on their stands and the helmets hung up as usual, right where Cindy always kept them. It wasn't until later that I heard about the accident."

"Wait a minute, wait a minute," I said hurriedly. "If you're right about the helmet, then you're also saying that she was riding without a saddle!" The idea that my father would have put the saddle and helmet back in their proper places while dealing with his wife's fatal accident was unthinkable.

"My stars, Sue-Ann. I guess that's what I *am* saying."

"But why?" I was asking it out loud and in my head, too.

"She did it sometimes . . . Myra began, then stopped.

"Did what, Myra?" I asked.

"It used to worry me to death, Sue-Ann, but sometimes . . . she told me that sometimes Mike would aggravate her so that she'd just hop on the nearest horse and gallop off somewheres."

"Mike?"

"I know she didn't want you to know, but Mike was always on her about caring more for the horses than she did for him. You know that he wanted her to sell that place and move somewhere else."

"I didn't know anything . . ." I faltered. I felt, at that moment, like the stupidest person on earth. Was I the only one in Pine Oak who didn't know that my parents were having trouble?

"I'm sorry, honey, that I had to be the one to tell you. But that was how it was. She had done well with her business and he was still working on high school teacher pay."

"But where did he want to go?" I asked.

"Oh, as to that, I don't think he knew that himself. Sometimes it was one place sometimes another."

"Well, look, Myra. I'm glad you told me. It's okay; I mean, I'm okay with it. I'll give you call in a couple of days about that lesson."

"You be careful, Sue-Ann, hear?"

"I will. Bye."

But I no longer wanted to ride. What I wanted to do was call the hospital in Forester, but for once, I didn't want to talk about my health. Because of my continual thyroid treatment, I had Dr. Will Morris' number on my cell phone at Number 6. I pressed the button. It rang twice, and when he answered, he didn't seem harassed as he sometimes did on busy days in the ER.

"Dr. Morris."

"Dr. Will," I said. "It's Sue-Ann McKeown."

"Ah, Ms. McKeown," he said, and I could see him in my mind: he was smiling. "If you can use the phone, you must not be hurt too badly this time."

"Funny."

"Well, if you're not hurt, you must have called either to ask me out or to give me the phone number of that gorgeous blonde co-worker of yours."

"Gina's too old for you," I answered. "And she's taken."

"So you keep saying."

"I won't ask you out, but I'll buy you lunch."

"Isn't that the same thing?"

"No."

"And it's not for hours."

"That'll give you time to get me some information."

"Aha. The plot thickens."

"I'm afraid so. Look," I softened my tone. "I've just learned something about . . . but you don't know anything about that, do you?"

"About what?"

So I quickly told him the story of my mother's accident, which had happened only days before I was supposed to come home from Iraq, and before Dr. Morris had started his internship. Then I let him know some of the questions I had and ended up asking him to see if he could find a few pieces of information for me. When I was sure he had the facts, dates, and times in his head, I told him I'd meet him at El Tapatia at noon sharp.

I was there ahead of time, trying not to gnaw on the end of my fingers. Gina was practicing a new song, so I told her I had an interview to do and would be back shortly.

El Tapatia was one of several Mexican restaurants in Forester, all of which seemed to be owned by a man named Paco. Paco, as usual, was sitting behind his own check-out desk, greeting customers as they came in and inquiring about how they found the food as they came up to pay. Hanging on the wall behind him was a portrait, done in oils, of himself riding a Paso Fino pony outside the gate of a rural *hacienda.* In the picture, his seat looked stiff, but I wasn't sure whether it was because he just wasn't a very good rider or because he hadn't been able to find a very good painter. Both, maybe.

Paco had no reason to do more than just nod and smile at me as I came in, and I realized that I had been in the restaurant only a handful of times, the last time being with Jack Stafford, when he had paid me that unexpected and unwanted visit in a last-ditch attempt to convince me to move back to Richmond with him. I remembered that we had just attended a Cowboy Mounted Shooting event at the fairgrounds—the first and only such event I had ever seen. It was there also that I had spoken to Krista Torrington for the first time. Then there had been the three Goth teenagers skulking through the stands like ghostly negatives. One of the three was dead now, and one—Becky Colley—worked for *The Courier*. So much change in so little time.

No beer is served in Jasper County on Sunday, so I had to make do with a Diet Coke, then a cup of coffee while I waited. I was about to ask the waiter for a second cup when I saw Will Morris enter the restaurant and look around. He was dressed in street clothes, which was a little disconcerting because I was used to seeing him in his green scrub smock. Another surprising thing was that he was with a companion—a tall, thirtyish woman dressed in a white shirt, white trousers, and sturdy, black shoes. Her straw-colored hair was tied tightly behind in a bun. She looked both austere and professional.

When Dr. Morris finally spotted me, he led his companion to my table and made the introductions without his usual banter.

"Sue-Ann McKeown, this is Peggy Haskins. She's an EMT."

The woman shook my hand and sat down. "I'm the one who brought your mother to the hospital," she said simply. Her accent placed her way out of Jasper County; possibly as far out as the Midwest.

Dr. Morris had done his work well. Too well, maybe. I wasn't sure that I wanted to hear what Peggy Haskins had to say.

And of course the conversation didn't take place as fast as I'm going to make it seem, and yes, we ordered something and some of us ate and we even sat around for a few minutes afterwards. I remember that Peggy visited the rest room once and that Dr. Morris kept touching the pocket of his shirt for the ubiquitous pencil he usually had at his fingertips. But he must have left it in his scrubs, so he pretended to be picking lint. Those are things I remember in the space of an hour and a half. Which is probably more than most people can recall;

after all, we're doing something all the time. And I'm sure we talked about many things: our jobs, our hobbies, our favorite Mexican foods, but I only remember the part that had to do with Cindy. And it went like this.

"We got the call sometime in the morning," Peggy began. "I can look up the exact time if you'd like. I was working with Jeff Switzer that day—he moved to Arizona a few weeks ago. Nice guy; very competent. I was driving and I had to stay on the radio because I wasn't sure where I was going—we don't get to Pine Oak very much. But we ended up making good time and parked in front of the house—there was a truck blocking the only lane that led around back. We ran the stretcher back there to where the arena was. There was a man sitting on the ground next to your mother. He had his head buried in his hands and your mother wasn't moving. She was lying with her head at an angle. It was resting on one of those long railroad ties that go all around that riding arena. Then I saw a horse and I wondered why it was loose in the ring. I saw a couple of other horses too, but they were in a pasture.

"Remember now, I had to see and register all these things in only a second or two, because as soon as we reached your mother, Jeff and I were both bending over, trying to get a pulse and giving her CPR. But I could tell that her neck was broken and no amount of CPR was going to do her any good.

"I asked the man—I guess he was your father— what had happened and he told me that the victim had gotten bucked off her horse and had landed there where she was lying. She had sand on her face and legs from where she had fallen. I saw a brush lying in the arena only a few feet away. I thought about using it to brush the sand off before we lifted her on to the stretcher, but we're taught not to touch things at the scene of an accident. I wiped the sand off with my fingers. When the sheriff finally got there, Jeff told him what we knew, then we got her in the ambulance and took off."

I listened to it all in silence. I had food in front of me but I'm sure I didn't eat any of it. "What . . . I began. "Um, what was she wearing, do you remember?"

"That's one of the things that confused me," said the EMT. "She was wearing shorts, a thin blouse, and sandals."

"No helmet?" I asked hopelessly. "No riding breeches, no boots?"

"No. I talked to the sheriff's deputy later, though, when he came to the hospital to get information for his report. There were marks in the sand—deep tracks, like—where it looked like a horse had spooked. I saw them, too, right next to where I found that brush. I mean, I'm sure there was no foul play. Is that what you're worried about?"

"If she had been wearing her helmet . . ." I began, then faltered.

"Helmets save lives," said the EMT. "But people can still die even if they're wearing them. Your mother fell at a bad angle. If she had been wearing her helmet and had lived she might have been a paraplegic, she might have had brain damage. We'll never know. Here's one thing, though."

"What's that?"

"It's odd, but I remember studying her face. Her eyes were closed and she had a little sand on her forehead. She looked pretty, and a lot like you. But overall, she looked peaceful."

"Peaceful?"

"Peaceful."

Chapter Eighteen: Flattop

Monday morning staff meeting, me presiding. The whole crew was present and alert. Outside the windows of the staff conference room, rain came down in sheets and most of us had gotten wet running from the parking lot. Randy Rivas, who was the last to arrive, was rubbing his wet hair vigorously with a towel that he had pulled from his workout bag. Annie Gillespie was paging through a white tablet on the desk in front of her; Becky was fidgeting with her nails; and Betty was murmuring something to Mark, who was studying the calendar in his appointment book. Gina was worrying over her own appointment book, which had gotten wet in the rain.

Cori Glenn, who was still carrying her left arm in a sling, sat next to me at the table. "Welcome back," I told her.

"Thanks."

I smiled at her and quipped, "Ready to get back to work?"

"I *been* workin," she said.

Everyone looked in Cori's direction.

"Whatcha got?" I asked.

Cori took a deep breath and began, "I went to see my brother in prison on Saturday," she said.

Eyebrows went up around the table. Cori noticed. She picked Annie to look at and continued. "Miz McKeown already knows this, she said. "My brother's name is Tywann and he's in state prison. He got sentenced to 20 years for nearly killing a couple of guys." She paused, then added, "While he was in Hardy."

"What?" Randy exclaimed.

"Your brother was in Hardy?" Annie asked. "When was that?"

"Five, six years ago. I ain't seen him much since then," she said, looking at nothing on the long table, "I'm on his visiting list, same as my mama and sister. Went a couple of times when he first went in, but after that it seemed like stuff kept happenin. Getting my degree, havin the kids, getting this job. But I finally went. I just showed up, unexpected." She looked up again, from one of us to the next. "I guess none of you ever had to visit folks in prison," she said, "but it's easier than you'd expect. You show an ID, they check your name off the Visitor's List, and then you go through this metal detector in Security. You get patted down, too, I guess so that they can be sure you don't have drugs or stuff to smuggle in. And after they're sure you're not there to do anything wrong, they let you go into what they call the Visitor's Park. But it ain't no park. It's just a staff cafeteria that they don't eat in on weekends. Square tables and plastic chairs. It's not like you have to sit across from whoever you want to see with a sheet of plexiglass between you. And you don't have to talk through a hole or use a telephone or anything."

No one at the table knew what to say, although they were listening to Cori with reporters' ears, trying to figure out where she was going. But Cori was faltering, not at home speaking for too long and to a group of people, even people she worked with every day. It was Gina who came to her rescue.

"How was your brother?" she asked.

Cori looked directly across to where Gina was sitting. "He, uh. I guess he was getting by, but he's changed so much."

"Grown up?" Gina prodded.

"Grown up, yeah. His voice is deeper, and he had tattoos. Lots of tattoos—even on his face. I mean, where can guys get tattoos in prison?" When she said it, it had seemed like a rhetorical question, but unexpectedly, Annie had the answer.

"Staplers," said Annie.

"Huh?"

"My ex is a doctor at the prison," she said, shrugging her shoulders just enough to be noticeable. "He told me once that the inmates steal staplers from wherever they can find them: the library, education classes, even the infirmary. They take out the tiny springs and stretch them out. They can get up to a dozen needles from one stapler spring."

"Ink?" Mark asked.

"From ballpoint pens mostly," Annie said. "But also soot from burned newspapers, plastic, whatever they can get."

"That's dangerous, though, right?" Cori asked.

Annie was careful with her answer, but it took no real thinking to make the connection between unsanitary conditions, shared needles, and disease. She opted to be kind by saying, "Sometimes, yes."

I headed off the subject by trying to get Cori's story back on track. "What did you all talk about?" I asked.

"Well, at fist mostly about Mom and Syreeta and the kids, but I could tell he wasn't too interested. Then I told him about my job and told him I was working on a story about Hardy. Then his look changed. I might have just told him that his sentence was over and that he could come home."

"He talked to you about when he was there?" Annie asked.

"All of it. After I left I wrote down as m   ᴵ could and I'm making it into a little story. I don't it's something we want to print, but it's some me to have. Anyway, he told me not to go there again. Told me that Mr. Sadberry was a sadistic motherfucker and that I was lucky the guy who ran me off the road hadn't killed me. He said I wouldn't be the first."

"So," I began, thinking quickly, "your brother was convinced that the guy who ran you off the road was from Hardy?" Remember that only Gina and I knew—thanks to Donny Brasswell—that I had already identified the driver.

"He knew it when I told him about the scarf or kerchief or whatever that thing is that everybody at Sadberry has to wear around their necks."

"He had to wear one when he was there?" Mark asked.

"Yeah," answered Cori. "And you know why?"

"Tell us," I said.

"Mr. Sadberry and his goons punish the boys by grabbing the back of the kerchief and yanking it up. Tywann told me that one time, one of the goons picked him up off the floor that way, so that he was dangling." She paused.

"Like he was on the end of a noose," I breathed.

"Like he was on a noose," Cori agreed.

The horror of that situation was lost on no one, and I when I looked around, I saw a circle of grim faces.

"Good work, Cori. Great work." I looked around the table at each face. "I think it's coming together," I told them. "Cori, get with Annie after the meeting and she'll fill you in on what we've pieced together while you've been out."

Cori nodded.

"Okay, who's next? Annie?"

Annie looked at her tablet, then at me. "I do have something."

"You've been poking around," I said.

"Like you suggested," she answered.

"Yep."

"Well, I poked through the morgue."

"Thought you might."

"Know what I found?" she asked me.

"Probably, yes. But you followed up on it and I didn't. Give."

"Okay, you had already given me a couple of folders you found. The one labeled H. A. Hardy was empty except for a note that said that Hardy used to be called Sadberry."

I nodded.

"And you had found the Sadberry folder, too, which told me that it was an orphanage. And the folder was full of stuff. Bad stuff. Stuff somebody had been working on for years."

"What kind of stuff, Miz Gillespie?" asked Cori."

"Rumors of abuse at the orphanage, a story about runaways, an investigation by the Child Services Department. Some of it was nitpicky stuff, but it all added up into something significant. And then there was a story about a boy who committed suicide. If you read between the lines, the article seems to indicate that it was more than just a suicide, but there wasn't any proof. I looked back at the other articles and saw that they were all written by a guy named Bill Rumsford, who was the editor at the time. So I decided to find him and ask him a few questions."

"Which, unfortunately, you couldn't do," I said.

"No."

"Why not?" asked Cori.

Annie answered. "He's dead. He's been dead for years. In fact, he died a long time before Mr. Dent was hired. When I found that out, something felt wrong, but I couldn't put my finger on it. So I went back to the morgue and looked through the files again. Something was weird. Almost everything in that file was put there

during Bill Rumsford's time as editor. Only a few things
from Mr. Dent and nothing from anyone who was here
between the two. So I did a little more digging and found
out about Flattop Scarborough."

"Who the hell—" asked Mark.

"Nice name," said Becky.

I didn't say anything. I was trying to suppress an ear-
to-ear smile listening to a good reporter's account of
how she worked—and how well she worked. It
reminded me of my younger days on *The Richmond Times-
Herald.*

"Jim Scarborough," Annie said. "But everyone
called him Flattop because of the way he wore his hair.
When Mr. Rumsford died, the owners of *The Courier*
needed someone to come in and take over in a hurry.
And Jim Scarborough was a cousin of the owners. He
did have some experience: he did some writing for *Stars
and Stripes* and spent a lot of his military time in
Communications. He grew up and went to high school
in Forester, so he knew the area well. And because Mr.
Rumsford's staff was already in place, you'd have
thought that the paper wouldn't miss a beat. Instead, it
seemed to wilt like a piece of wet spaghetti.'

"For how long?" asked Randy Rivas.

"For as long as he was editor," answered Annie. "I
looked through some of the old editions of the paper
that he worked on, but he was such a bad record keeper
I actually had to go to the main library in Forester to find
some of them. In a nutshell, his stuff was boring. Long
articles on local commissioners, deer-hunting adventures
. . . right-wing stuff, but not as bad as Cobra Conlon's
blather."

"Did you find anything about Hardy?" I asked.

"Yes. He loved it." Annie took out photocopied
sheets of an old newspaper article and passed one to

each person at the table. It was entitled, "Hardy Is Good For Jasper."

"Not much with titles, was he?" scoffed Betty, who had written a boatload of them in her time.

"Anyway, you get the idea. A complete reversal from Rumsford's pieces. But there was something still nagging at me, and it wasn't until I went back through the files again that I realized what it was. Assuming that Rumsford kept good files—which he seemed to—why was the Hardy folder empty? It took me a while to figure out that Rumsford died just after the suicide, but *before* Sadberry changed its name to Hardy. So now I had a new question."

"If Flattop Scarborough didn't keep the fiahls up to date . . . Gina began, obviously trying to reason out what Annie was moving toward.

"And Rumsford was gone . . ." I continued, trying to do the same as Gina.

"Then who created that file folder?" Mark said triumphantly.

"Yes. Good one, Mark," said Annie. "Did Flattop create it and later decide not to put anything in it, or did he get too busy, or what?" She looked first at me, then at Gina, then quickly at everyone else around the table. "That's what I decided to ask him."

"You found him?" I cried.

"I did. It wasn't that hard; there aren't many Scarboroughs in Jasper County. He lives with an unmarried daughter in an old farmhouse way on the other side of Forester. He's in his seventies now, and totally bald. He had a stroke a while back so that he's confined to a wheelchair and the right side of his face is slack. He can still talk okay; he slurs his words a lot but when you hear him you shouldn't have any trouble understanding what he's saying."

"How can we hear him?" asked Cori, looking towards the door as if Flattop might be lurking just outside.

Annie's answer was to pull a mini-recorder from the bag by her chair and put it on the table in front of her. "I recorded our entire conversation. Want to hear it?"

We did.

She thumbed the Play button.

We can pretend here that we are listening to the tape. That's fine; it's normal. But what we're really doing is reading an edited-down version of the transcript of the conversation—one that Betty typed out later in the day. A full transcript would be rife with pleasantries and non-sequiters and fraught with uhs and ums and you-knows. If it's any consolation, we edited it down even further before the article appeared. Annie's voice is educated-Southern and she knows how to use it. Flattop Scarborough speaks in a loud mumble, if that's not an oxymoron. Kind of like a sleepy bear.

COURIER: Mr. Scarborough, I'd like to ask you some questions about your days at *The Pine Oak Courier*.

FLATTOP: Call me Flattop. People alluz did back then.

COURIER: Flattop it is.

FLATTOP: So all y'all down there haven't forgotten me yet, eh?

COURIER: Not by a long shot.

FLATTOP: Didn't have no good-lookin young gals like you at the paper back when I ran things. Had a couple of old bats, though, haw haw. Had to fire em.

COURIER: They were bad reporters?

FLATTOP: Office staff. They was good enough, probly, but too tied on to the way things was goin before I got there. I had to get my own people in fore I could get comfy.

COURIER: I can understand that.

FLATTOP: Trouble was, the new ones wasn't no good neither. Had to do most of everything myself.

COURIER: It was harder back then.

FLATTOP: Wasn't that long ago, missy. We had computers; called em word processors but they did the job. Got the old paper out every Saturday. How many days a week you all come out now?

COURIER: Two, working on three. Plus we're thinking of doing an on-line version.

FLATTOP: On-line. Yeah. Lotta people on line now I reckon. Can't see how ye'd get any revenue, though.

COURIER: We're still figuring it out. But if I'm the reporter, why is it that you're the one asking the questions?

FLATTOP: Haw haw. Can't get the reporter out of my blood, I guess. Go on, fire away.

COURIER: Well, one thing I want to ask you about is the H. A. Hardy Juvenile Center?

FLATTOP: What about it?

COURIER: Are you familiar with it?

FLATTOP: Why shouldn't I be? I was the editor-in-chief of *The Courier*, right? Hellzapoppin, woman, I had to put out some fires about that place.

COURIER: About Hardy?

FLATTOP: Sure about Hardy. The editor before me—Bill Rumsford his name was—seemed to have some kinda vendetta against the owner. Accused the place of bein everythin from a slave camp to a drug den.

COURIER: Any truth to any of that?

FLATTOP: Hail naw.

COURIER: How did you know the stories were false?

FLATTOP: I just asked Marcus, face to face.

COURIER: You knew him?

FLATTOP: Hellzappin, woman; we went to high school together. Not much of a reporter if you can't find that out.

COURIER: I did find it out.

FLATTOP: Yeah?

COURIER: Just now.

FLATTOP: Haw Haw. Feisty, ain't ye?

COURIER: Maybe a little. What else do you know about Hardy?

FLATTOP: What else is there to know? Marcus Sadberry provides a valuable service to the community. Givin delinquents a place to live instead of goin to prison. Lot of them boys, their *parents* are in prison, or they don't have no parents at all. All they need's a little care and a little discipline.

COURIER: You know the other paper in town, *The American*? It seems to agree with you. About Hardy, I mean.

FLATTOP: Haw. That's Wiley Conlon's rag. Calls himself Cobra now I've heard. Worked for me a couple of months just before the paper got sold. Picked my brain, he did, then went out and started his own paper. Read a few of his issues, not many. Seems like if Rumsford was way too far in one direction, Wiley took off too far in another. Oh, I guess I agree with all the things he says about the President, him bein a Muslim and all, but what can you do about it? Kill him? You can't jus go around killing the President of the United States.

COURIER: No.

FLATTOP: Ain't heard from Wiley since the paper was sold. Marcus Sadberry neither. I kinda woulda expected Marcus to keep in touch. Guess I've had my day, eh?

COURIER: At least you had it.

FLATTOP: That I did. Maybe I'll give old Marcus a call—

Annie pushed the button to stop the tape.

I looked at her but all I could say was, "Jeez, Annie." Then I added, "But did you find out about the missing articles from the Hardy file?"

Annie smiled at me. "Stay tuned," she said. "Tomorrow. You and me, same time same place."

Hellzapoppin.

Chapter Nineteen: The Purple Pen Lady

Rain had been battering the tin roof all night and forming puddles in the paddock. I didn't even need to look outside; Torrington's pirate radio station told me more than I wanted to know. I had awakened to Electric Light Orchestra singing "It's raining all over the world," and I believed it. This was followed by the Beatles, singing,

> *If the rain comes*
> *They run and hide their heads*
> *They might as well be dead,*
> *If the rain comes.*

Gina was already up and I could smell coffee brewing in the kitchen. I used the bathroom and was putting on some old barn clothes when the Beatles song ended and DJ Smokestack's voice came out at me through the speakers.

"Splish splash, everybody! This is WWET, your all-weather radio station playing you twenty-four hours of continual weather forecasts."

I went into the kitchen, where Gina was sitting at the table with half a cup of coffee in front of her. She had another radio tuned to the same station. Stereo in small towns. I kissed the top of her head and poured myself a cup.

Smokestack was still talking. "Hey you all, I need some more rain songs. Otherwise I'll have to play 'Raindrops Keep Fallin on My Head' or maybe 'Rainy Days and Mondays.'"

Gina spoke up, "Ah kinda lahk ;Rainy Days and Mondays.'"

"Rainy days and Tuesdays," I answered.

"Here's a tune you've all heard before. I mean, you've heard it if you're old." To Smokey, anyone over thirty was old. I remembered hearing the song in college. It was by Chi Coltrane, a blonde singer songwriter that looked a little like Gina.

> *Thunder and lightning*
> *I tell you it's frightening*
> *And you're in control.*

And as if on cue, I heard thundering in the distance. But when the song was over, it wasn't Smokestack's voice that came on the air. It was the reptilian rasp of The Creeper.

Imagine that you had a big ball—a ball as big as you are—and instead of air, it was filled with a voice. Then you punctured the ball with a sharp, thin knife and the voice come hissing out. That's what The Creeper's voice sounded like.

"*She's wrong, there*," he hissed. "*I'm the one in control. I control what these silly little disk jockeys play on your radio, yas I do. Because I am old. Older than you can imagine. I control the music you listen to and the type of radios you buy, the kind of books you read when no one else is around. Somewhere under your bonnet, you know this. But what you don't know is that The Creeper controls the weather, too. Ha ha ha ha ha.*"

"He sounds creepier than usual," I said.

"Umm."

"*The Creeper* likes *the rain*," The Creeper continued. "*He likes looking out his tower window and seeing it pelt the earth like wet buckshot. He likes the puddles it makes and the sounds that the new-born frogs make. Frogs like the rain, yas. Horses like it, too. They like to splash and roll around and look at their faces in the puddles. But when The Creeper looks into a puddle, he sees nothing but time.*

And it's not good to have nothing but time. Time and only time. The rain talks to you if you listen to it. It says, 'Come out, come out, wherever you are.' And you should listen. If it rains every day and every night you couldn't play baseball, no, but it doesn't mean you have to stay in bed like bears. You could write and you could sing and you could solve crimes."

"If Ashley wants to see us, whah doesn't he just call?" Gina asked, as the first bars of "The Rain Song" by the Bangles replaced The Creeper's voice on the radio.

"He hates the phone."

"We should go," Gina said.

"You go," I said. "I've got to meet Annie at the office."

"First things first," she said.

And, in a rainstorm, on a farm, with horses, the first thing is to clean stalls. While Gina went into the barn to mix up the morning feed, I splish-splashed through the puddles of the paddock pushing a rusty wheelbarrow that contained a manure rake. There were three stalls and three horses, so unless we wanted to let them out in the thunder and lightning, we had to go into the stalls and clean around them. It was particularly bad when they had to be in all night, which they had. Alikki grumbled some and Emmy pretended to be a little wild, shaking her head and stamping a little. I had to tell her that was not correct, but both she and Alikki seemed to feel the steadiness of Irene, our alpha-mare, who usually kept both of them in line. The fresh scent of Irene's thick mane woke me up as much as the coffee had and made me glad, for the umpteenth time, that I had returned to Pine Oak. There was not much good about a rainstorm that had lasted through the night, but at least it hadn't been cold enough to have to put on their heavy blankets.

With two of us working, we soon had removed the manure and replaced the bulk of the wet, smelly hay with fresh. The Creeper was only half right; horses liked rain okay because it cooled them off on hot days. But some horses were so frightened of stormy weather that they might stand stock-still in the middle of a field, hanging their wet heads and waiting miserably for the storm to pass.

I had never seen a horse hit by lightning; neither had Gina, but my mother had heard stories and was terrified that one of hers would be next. She instilled in me the mathematical certainty that thunder equaled lightning equaled horses in their stalls. And they didn't hate it that much to be in these square jail cells. It gave them a chance to sleep a little more, knowing that they were safer from predators than they would be if they had been out in open pasture. I made sure to pile a bit of extra hay in the center of each stall in case they wanted to lie down.

"Did you get wet enough?" Gina asked me when we finally trudged back to the house. We both took our muddy shoes off and left them on the porch.

"Wet enough to have to take a shower," I told her.

"Can ah watch?" she asked playfully.

"You can help," I told her.

I drove to *The Courier* office though the still-pouring rain. Gina had made arrangements to go out to Torrington to see Ashley. The office was open; it always was on weekdays even if most of us were out doing other things. Bobby DuPre was sitting behind the receptionist desk doing some proofreading for Randy, who was in his cubicle typing up whatever he was working on. Annie was in her office with a woman I had never seen before, but I could only see the back of her head from where I stood. Gray hair, tied up in a tight bun. Granny hair. I waved at Annie as I closed my umbrella and left it by the door.

It took me only a minute or two to get myself a cup of coffee and settle in behind my chair. Rainwater dripped down the outside of my window like molten glass. Then Annie was standing in my doorway, ushering in her companion, who, in fact, looked like someone's granny. Although she was obviously in her 70s, she hadn't turned to fat or shriveled up like a lot of the older women I knew. Her clothes were from the seventies, an era that was never in fashion in Jasper County: a blue, flower-print dress worn over a pair of loose yellow slacks, a kinda-matching yellow sweater, and sandals worn with gray socks. She also wore a big, friendly smile.

'So you're the new editor," the woman asked before Annie could make the introductions. "My name is Alice Wilkins."

"Ms. Wilkins," I said, standing and taking her outstretched hand. "Sue-Ann McKeown."

"Oh I know who you are, Miz McKeown. But you can call me Allie. That's what Mr. Rumsford always called me. I guess he was the only one who called me that, but somehow I feel like I'm back in the good old days."

"Are you talking about *Bill* Rumsford?" I asked.

"'Course," the woman said, taking a seat in one of the chairs facing the desk.

"Miz Wilkins was office manager at *The Courier* for over twenty years," said Annie, taking a seat behind her.

"Office manager? Twenty years?" I suspected that Annie had done something special. But then again, she had a good boss.

"It wasn't always here in this building, of course. We used to be over on Fifth Street, where that big flower shop is now." She looked comfortable in the chair and I realized that she had probably sat in a similar chair in a similar office thousands of times in her career at *The Courier*.

"What did the office manager do back then," I asked.

"Oh, a bunch of things," she enthused. "Answered the phone, of course, made sure there was always good coffee brewing, ordered supplies . . .

"Did you sell ads?" I asked.

"Once in a coon's age, maybe. Mr. Rumsford usually had someone doing that on commission." She looked around my office, at the intercom, the new flat-screen computer screen, the photos on my walls depicting some of the stories I had worked on in Richmond and Iraq. "Maybe there wasn't as much to write about back then," she continued, "but, my, it was an exciting time for me. I learned so much about the newspaper business I might have been working for one of those big-city newspapers, like *The Dothan Eagle* or what not."

I started to say something, but Alice seemed to be on a roll. "Oh, there weren't many of us then; just me and Mr.Rumsford and a typist, and whatever reporter we could get at the time. Mr. Rumsford wrote most of the real stories; most of the other stuff was unpaid from people in the community. One of the pastors would write up the religious news, the football coaches would take turns writing about the local games, the bowling alley would send in scores from the week . . .

"The bowling alley still does that," I told her.

"I used to bowl once upon a time," she said. "I won the trophy for most improved bowler once."

"Did *The Courier* have a team then?" I asked.

"Oh, I don't think so. I just liked it. I liked seeing the people and being part of the bustle. But after I left the paper, I moved to Hanson's Quarry with my daughter and her husband. The bowling alley's too long a drive and I really don't have the money any more."

I sat back in my chair and studied the elderly woman. Her accent placed her as Jasper County born and bred, her clothes were, well, interesting—the clothes of a woman who didn't kowtow to fashion. But it was her demeanor that struck me the hardest. She was a happy, confident woman who spoke with no reluctance, and I suspected that it was simply being back in the place in which she had toiled for so long that was bringing back happy memories.

"What can tell me about Mr. Rumsford?" I asked.

"Mr. Rumsford? Why, he was a wonderful man. A true newspaper man. Not like that foolish man that replaced him.

"Are you talking about Mr. Scarborough?" I asked.

"Hmmh. Some of us had a different name for him."

"I may have heard some of them," I laughed. "Listen, Miz Wilkins. I mean, Allie, Miz Gillespie has probably already asked you this, but did you follow the stories that Mr. Rumsford was working on?"

"Follow them how?"

"I mean, were you familiar with what he was doing? Did he talk to you about the stories he was writing and what he was trying to accomplish?"

"Miz McKeown, I knew everything that went on in that office—and maybe in that man's mind, too. I kept the files in the back room, don't you know?"

"You maintained the morgue," I said.

"The morgue, the archives, whatever you want to call it nowadays. Sure, that was my job, too."

"You were the one who arranged all the old files?"

"I was the one who *started* those files," she said firmly. It took me an age and a half to get everything right, but Mr. Rumsford hired me because I was a stickler and I didn't want to let him down. I made sure we had half a dozen copies of every issue we ran and I sent some out to the bindery at the end of the year. And 'cause I was the only one who knew what was in em, I did whatever research Mr. Rumsford needed done from those files."

"You're the purple pen lady, aren't you?" I asked, smiling.

She smiled back at me. "I always used a purple pen, yes. That way I could tell it was me who'd done something—and everybody else could tell it, too."

I glanced over at Annie, who was following our conversation with her own slight smile, letting me find out for myself what she wanted me to know, but ready to jump in if I slipped off track.

"Here's something else Miz Gillespie has probably already asked you: what do you know about the H. A. Hardy Detention Center?"

"Ha! Hardy, Sadberry, it's all the same. Mr. Rumsford knew enough to blow the roof off the place, but he could never get any proof."

"Proof about what?" I asked.

"All that abuse that went on. Probably still goin on long as that Sadberry man is in charge."

"How did you hear about the abuse?" I asked.

"Everybody heard rumors of what went on in there," she said carefully. "Sometimes a kid would get out somehow, and claim he'd been beaten up by the staff, but Sadberry always had one of the other boys confess that *he'd* done the beating up. Couple of times one of the kids ended up in the hospital, but same story. He fell down from a tree or some such. Back when it was an orphanage, we had some complaints from foster parents, telling horror stories about things their adopted kids say they went through. But there's no way to prove any of that. Even when it was an orphanage, it had a reputation of taking in only the 'bad 'uns,' so people in the town didn't pay much attention." Alice looked from me to Annie and then back again. "But then there was the death of that poor boy."

"Allen Tilley," I prompted, but I don't think she needed prodding.

"You've got it right," she said. "Are you investigating that after all these years?"

"Somebody's got to, don't they?" I asked.

"Mr. Rumsford would be proud."

"I'm glad," I said sincerely. "What can you tell us about Allen?"

"Wasn't much to know, at least according to Mr. Sadberry. He was a local boy, what, sixteen years old. Small boy from what I heard. Frail. His parents were both dead and I guess he didn't have any other relatives. Found hanged in his closet."

"Who found him?" I asked.

"If I remember right—and I do—one of the Watchers. His roommate was gone that night. A little too conveniently gone if you ask me—and you haven't."

"How was he gone?" I asked.

"That's what Mr. Rumsford wanted to know. But Mr. Sadberry said that he had gone to a foster home the day before."

"Could Mr. Rumsford verify that?"

"No. And the boy never showed up again."

"He never—"

"That's right. The boy disappeared right into thin air."

I shuffled through some notes I had on my desk. "I found one article that mentioned that roommate," I said. "Something Krebs."

"Joseph Krebs," Alice said decisively. "I've remembered it all these years. Mr. Rumsford tried to locate him for weeks, but then he had that heart attack."

"I didn't know about the heart attack," I said.

"Happened in Forester," she said matter-of-factly. "He was driving back from covering an ag show when it hit him. He managed to pull off the road, but he died right there in his pickup." There was a real sadness in her features as she related these facts, but she quickly shook it off.

"It wasn't such a surprise," she sighed. "Mr. Rumsford was a big man. Over six feet, and he liked his food and drink the way grass likes sunshine and water. He wasn't really fat, but toward the end he had started putting on some weight. He liked smoking cigars, too. And all the pressure he had on him—trying to take on the sins of the whole county. It couldn't have been easy for him."

"Is that when they brought in Mr. Scarborough?" I asked.

"Pretty soon after," she said.

"And did Mr. Scarborough try to follow up on the Allen Tilley case."

"Hmmph."

"No?"

"Oh, he talked to Mr. Sadberry all right, but it seems like they were pally wallys. If it had been up to Flattop, Sadberry would have gotten a medal, but it didn't matter. Not too long after Allen Tilley died, the state stepped in and shut the place down."

"Now you're telling me something I don't know anything about," I said.

"You don't know because Flattop wouldn't print anything negative about his old chum. He just wrote this teensy little article about Mr. Sadberry wanting to pursue other interests. Hmmph. Truth is, the state kicked him out of the orphanage business. And good riddance, too."

Annie joined the conversation at last. "I didn't know about that either," she said. "And I went through every issue of *The Courier* for a couple of years. Then she added, "Of course I had to get those old issues from the main library in Forester."

"I was wondering why the Hardy folder in the archives was empty," I said.

"It was empty because Flattop never printed anything about Hardy," she said."

"But you made a folder for Hardy anyway, and you wrote that reference to Sadberry on the inside?"

"Did I do that?" she asked. "Sounds like something I might have done at that. I was a pretty sneaky old bat wasn't I?"

"You were a valuable newspaper woman," I told her sincerely. "Without your help, I'm not sure we would have ever found out about all this."

"I had hoped." And then she stopped. Suddenly, she seemed to be blinking back tears. "I'd hoped that someday someone might look through those old files and see . . . Oh, I don't know. I'm just an old woman ranting about nothing."

"Thank you for your work for *The Courier*, Allie. You did a fabulous job."

"Do you think that Mr. Rumsford . . ."

"Allie, I don't think anything. I *know* that without you, Mr. Rumsford would have been lost."

"Thank you, Miz McKeown. And are you going to nail that bastard Sadberry?"

"Yes I am, Allie. Me and Miz Gillespie and Mr. Rumsford and you. We're going to nail him."

When we were finished talking, I asked Randy Rivas to come into the office. "Randy," I told him. "This is Alice Wilkins. Call her Allie. She was the office manager here for twenty years. Will you show her around the offices? There's probably been a lot of changes since she was here."

"Glad to." Randy was both handsome and gallant— the perfect person to usher Allie Wilkins through *The Courier* offices.

As he led the excited Allie Wilkins through the various sections of *The Courier*, I turned to Annie. "Incredible work, Annie. How did you find her? What made you even *look* for her?"

Annie stretched out in her chair, putting both her arms behind her head and leaning back. "You were the one who gave me the idea," she said.

"Me?"

"You and Ginette, but especially Ginette."

"How so?" I asked, genuinely puzzled.

"Ginette was the office manager when Mr. Dent was here," she began.

"Yes?"

"And she was in love with Mr. Dent."

"I'll grant that," I granted, grudgingly.

"And now you're the editor," she said, "And she's in love with you."

"So that . . . ?"

"So I wondered if Bill Rumsford's office manager was in love with him. Well, guess what?"

"You think?" I asked, looking out the door as Randy showed Alice the computer where Betty now did what used to be done as hands-on paste-up. But my question was redundant. Alice Wilkins' devotion to her boss was way more than just an employer-employee one.

Annie just raised her eyebrows.

"That was brilliant, Annie," I told her. "Remind me to give you a raise,"

"Give me a raise," she said.

"I mean, sometime after this recession is over."

"Count on it," she said.

Chapter Twenty: Will

I spent the next hour doing editor stuff. I carefully went through the story that Randy had been working on: at least two high school athletes had admitted getting high on bath salts they had bought at convenience stores or truck stops. I assigned Becky to take pictures of the displays of bath salts in the places we knew sold them. I talked to Bobby for a while on how the morgue filing operation was coming and gave Betty a pep talk on using our new computer equipment to completely eliminate the need for pasting up shoppers—those pesky advertising supplements that were stuffed into our Thursday edition.

The rain was finally letting up as I left the office and drove to the County Courthouse in Forester. I had a few questions that only a look at public records would satisfy. I was anticipating a long, arduous, and fruitless process filled with red tape, but it had to be done. Luckily, I don't have to bore you with it by describing it all here. All I have to say is that it took a little less time than I thought it would and I had to speak to fewer people with almost no red tape. And fruitless, my no. I was making photocopies of the results of my research when my cell phone buzzed. I recognized Gina's number.

"Gina. What's up?"

"Where are you?" she asked.

"In Forester. I'm looking up some things at the courthouse."

"About Hardy?"

"About a lot of things."

"Fahnd anything?"

"I did, yes."

"Ah talked to Ashley."

"Anything happening?"

"A lot. But we need to talk."

"You mean, like, not on the phone."

"Lahk that, yes."

"Have you had lunch?" I asked.

"Ah could probably eat somethin."

"Eat Now?" I suggested.

"Too crowded. Someplace smaller and quieter."

"What about the Burger King down from Walmart?"

"Good. Let's meet there in an hour."

"I'll be there," I told her, and we—figuratively—hung up.

It took another few minutes for me to finish with the records, but I still had one more stop to make. Luckily, Monica Sorenson's law office was located just around the corner from the courthouse. A converted red brick home, it simply took its place in line beside similar converted houses: a real estate agency, a physical therapy center, and the like. A sign on the well-kept lawn stated in a stately font: Sorenson & Gallardo, Attorneys at Law. I walked up a set of flagstones, opened the front door, and walked in, almost knocking Monica down in the process. The lights were off and she was carrying a brown briefcase—obviously about to go out the door.

"Sorry," she said, "but I'm—oh, Sue-Ann. Come in."

"It looks like you were just going out," I said. "Do you have to be in court?"

"No, not today. In fact, I'm taking the rest of the day off. Come in. I'm glad to see you." Monica switched the lights back on and I could see that she was dressed impeccably in a white, long-sleeved blouse, longish beige skirt, and black shoes with low heels. She was carrying a London Fog overcoat—the rain had stopped and it was warming up outside. "Come on back. Sorry about the mess. My secretary's out today and my partner's in court in Tallahassee."

"I should have called first," I said. "But I was just over at the courthouse and—"

"No problem. Step in and have a seat."

The room she led me to looked pretty much as I would have expected a small-town lawyer's office to look. Two walls were taken up with shelves of law books. There was a rather small but expensive-looking desk and three leather-covered chairs—the one behind the desk swiveled, the two in front didn't. Monica put her briefcase down on the floor, hung up her coat on a peg behind the door, and sat down in one of the visitor chairs. I didn't know whether this meant that she was treating this as a social visit or that she didn't have time to discuss legal problems on her off time or neither or both. In any case I sat on the other visitor chair and decided to make it short.

"Listen, Monica. Do you know if my mother made a will?"

Monica ran her hands luxuriously through her curly brown hair, then kicked off her shoes as if glad to be off the clock for a while. "I'm pretty sure she didn't, Sue-Ann, But if she did, she didn't give it to me."

"Did she ever talk about making one?"

"She did, yes, but she said it like somebody else might say that they'll travel to Sydney someday. She always seemed to be too busy to actually sit down and do it. And, you know, with you living out of state, she wasn't really sure what to do about her horses."

"I guess that would have been a problem."

"You didn't find a will among her papers?" she asked.

I flashed back almost two years to just after I had returned home from Baghdad, burned out and sick from a disease I had never even heard of. Before I got myself together enough to actually go through Cindy's papers, vandals broke in the house and trashed it. Papers and folders everywhere. I tried to go through it all carefully, but there was a chance I might have thrown it away by accident, although I didn't feel like telling Monica that. Instead, I just replied, "I didn't, no."

"Have you asked your father about it?"

"He's living in Italy now, but I think his name was on a lot of their community property."

"The spouse generally inherits if the deceased is intestate," she said. "Why? Do you think there was a problem?"

"No, nothing like that. I was well provided for."

"Have you thought about making a will yourself?" she asked.

"Me?" I was taken by surprise.

"Everyone needs a will, Sue-Ann. I'm not trying to be a lawyer here; just a friend."

"No, no," I replied hurriedly. I had suddenly realized that making a will of my own seemed like the best idea I had heard in years. "Is there a form or anything that you can give me? I mean, kind of a will template?"

"Sure. Hold on a minute." Monica got up and padded barefoot across the rug to a filing cabinet, where she quickly found a folder and pulled out five or six sheets of paper stapled together. "Here take this." She handed the sheets to me and sat down again.

"Should I make a copy and bring it back?" I asked.

"I have plenty," she smiled. "You can get stuff like that on line, but that one there I put together specially for my clients."

"Thanks, Monica. What do I do when I actually get a will finalized, anyway?"

"Keep it safe. If you use a lawyer, give her a copy."

"I will."

"I need to ask you this, Sue-Ann, and I know it's none of my nosy business, but I read that article in *The Courier* about one of your reporters getting run off the road and you all getting a brick thrown through your window. Do you think you're in danger? Is that why you're thinking about wills?"

"I was in Iraq, Monica, and I didn't think about wills then. Maybe I was too stupid then. And there's a lot of different kinds of danger in the world. As far as the brick goes, it was scary, but I'm not too worried about it. The tables are about to turn."

"You know who did it?"

"I do know, but I can't say anything about it right now. News at ten."

"You're not a news anchor," Monica said.

"Yeah, but I always wanted to be." I stood up. "Have you heard from Joe Rooney again?"

Monica smiled. Was it a shy smile or was I seeing it wrong? "It's only been a couple of days Sue-Ann."

"Oh, right." So much had been happening that it seemed like weeks since Gina's performance at The Red River Saloon. "Anyway, good luck with that. I'll get back to you on this will thing. I will."

~ ~ ~

When I arrived at the Burger King, Gina's car was not in the lot, so I ordered a fish sandwich and a coffee and settled down in a corner booth with a folder of newly photocopied documents. I was so engrossed in what I was reading that when Gina arrived, my coffee had grown cold and my sandwich was untouched. She greeted me like a colleague.

"Sorry ah'm late," she said.

"Hey," I said, looking up at her. "You going to order something?"

"Ah'll get somethin later." She sat down across from me in the booth, her back to the window. "Show me what you've got."

"You first," I told her. "What did Ashley want?"

"A coupla things," she replied. "First off, Carlos called his mother again."

"Did he say where he was?" I asked.

"No, but we *know* where he is, Sue-Ann. What we didn't know was whah he ran away in the first place."

"And we do now?"

"Raht. He watched one of the guards beat a boy half to death. Didn't get him no medical attention or nothin. Just shut him up in a room to let him heal by himself."

"So that's why there haven't been any scandals there in the last couple of years. They just don't report injuries any more."

"Raht."

"Why was the boy beaten up, did Carlos say?"

"No, but ah kin guess."

"Sex?"

"Bingo."

"Maybe we should get Carlos to Torrington," I said.

"Ah agree, Sue-Ann, but Ashley's got to be sure that the boy's not a risk to the Compound. Raht now, Carlos is safe where he is."

"You think?" I asked, not convinced.

"Ah do," she said. "For some reason ah lahk that Red Rivers guy."

"He likes your music."

"It's more than that. But you and ah'll go out there soon. Maybe take Clarence with us. See if we can talk to the boy ourselves."

"When?"

"Tomorrow? As soon as we can, anyway. But there's more trouble fixin to happen. Jeremy was out in the woods the other day, pretty near where him and Clarence and Sandra Murillo were out balin pine straw. He saw Joey Bickley."

"Did Joey see him?"

"Jeremy doesn't think so, but Joey had a rifle and he appeared to be lookin for somethin."

"Or some place," I said.

"Raht. The only reason he didn't fahnd Torrington was because it started to rain so bad that he had to pack it in. But he'll be back out. Without a doubt."

"What does Ashley think?" I asked her.

"He's not sure. He's thinking of letting Colonel Frogmore handle it."

"That doesn't sound good."

"You think Frogmore's his real name?"

"I guess that's something . . . I began, but stopped. "Wait. I need to tell you what I've been doing this afternoon."

"Oh, raht. Does it tie in?"

"Some of it, maybe. Listen, after I left the courthouse, I spoke to Monica Sorenson."

"That lady that was at the Red River Saloon the other naht?"

"Yes. She's a lawyer and she was a friend of my mother's—although I don't think she was my mother's lawyer, if that makes any sense."

"Go on."

"She's pretty sure that Cindy didn't make a will."

Gina listened silently, not knowing where I was going. I wasn't sure I did, either.

"At the courthouse, I went to property records and looked up the deed to the house and the farm. Cindy had it put in my name only a few weeks before she died."

"That doesn't make any sense, does it?" Gina asked.

"I looked up the deeds of those two rental houses Cindy left me. Same thing, and on the same day."

"I don't lahk where this is goin, Sue-Ann."

"Neither do I, but while I was at the courthouse I also wanted to find out something else—something related to Hardy." I shuffled through the papers in my folder as I continued. "Remember the boy that died at Sadberry Orphanage?"

"I remember all raht, but I'm not sure about his name. Wasn't it Allen somethin?"

"Allen Tilley. And Allen had a roommate that just happened not to be there on the night that Allen died. His name was Krebs. I couldn't find anyone with that name in the phone book so I decided to do a search on Krebs in the property records."

"And what did you fahnd?"

"Not a thing. Which isn't really that curious because he might have left town after he was adopted—or even adopted by someone who lived out of town. But then I had another idea." I placed a photocopied sheet of paper in front of Gina. She read for only a couple of seconds, then: "Sue-Ann, is this what ah think it is?" She got a pair of glasses out of her purse and continued to read.

"It is," I smiled.

Gina looked up. "Pardon mah French, girl, but for fucking out loud, this is *it*."

"It is," I smiled. I looked into her beautiful face. Then, through the window, I saw something that shouldn't have been there. A white Camaro was cruising by slowly and I saw a face looking out at us.

"Gina," I said. "The white Camaro."

She spun around to look. "Where?" But it had gone around the building. "Are you sure?" she asked.

"I've seen that Camaro a hundred times," I told her. Had the driver seen me looking at him? Was he spying on me? Or on Gina? "I think we need to call the sher—"

I began, but stopped dead when I saw that the Camero had simply driven around the building and was making another pass by our window, faster this time. The passenger-side window was down and the driver's hand was stretched out, holding a long cylinder.

"Get down!" I screamed. I jumped from my chair and threw myself onto Gina just as the boom of a shotgun blast sent glass splinters flying everywhere.

I heard screams and the sound of scampering feet as the employees panicked. I felt Gina's hair beneath my chin and I heard her soft moan beneath me. I opened my eyes and lifted my head. Gina's hair was streaked with blood.

"Gina!" I tried to sit up but knocked my head on the underside of the formica table. My inertia had carried us both to the floor and partially protected us from falling glass. Not totally, though. I felt half a dozen prickles where tiny shards had lanced into my flesh and my right shoulder had a nasty, stinging gash that I really didn't want to look at too closely. It was Gina I was worried about though.

She struggled beneath me. "Get offa me, ya big lummox," she managed. I got up, cautiously. The bottom portion of the window had been blown completely out and the top half was hanging precariously.

"You've always wanted to say that to somebody, haven't you?" I asked.

"Said it to everybody ah've ever been with," she said groggily. "Damn, Sue-Ann. You shoulda tried out for the football team. You all raht? What happened?"

I helped her up from the floor and away from the hanging glass in the window. No one else had been hurt, but only because we had been the only two patrons in the Burger King. The employees had fled to the kitchen, I looked outside, but the white Camaro was gone. I examined Gina as carefully as I could, but except for the blood in her hair and a long cut on her right thumb, which she may have sustained just trying to get up from the floor, she seemed unharmed. But my tackle had dazed her. When she recovered, she looked at my face and muffled a scream.

"Sue-Ann," she cried. "You're all hurt.

"You're the one with blood in your hair," I told her.

Gina felt around in her hair and her hand came back sticky with blood, but she shook her head. "It's *your* blood, silly," she said."

"Mine?"

"You've been shot!"

I reached up into my own scalp and felt the wound, which was a thin crease, but painful, and bleeding profusely. The blood must have dripped down into her hair as I held her tight under the table. "Looks like I got grazed by one of the buckshot pellets," I said. "It could have been worse."

"But what happened, Sue-Ann?"

"It was the guy in the white Camaro," I told her. "I saw him holding something out the window. Must have been a shotgun."

"You saved mah lahf, Sue-Ann. You saved me from getting my fool head blown off and guess what. Ah love you more than it's possible to love anyone. I'll love you forever, even if you dump me." And she grabbed me and held me and kissed me and I was glad. We were both still alive, and I was glad about that, too. And when she pulled her face back it showed more than a few traces of my blood.

"Um . . ." The voice came from over our heads. We looked up from the floor and saw a middle-aged black woman wearing a Burger King uniform looking down at us.

"She loves me," I explained.

"Girl, I'd love you, too, if you'da saved my fat ass like you saved her skinny one. I saw what you did, but I still don't believe anybody could move that fast."

"I was on the Olympic team," I said.

"Well, whatever. Who was that and why did they shoot at you?"

I answered both questions with one word: "Enemies,"

"We called the cops and the ambulance, too."

"Thanks," I said. "I think we might need both."

We spent the next few minutes wiping blood off ourselves with Burger King napkins and a couple of paper cups filled with water. We had found a table on the other side of the restaurant that was glass-free and were sitting next to each other in a booth. Before we were finished cleaning up, a Sherriff's Department car pulled up outside and Billy Dollar rushed in.

"Sue-Ann!" he shouted as a greeting, "What the Sam Hill happened here?"

"Remember that guy who threw a brick through our window the other day?"

"This wasn't done with no brick," he said.

"Probably a twelve-gauge shotgun," I said. "One of the pellets just missed going into my skull. Wanna see?"

"You're in shock," Sue-Ann," he said.

"Probably," I agreed. "But you need to get that guy in the white Camaro. His name is Neely something. Neely Burks."

"Got it." Dilly rushed back to his car and made a call back to the switchboard. That set me free a little. I could relax a little. But relax is a relative word. It's easy to talk about now, but at the time I felt like someone had just drained a gallon of adrenalin from my body and left me alone in a room with a thousand gremlins. I was shaken and, I realized all at once, in pain from a dozen cuts. Napkins—wet and red—were piling up on the table in front of us as the ambulance finally arrived and two EMTs rushed in. I recognized one of them as the very woman who had responded to my mother's accident.

"Hey, Peggy," I managed.

With my hair sticky-red and my face all streaked, I don't think she recognized me. Her mouth was a thin line. "We need to get you on the stretcher." she said.

"I can walk," I told her "In fact . . .

"Git on the damn stretcher, Sue-Ann," Gina said loudly.

I got, although I still don't think it was necessary.

Peggy the EMT looked at Gina, trying to tell what blood came from where. "What about you?" she said.

"Ah'm all raht," she said. "You git her to the hospital. Ah need to git our things together and make sure her car's locked. Ah'll follow as soon as I can."

"You can come with me if you want." It was Dilly Dollar, who had rejoined us after calling in.

I had gotten on the stretcher and Gina was holding my hand. She kept it tight in hers until I was in the ambulance and they had closed the doors between us.

I know you were all expecting Dr. Will Morris to be standing outside the Emergency Entrance with a clipboard in his hand and a pencil in his mouth. I was, too, but it didn't happen. Instead, a thin guy and a husky gal in blue smocks took the stretcher from the ambulance and wheeled me into the ER.

"Are you doctors?" I asked.

"We will be. Why, are you sick?"

"I'm cut," I said. "And shot."

"Tell us," said the woman, who I guessed was in her mid-twenties. Brown hair tucked out of the way in a tight bun. "There was a pile up out on I-10 and we're a little overbooked right now. Are you allergic to any medicines?"

"No."

She produced a couple of pills and a paper cup of water. "Mild pain killers," she told me. I downed them and put the empty cup beside me on the examining table.

As they removed my clothing and picked small shards of glass out of my flesh in a few places, I told them about the shotgun blast and the falling glass.

"You'll have a thin scar on your scalp," the man said in a mild, all-business voice. "The bleeding's stopped, but I'm going to put some antiseptic on it. It might burn a little."

It burned more than a little, but I was more worried about my arm. The husky woman had been cleaning around the wound, looking closely for any remaining glass. "This cut is going to have to have some stitches," she said. "Hold still; this might pinch a little," and before I knew it, she had given me an injection of what must have been a kind of numbing drug. The two worked smoothly, as if they were a team that had been together for a while. I even wondered briefly if they were married.

"Yowch!"

"Sorry."

By the time Gina and Dilly Dollar showed up, I felt like I'd been picked apart and taped back together with band-aids. I probably looked like it, too.

"You okay, baby?" Gina asked, not paying any attention to Dilly, who shuffled in a couple of steps behind her. "I got here as soon as I could."

I got up to hug her, but winced because of my right shoulder, which was stitched and had a bandage around it. I broke the hug reluctantly. "Well, except for my arm, I feel surprisingly good." And I did. Whatever blood I'd left on the tile floor of the Burger King had been replenished by my beating heart. So had the blood I'd left on Gina, and when I looked at her my heart beat faster. That's not a lie; that's really something that happens when you're in love with someone and you're lucky enough to be near her and talk to her and even touch her if you want. And if you've just gone through a near-death experience with her.

"Billy," I turned to him. "Did they find the white Camaro?"

"Not yet, Sue-Ann," he said grimly—and Dilly is not a grim man. "But we'll find it."

"Where's Joey?" I asked. I had gotten so used to him showing up when he wasn't wanted that I was more than a little surprised that he didn't show up on the one time he was.

"He's doing training today. Classroom stuff that we have to suffer through every year. I'm scheduled for next week."

"I told Joey about Neely Burks the day after he threw that brick through our window. Why didn't he arrest him then?" I looked to Billy for the answer, but he shrugged.

"This is the first I've heard about it," he said.

"That makes no damn sense!" Gina exclaimed. "If Joey knew that the man was a danger, then whah—"

I cut her off. "Gina!" I cried. "My papers. The ones from the courthouse."

"Ah got em, Sue-Ann. They got shot up some, but ah got em."

"We need to go, then. Billy, do you have any more questions?"

"I got everything I need from Ginette on the way over."

Gina looked toward the two nurses, who were cleaning up the mess that came from me. "Is she fahn to go?" she asked.

"She's okay," said the woman. "But she needs to take it easy for a day or two. Don't use that arm much. Watch those stitches don't come loose. Otherwise, you be back here in ten days."

Bill Dollar drove us both back to Burger King, where we got in our separate cars and drove home. I drove in front and Gina behind, to keep an eye on me.

At home Gina took a shower while I washed myself carefully with a warm cloth, being careful not to wet my bandages. Gina's own wounds were minor; even the cut on her thumb was superficial. After she had dried her hair, she went into a closet and pulled out six polo shirts on hangers. They were dark green and each had a name in italics over the right breast: *Ginette, Sue-Ann, Bobby, Betty, Krissy,* and *Randy*.

"You had bowling shirts made?" I asked. I turned one of the shirts around and saw the sewn-in image of a bowling ball sandwiched between the words '*Courier* Crushers.'

"Ah did, yes. Ah took the money out of our advertising budget."

"You're not thinking of bowling tonight, are you?" I asked.

"*Ah* am, you're not. Ah got to, Sue-Ann. We're bowling Joey's team tonaht."

"What about your thumb?" I asked, eyeing her bandaged digit."

"Ah'm a southpaw, remember?" she said.

"Oh, right."

"Ah'm not sure if Randy's finger's healed or not, but can we bowl with only four?" she asked.

"Sure. They'll just use my average."

"That's all right, then," she said. "Let's go and kick us some butt."

It had been a long day, and it was about to get longer.

Chapter Twenty-One: 300

Gina insisted on driving us both to the bowling alley. It was one of the first times we had been in a car together and it felt cozy, even intimate, but a little frightening. I was drooping from the excitement, the cuts and bruises, and the pain meds. I had thought about staying home, but I really didn't want to be in that house by myself. And we had a lot to talk about and several situations to resolve. The first of these was the growing problem of Joey Bickley, whose prying into our affairs and the affairs of Torrington was getting serious. It didn't make it any easier when I spotted his dark blue Ford F-150 pulling into the parking lot at the same time we did.

"It's Joey," I said as Gina parked the car.

"Ignore him," she said.

That wasn't so easy. He parked next to Gina's PT Cruiser as Gina was locking up her side of the car.

"You picking up hitchhikers these days, Cartwright?" he asked.

"Only good-lookin ones," she replied. "Nothin you need to worry about."

"Yeah, well—"

But we had both turned our backs on him by then and were walking towards the entrance to Hi Score. I was wearing a Braves baseball hat that covered most of my scalp wound and a light windbreaker that hid the other bandages, large and small, on my arms. This was one day I wasn't slowed down by having to schlep my bowling equipment, and Gina used a house ball and rental shoes, so all we carried were our purses and the new green bowling shirts.

We were early and the place was almost empty. Two earlybirds sat at one of the tables drinking beer and munching from a bowl of nachos and cheese. The place gave off its mysterious, twangy scent of onion rings and lane oil. Doesn't sound appetizing? In a bowling alley it's irresistible.

Evidently, Gina thought so too. "Sue-Ann," she said, "Ah'm hungrier'n a hog."

"Umm, me too." I remembered that the sandwich I had ordered at Burger King had gone untouched, except maybe by buckshot and flying glass. With nothing to set down except our purses and the shirts, we checked to see what lanes we were on, then headed for the concession stand.

"Lemme have a cheeseburger all the way, an order of them nahce onion rings, and a pitcher of Honey Brown," Gina said, then she added, "And whatever mah friend wants." I was beginning to think that Gina had taken to the bowling life with surprising gusto when I saw Joey approaching us again across the dark gray expanse of carpet.

"Driving her around and treating her too, huh Cartwright?" He looked me over, taking in my cap and windbreaker. "Looking more butch than usual today, McKeown."

Gina had had enough. "Joey," she said. "Shouldn't you be out looking for that white Camaro instead of followin us around and makin stupid comments?"

Joey looked puzzled. "White Camaro? You mean Burks? You think he's going to chuck another brick through your prissy little window? I mean *if* he threw that brick in the first place, which he probably didn't."

"Damn it, Joey," she replied loudly, "the man almost blew our fucking heads off this afternoon with a shotgun. Don't you ever check in with your office?"

His face went as grey and as blank as the carpet beneath our feet. "What the fuck you talking about?" he said. "You'd say anything just to—"

Gina shouted at him before he could finish his sentence. "Don't say another goddam word until you check in with Bill Dollar or Tequesta or the damn Sheriff himself."

"If you're pulling my leg, I'll—"

"Just do it!"

Joey fumbled around in his pockets for his cell phone, let out a few choice curse words when he couldn't find it, then stormed up to the desk, where one of the older members of the Highsmith clan—Jake?— was talking on the phone. Joey didn't wait even a second before snatching the phone from the man's hand. I could make out the words "police emergency" leaving his lips as he pressed the disconnect button and dialed again. After what was probably a ring and a half, he spoke briskly into the mouthpiece, then just listened. His face went from displeasure to shock to red-faced anger, as if his heart was pumping blood for the benefit of his skin only. He asked a few questions, listened, asked a few more.

I turned away. Gina had given the woman at the concession some money and received our pitcher of beer in return. Isn't capitalism great? Gina hoisted it carefully and motioned me to a table behind our two lanes—5 and 6—pretty much in the middle of things.

The lanes were turned off and one of the Highsmith siblings was operating a machine that looked like a cross between a robot and a desk printer. It had wheels in both gutters and was connected to a power source by an unwieldy-looking black cord that must have been at least a hundred feet long. Highsmith—Jimmy I think it was—made sure it was centered in the gutters, then pushed a button on a remote-control device he held in his hand, and down the lane it went, stripping off old oil from the lanes and sucking it into a reservoir. It stopped a few feet from the pins, then made its slow way back, laying down a thin layer of new oil in a strictly programmed pattern on the surface of the lane. Jimmy then hefted it out of the gutters of that lane, moved it to the next, and the process went on.

Almost before we had settled down in our plastic chairs, Joey Bickley came storming over from the main desk and glared down at us.

"Ah'd ask you to join us, Joey," said Gina. "But ah don't want you to."

"What the hell have the two of you done!" he shouted so loud that both Highsmiths—as well as the nacho-munching couple—turned to look at us.

"What do you mean?" I said evenly.

"I was watching Burks. I had him in my sights. I was going to nail him, and you had to go and set him off. What did you do, call him up and tell him you had something on him? How did he even know where you were, anyway?"

"I don't know." Actually, I was pretty sure I *did* know. I suspected that Flattop Scarborough had followed up on his wish to call his old friend Marcus Sadberry and innocently tipped him off on what *The Courier* was up to. But that was none of Joey's business so I kept silent.

"And how did he know that the two of you were together?"

"I don't think he did know that," I said. "He got lucky. Have they caught him yet?"

"The bastard's disappeared."

"Did they check Hardy?"

"Of course they checked fucking Hardy. Sadberry says he hasn't seen him today. And yes, they checked. The car's not there either."

"His mother?" I asked.

"Same thing."

"Well," said Gina, sipping from her beer glass, "maybe he'll show up here and you can conk him with a bowling ball or something."

"Blow me, Cartwright."

"Not till you call me Ginette," she said.

"I'm going to have a good time beating the shit out of you and McKeown tonight," he said, motioning with his jaw toward the lanes.

"Twenty stitches on her bowling shoulder says that McKeown's not bowling tonight." I told him.

"And a crease down the middle of her scalp the size of the Panama Canal," Gina chipped in.

Joey just stared at us for a few seconds, his face a changing mask. Now it was hard to tell if he was furious or just furiously pensive. "If I find out that you two have been hiding that kid that escaped from Hardy, I'll—"

"You'll?" Gina said.

"And I'll tell you something else, bitches," he said, his voice dropping a few decibels as a few more bowlers came in and put their bags down at the next table. "I'm going to find out about the truth about the two of you, but first of all, I'm going back in those woods behind your place and find out whatever the hell's going on out there. Don't think I didn't see the purse in Clarence's truck the other day."

"Probably his mother's," I answered. 'But you know, maybe Clarence is secretly a crossdresser."

"We'll find out who'll have the last laugh," he scoffed.

I turned away and drank beer. Gina was looking over the score sheet. She looked up. "Bring it on," she said.

We heard Gina's name called and we left Joey and went up to the concession stand to get our food. "Easy for you to say," I said.

"Ah've got an idea," she told me, "but it maht be dangerous."

"Tell me."

And by the time we had finished eating and she had picked out a ball from the rack and the team was preparing for shadow bowling, she had let me in on her idea.

"I don't like it," I said, shaking my head.

"Neither do ah."

"We don't really have any choice, though, do we?"

"No."

Gina got her cell phone and went outside. It was a few minutes before she came back in and by that time the rest of our team had arrived and were busy changing into their bowling shoes, putting on the new shirts, and making sure that their resin bags were handy. Gina greeted them all with a smile, then looked at me and simply nodded.

Okay. All I had to do was sit tight and wait. In the meantime, I took better stock of my surroundings. The entire *Courier* Crushers had shown up for the match. Krissy Jablonsky and Betty Dickson had arrived together and I wondered again if they were actually a couple. Big-boned Krissy, with her unruly shock of reddish-brown hair tied back in a ponytail was almost larger than life while dowdy Betty was, well, it was sometimes difficult to tell if Betty was in the room at all. It took all kinds to make a couple, I supposed.

We had good news when we learned that Randy Rivas' sprained finger was healed enough so that he could bowl in my place, and I watched as Randy sent his practice ball down the lane. Oddly, Randy bowled more like an ice skater than the college baseball player he had been. His approach was almost dainty, and his release careful and precise. His ball traveled down the lane with the proper spin and trajectory, but slower than I would have expected and without the pin action that would have brought him from a C bowler to a B. But Randy would be bowling his first games of the season, so he would be bowling for average and his scores almost certainly wouldn't affect who won or lost the match.

In a handicap league, every team starts the night nearly even. Different leagues or houses have different ways of determining handicap, but the idea is to give less talented teams a chance to win. In the easiest scenario, someone who averages 200 would have no handicap at all while someone who averaged 150 would have 50. So it would be the team that bowled the highest over their average that would win the game or the match.

I glanced at our score sheet as Gina finished lacing up her red and white rental shoes. Her average was only 98, but she had bowled only a few times in her life. She would get better, I hoped. Betty Dickson, who threw a very slow ball in a straight trajectory (although not necessarily straight at the headpin), came in at 129, and would probably stay at that level not only through the season, but throughout her life, like some dressage riders I knew that had been competing in Intro classes for years. Krissy, on the other hand, had potential, although I'm not sure any coach in the business would look forward to trying to straighten out her jangly movement and convince her to give up the back-up motion she put on her too-light ball. Like Gina, Krissy was a lefty, but she threw the ball harder than anyone on the team and sometimes got good pin action as a result. My average on the sheet was 164, but I wasn't sure how high (or how low) I was capable of bowling after being away from league bowling for so many years. My average, of course would not count in tonight's match.

Bobby DuPre, our anchor bowler, even in his mid-sixties, had turned out to be one of the best bowlers in Jasper County. Smooth and precise in his delivery, he threw the ball out neither too hard nor too slow, with a spin that carried it out to the nine board and back in to the pocket. It would have been textbook bowling if we had been back in the 1970s, but the advent of resin bowling balls, high-tech construction, and wrist guards, had turned bowlers into virtual robots capable of cranking out double the number of revs Bobby got. Their balls delivered more pin action, but were way harder to control. Bobby's previous week's scores put his average at 194, but gave him almost no handicap.

Our opponents were called, I swear, Joey's Jerks. They consisted of Joey Bickley, two brothers who went by the name of Big and Little Small, a thin man in his early thirties named Mouse, and an older woman who was simply referred to on the score sheet as MM. I was nonplussed when I realized that they were my father's initials. When Krissy threw her last practice ball, I leaned over and asked her "What does MM stand for?"

"Mouse's Mom," she said.

I studied the score sheet, which had everyone's averages and handicaps posted on it. We had the player with the least handicap but also the one with the most. Joey's Jerks, on the other hand, were all averaging in the 160s except for MM. who was 145. On paper, of course, it was even, but someone had to win.

Randy Rivas, as friendly as a mutt with a new home, sat down beside me. "Gina tells me you're not feeling well tonight," he said. And it was only then I realized that he and the others had not heard about the shooting and my injuries. It was just as well; why worry them at a time that they were enjoying their leisure—time that most of them looked forward to all week.

"I'm okay, Randy. I'll tell you about it tomorrow."

"Tomorrow?"

"I realize it's not one of our usual days for a staff meeting, but something's come up."

"Something good?" he asked cautiously.

"I hope so. Now let me see some strikes."

All bowling matches are interesting if you know how to watch them, but I believe that even visitors from countries without bowling alleys could be entertained at Hi Score leagues. For one thing, Mouse and his mother pretended not to know each other. In fact, MM pretended she wasn't even on her own team and spent most of her non-bowling minutes hanging out with the women on the Willow's Florist team. Mouse himself seemed to be a gadfly, rushing to one lane after another, adjusting his glasses, and extemporizing on whatever was on his mind.

Big Small wore a Bluetooth headset throughout the match, looking like an overweight mechanic who had been picked up by aliens and given a surgically implanted homing device. As far as I could tell, he never spoke on the microphone the entire night, nor did he seem to be listening to music. His brother Little looked exactly like him—an overweight mechanic with a pot belly—only two inches smaller up, down, and all around. Instead of a headset, he wore a noose around his neck connected to about a foot of rope.

Now it's not likely that I'm going to sit here and describe every shot that every bowler took, making sure to mention how close they came to each missed spare and what the sound reminded me of whenever ball struck pins. But it's important that I give you an idea of the personality of the match. The feel of the way things went and why. The truth is that—on that particular night—Joey's Jerks didn't have as much chance as an armadillo trying to cross the interstate at rush hour.

And the reason was Joey Bickley himself. Out of sorts because of the news of the shooting and incensed to be bowling against my team, he simply tried too hard.

Joey, who already threw his heavy ball harder than I had ever seen anyone throw one, seemed to think that harder was better. It isn't, because the harder you throw a bowling ball, the less control you have. Sure, if you hit the heart of the pocket you're going to get a strike 90 percent of the time, but this is true whether you throw it 50 miles an hour or 5. And if you hit the headpin dead on, you'll leave a split the same number of times; the only difference is that the other pins will go down more quickly with a fast ball.

Joey got off to a bad start. His first ball hit the headpin but still left a difficult spare, which he missed. And from there it was downhill. And one of the reasons was Bobby.

When Bobby bowls, he is all bowler. There is nothing around him except the pins, and he probably knows more about those pins than anyone at Hi Score except maybe the Highsmiths. Sometime in the first half of the first game, Bobby was at the line studying a full rack. Just as he was about to make his first step to the line, Joey grabbed his ball and made his own ungainly approach on the next lane in an attempt to salvage a spare from a bad first hit—a gross violation of bowling etiquette. He failed. Luckily Bobby managed to stop his own approach in time, but his concentration had been broken. When Joey came back to the ball rack Bobby had a few words with him that Joey took badly. I didn't hear all of it, but I did manage to hear Bobby's final words.

"When you know as much about bowling as I do, you can tell me what you can do and what you can't."

Joey growled and walked away, but that set the stage for the rest of the match. As Joey got worse and worse, Bobby got better, and by the middle of the third game, *The Courier* Crushers were so far out in front of Joey's Jerks that they all would have had to strike out from the fifth frame to even have a chance. They didn't.

And to add insult to injury, the sixth frame of the last game saw Mouse, MM, Big Small, and Little Small all have strikes. If Joey would have struck too, no damage would have been done and there would have been daps all around. But Joey left two pins, which immediately made his teammates virtually go nuts, putting their hands around their own throats in choking gestures, because in bowling circles, being the only one not to strike in a frame means that you have been hung. So not only did Joey have to buy each of his team members a beer, he was required to put on the noose.

"Nahce tie, Joey," Gina told him.

"Fuck you, Cartwright. Any time you want to go one on one, let me know."

"Whah don't you go one on one with Bobby?" she asked.

"Fuck that old asshole, too," he said.

"Isn't that called buggering?" she asked.

But the rout wasn't finished. Gina was bowling a bit better than I had seen her and ironically, it was because of Joey. She was throwing it harder, although not as hard as Krissy, and throwing it harder made her concentrate more on throwing it off the correct foot. She was even managing a little finishing slide. I was proud of her.

Randy was going pretty well too, despite his still-sore finger. His first two games were in the 150s and he was well on his way to another in the same range. Betty was bowling her average and Krissy was too, although in an unconventional way. Her average was 156 going in, but she began the night with a 199 and followed that with a 120. I had done the same myself enough times to know how if felt.

But Bobby was bowling out of his mind. His first two games were 188 and 196, but he started the third game with a six-bagger. They weren't all perfect hits but they all went down. His strike in the seventh was a little light, but it somehow carried the five pin, and the one in the eighth was even lighter but resulted in a lot of mixing—pins jumping around on each other before toppling. The ninth ended by Bobby throwing a perfect pocket hit that seemed to make all ten pins instantly disappear.

By this time, Joey was almost comatose with fury. His strength had given out, too, so even though he tried to throw his ball through the back wall with every turn, his mph was way down. And so was his score. 95 going into the tenth on an open frame made it so that his highest possible score would be 125, his lowest 95.

Yet even Joey knew that Bobby was working on a perfect game, and like the teammates of a baseball pitcher who was doing likewise, no one said anything, everybody pretended that nothing special was happening.

And when Bobby stepped up to the line in the tenth, everyone was silent. Yet Bobby stepped back, put his ball in the rack, and motioned for Joey, his anchor counterpart, to go first. Bobby sat down to watch him, drying his sweaty hands on his towel that most bowlers carry in their bags along with their resin and shoes. The resin bag that Bobby used was a pretty one, too. Garnet and gold, looking a lot like a flattened pin cushion with the word Storm silkscreened across the center. Storm also made the ball Bobby was throwing and I made a mental note to get one for myself.

Joey managed a spare on a 2-10 baby split, which saved him at least a little face, then struck on his last ball to score 115, his lowest game of the year.

Then Bobby walked out onto the approach. He addressed the pins just as he always did, left foot slightly forward. Then he made his series of four steps—almost like dance steps—right foot, left foot, right foot, and slide on the left as his body turned and he released his ball from the center of the lane. It flew almost straight at the gutter before catching some friction at the nine board—which I suspected was the mark he aimed at—making a spinning left turn, and connecting to the right side of the headpin for another perfect strike. Simultaneous with the hit, Bobby pumped his right fist like he was punching Joey in the stomach.

The same thing happened on his second ball. Perfect strike, perfect fist pump.

By now, everyone in the bowling alley was gathered together behind our lanes to see the outcome. Bobby ignored them. He stepped to the line, pumped, started his four-step approach and made his release, then immediately went down into a crouch, his hands over his face. I saw it too—the ball traveled to the left of the nine-board before it made its turn toward the rack. I think that Bobby and I both groaned, but Bobby realized something before I did and straightened up. As the ball approached the pins, he turned his body slightly and instead of pumping with his right fist, he threw a pretend fastball with his left hand and screamed "Get it!" at the pins. Sure enough, the ball hit the 1-2 pocket on the left side of the headpin in a perfect Brooklyn smasheroo. All ten went down instantly and Bobby had his perfect game.

A clamor went up from the crowd as every other bowler in Hi-Score began clapping. It wasn't often they saw a 300 game, even in this hi-tech era. Bobby finally turned back around and smiled sheepishly. Then he said, "Whew!" and pretended to wipe his brow with the back of his bowling hand.

As Bobby was putting his ball back in his bag and changing shoes, our whole team crowded around him and said nice things and patted him on the back. And not only our team. It seemed like the entire Tuesday night menagerie went over to congratulate him. Mouse, Biff and Baff Hoke—their scraggly teeth on display in their smiles—members of the Highsmith clan, etc. The exceptions were Joey Bickley, who had packed up quickly, and Cobra Conlon, who had sidled over to Joey for a conversation. Both glanced my way from time to time and Cobra pressed his lips together and nodded.

This boded no good either for me or Gina, so when Joey headed for the door, I broke away from the celebration and intercepted him.

"Thanks for the match," I told him. "You'll do better next time." Although this was standard bowling etiquette, I really didn't mean it. I was just fishing for a response. It came in almost a hiss.

"Next time?" he spat. "Next time you might not be around."

"What's that supposed to mean?" I asked.

"It means that I just told Conlon all about you and Cartwright. I also told him about my idea of you hiding that kid."

"Joey," I began hesitantly, "You can't—"

"I can do anything I want," he said and tried to push past me. I wouldn't budge.

"Joey," I said, deliberately and noticeably taking a deep breath. "Joey, do you really want to know about Gina and me?"

"I already—"

"Maybe you do and maybe you don't," I said carefully. "But if Conlon publishes something like that in his paper, people might believe it. I'll probably lose my job. Gina will lose hers. The paper will go under and other people will lose jobs, too. Is that what you want?"

"It's exactly what I want."

"Joey," I continued. "What if someone wanted to publish something that *you* wanted to keep secret?"

"Ha, I don't have any secrets," he said.

"Everyone has secrets, Joey. But just because I might know something embarrassing about someone doesn't mean I have to go around blabbing to everybody about it."

"What are you talking about?" Joey had to stand aside to let a couple of the Willow's Florist women leave.

"You want to know about me and Gina? You want to know about Carlos Murillo? You want to know about what I've got hidden in the woods in back on my farm?"

"Yeah."

"I'll tell you, then."

Joey put his bowling bag down on the carpet and looked at me. "Yeah, go ahead then."

But people were leaving en masse now. "There's too many people here. I'll meet you at your house."

"My house?"

"I know where you live from that time you arrested Cletus Donnelly."

"You're really going to come over?"

"I am, but you've got to promise me not to let Conlon print what you told him."

"I'll think about it, but it better be good."

I was almost obsequious in my reply. "Thanks, Joey. I really appreciate it. And it'll be good. I'll see you in a little while, okay?"

He looked dubious. "Okay, but if you don't show up—"

"I'll show up. We're talking about my future here."

After Joey left, I looked around and saw that Gina was one of the only bowlers left in Hi-Score. She approached and looked at me questioningly.

"Let's go home," I said. "I've got to get my car."

On the way home, we talked a lot, but I'm not going to tell you what we said.

Chapter Twenty-Two: Trojan Horse

I didn't even bother going in the house before getting in my Toyota, pulling onto the old dirt road, and pointing its muzzle toward Sawdust Street. I had made the ten-minute drive only once before and under very different circumstances. I couldn't help but remember, though, that on that previous visit I had been shot with a crossbow and almost beheaded with a sword wielded by a crazed ex-mental patient. I hoped my luck would be better this time, but it was hard to be sure.

Sawdust Street was as typical a residential street as could be found in Pine Oak. Two- or three-bedroom houses spaced out on both sides of the street, some with red brick facades, others with white shingle siding, most with tin roofs. Sidewalks or flagstones led from narrow driveways to the front door. Lots of trees and landscaping. Thick hedges of viburnum, wax myrtle, and azalea. Joey's house was surrounded by a boxwood hedge that, like him, was tall and thick. Neither it nor his lawn had been cut lately, but a handsome man who has not shaved for a couple of days or has a shaggy head of hair is still a handsome man. It was a place for a wife, husband, and maybe one or two kids. A house where a tricycle on the sidewalk would not have been out of place. Yet Joey was single; to my knowledge he always had been and I wondered why.

I pulled into the driveway and parked behind his big Ford. I had nothing to steal, so I left the door unlocked and closed it firmly. Then I walked quickly up to the door. A car drove by behind me and pulled into a driveway a few houses down. Another bowler just getting home? I knocked on the door, then immediately turned the knob and walked in.

Joey was halfway between the door and a sofa, but stopped as I came in and closed the door softly behind me.

"You just barge in like that on everybody, McKeown?" he asked. Yet his voice was not as sarcastic as usual, his manner a little puzzled; as if he had not really expected me to show up. And it was obvious that, now he had me where he wanted me, he didn't quite know what to do with me.

"I knocked," I said simply. "Why, are you expecting someone else?"

"Just tell me what you have to tell me," he said.

I put my purse down next to a Barcalounger and sat down in its expansive comfort. "What do you want to know?" I asked. "Or maybe I'm the one who should be asking the questions."

"What are you talking about?" Joey retreated to the sofa and sat down so that we were staring at each other across the room. He was still wearing the street clothes he had bowled in, and that he had presumably worn to his training session earlier. Dark blue slacks, a tan, long-sleeved shirt, and black clodhoppers.

"Why didn't you arrest Neely Burks after I told you he threw that brick through my window? And ran Cori Glenn off the road? Is that supposed to be good police work? Did you talk to the Sheriff about it or did you just decide to ignore it? I mean, just because I told you it happened, did that make it not true?"

"I've got my reasons. I told you I was watching him. Then that damn training session—"

I deliberately interrupted him. "And where is he now?" I asked pointedly.

"You mean after you did whatever the hell you did and made him run?"

"All I did was a little research. I was doing my job; I'm not sure you can say the same."

I got up from my chair and started walking around the room. It was, not surprisingly I suppose, a sparely furnished room. In addition to the sofa and Barcalounger there was a TV stand against the wall near the front door. It held a relatively ancient-looking TV, a CD player, and a short stack of DVDs of the kind you can find in discount bins at Wal-Mart for a couple of bucks. I browsed through them as blithely as I could. Episodes of *The Andy Griffith Show, The Three Stooges, Beverly Hills Cop*. I carelessly dropped them back on the stand with a clatter. I studied the only photograph on the wall: a picture of a couple in their sixties.

"Your parents?" I asked.

"None of you're goddam business," he responded. "Sit down and leave my stuff alone."

"Remember the Trojan horse, Joey?" I asked, picking up a weeks-old *TV Guide* from the arm of the couch where Joey was sitting.

"Was it a TV Show?"

I dropped the *TV Guide* back on the couch and walked back toward the TV. I switched it on and off just to hear it click. "It was part of an old Greek poem by Homer. *The Iliad*. You'd like it because it's about armies and war. The Greek army was outside the gates of this city called Troy, but they couldn't get in because it was too well fortified. Kind of like The Green Zone in Iraq. But one morning the people of the city looked outside the walls and they didn't see any more Greek soldiers, just this gigantic wooden horse. Do you remember now?"

"Yeah," he said. "They stupidly brought the thing inside, but it had soldiers in it and those soldiers got out and . . .

I took a step toward the front door and finished the sentence for him. "And opened the gates."

And with that, I turned the knob of the front door and stepped back.

Like a mob of robots, six soldiers dressed in camouflage filed quickly into the room. There was a sudden rush of sound like many boots in a stairwell at the close of the workday. The faces of the soldiers were streaked black in patterns of their own choosing and all held assault rifles. The first two into the room were Carol Frogmore and Jeremy. Joey let out a bellow and tried to push himself to his feet but Carol was too quick for him and butted him in the chest with her rifle. "You must remain seated," she said.

Jeremy took his position at the left wall while Carol stepped to the right. Four other soldiers I knew only vaguely stationed themselves variously around the room.

"Who the fuck are you people?" Joey asked loudly. I was glad his service pistol wasn't handy because I think me might have tried to use it.

A seventh visitor, wearing a colonel's uniform without a nametag entered the room after the first six had deployed. It was James Frogmore. His face was not painted like the others, but then again, he wasn't insane. His mien, however, was very serious. Behind him strode Gina, looking like she had just showered and dressed for an important occasion. Then I realized that she hadn't had time to do either; she always looked that way. She was even still wearing her new green bowling shirt.

"Hey, Joey," she began. "Ah heard you were havin a party so ah showed up. Hope you don't mahnd." She closed the door behind her and carefully locked it. Then she walked over to my side and gave my hand a little squeeze.

Joey was speechless. I give him credit because I think I would have peed my pants. Painted-up Torrington soldiers are super scary; I was afraid of most of them even when I sat with them at the dinner table.

Joey roused himself when Col. Frogmore stopped in front of him and looked down. "You are Sergeant Joseph Bickley of the Jasper County Sheriff's Department. Is that correct?"

"Who wants to know?" Joey blustered. "I'll have every one of you assholes arrested for trespassing."

Carol Frogmore stepped forward and raised the butt end of her rifle but her father stopped her with a gesture. "Carol, please," he said.

Joey looked at the tall, thin woman as she moved reluctantly back to her position. Then he looked at me and Gina and growled. "Who are these people, McKeown?"

"Your worst enemies, ha ha!" said Jeremy loudly from his corner, but the colonel made a motion for him to keep quiet. Then he spoke in a rational voice, kind of like the way a doctor speaks to a patient. Then I remembered that Col. Frogmore *was* a doctor.

"I understand that you're curious about what Ms. McKeown is hiding in the woods behind her house," he began. "Well, that would be us."

Joey sat up. "What? Some type of military installation?"

"Something like that, yes."

"*Real* military?" Joey persisted.

"Let's put it like this," explained Col. Frogmore. "Our existence is sanctioned by the military and we have access to military files and intelligence. But if anyone— you, for instance—tried to get information about us, it would be as if the Berlin Wall were thrown up again, with you on one side and what you wanted to know on the other."

"So they'd say they never heard of you."

"Our existence would be thoroughly denied and you would be placed on a watch list."

"Why?" Joey asked, still surly.

"It's very simple, Sgt. Bickley. The work we do is important and the military establishment does not want our Compound to be compromised. We who live there live there in secret. You wanted to find us, but we do not want to be found. Can I make it any more clear?"

"Probably not. So what are you going to do now, shoot me?"

"Let me, Daddy!" Carol said.

"Don't be preposterous, Corporal."

"Let me at least shoot him in the leg," she begged.

"The middle leg!" piped up Jeremy from the other side of the room. There were snickers from the other soldiers, even a mild guffaw.

Joey looked askance at Jeremy, then turned his eyes to Carol Frogmore. "Your name really Carol?" he asked.

"All things are false until they are revealed to be true," she told him stonily.

Joey blinked. So did I.

"We're not bad people, Sgt. Bickley. We're part of the good guys. Everyone here has been in combat, fighting for this country. But now we insist on being left alone."

"And what happens if I decide not to?" Joey said, only half belligerently.

Col. Frogmore sighed. "Then yes, someone probably will shoot you, even if I tell them not to. But it's not going to come to that. Do you remember my just telling you that we have access to military records?"

"I have a very good memory."

"Then it won't surprise you to know that we have access to your own military records."

"My own? But I never served in the . . .

"According to our records, you enlisted and were given a dishonorable discharge for beating up the captain in charge of your unit."

"That's a lie!"

"Of course it is," said the colonel blandly. "But it will certainly be confirmed if anyone—like say, the Sheriff—asks about it. Then he may ask you why you didn't put this on your employment application."

From the sidelines, Carol Frogmore piped up, "Then it's out on your rear, goodbye career!"

More snickers from the others in camo.

"So what do I have to do?" asked Joey with angry resignation.

"All you have to do is leave us alone, Sgt. Bickley. Don't go out in those woods again—for your own safety and for our own. If it makes you feel any better, there is no illegal activity going on. No drugs, no receiving of stolen goods, no human trafficking."

"And what does McKeown here have to do with anything?"

"Ms. McKeown and Ms. Cartwright are very important members of our organization."

"Does it have anything to do with McKeown being in Iraq?" Joey asked.

"Ms. McKeown was in Iraq and you were not," replied the colonel, without answering the question. "You were, I believe, rejected for having flat feet."

"But you said—"

"I said that we had access to military information and that we could cause that information to change at any time. Our second topic, though, concerns Ms. McKeown. If she and Ms. Cartwright are more than friends it is not your business. It is not *anyone's* business.

"But—"

"There is no more discussion on that subject," said Col. Frogmore firmly. "You will leave their private lives to them. If you have told anyone about your suspicions—about them or about our compound—you will tell them—immediately—that you were mistaken and you will be very persuasive."

"Oh, Joey can be persuasive about *some* things," Gina said.

"Good then," said Col. Frogmore. He was going to say more but one of the grunts had noticed a set of chairs around a table in the dining room and had brought one out for Gina and for the colonel. He tried to get Carol Frogmore to sit in another but she shoved him away with the butt of her rifle and gave him a nasty glare. I had relaxed into the Barcalounger; my injuries of earlier in the day were taking their toll. The stitches in my shoulder ached and my head was burning like someone had conked me with the edge of a hot iron. I had done my part and I was grateful to sit and relax for a while and see how this little adventure would play out. The first act was complete. The second was about to begin.

The colonel took a seat and nodded to the soldier who had brought it in. Then he turned back to Joey Bickley. "Now let's talk about Carlos Murillo," he said.

Joey jerked up straight on the sofa. The idea of getting to his feet crossed his features but he looked in Carol Frogmore's direction and let it go. "What do you know about Carlos Murillo?" he asked.

"More than you do," replied the colonel.

"You know where he is?"

"Yes. He's living in a trailer in back of the Red River Saloon."

"Red River . . ." and without warning Joey started to laugh. 'Well, shit. You can't get no safer that that. No wonder I couldn't get a lead on him."

"Are you acquainted with the owner?" asked Col. Frogmore.

"Knew him when I worked at the prison," Joey replied. "He didn't like it no better there than I did." He laughed again. "I'd like to see Sadberry try to take him away from *there*."

Now it was the colonel ho looked flummoxed, although he covered it quickly. "I thought you *wanted* Mr. Sadberry to find the boy," he said thoughtfully.

"I guess you don't have access to as much as you thought you did," Joey said.

I spoke up from the depths of the Barcalounger. "I do, though,"

Col. Frogmore turned in my direction. "You can explain, Ms. McKeown?" he asked.

"I'm Sue-Ann," I said. "I went to the courthouse today to do some research on Hardy. Burks must have been following me and figured something was up."

"What kind of research?" asked Joey.

I stretched my neck and felt a couple of little pops, which were kind of soothing. "I read everything I could find about Allen Tilley," I told them. "He's the boy that was found dead back when Hardy was called Sadberry Orphanage. The editor of *The Courier* seemed to think that the official story was bogus, and I believed him. There were just too many coincidences; too many holes in the story. Like the fact that Tilley's roommate just happened to be adopted that day. And that no one ever saw him again. I decided to try to find him. So I went to the courthouse and asked for any information I could find on Joseph Krebs. He would be a year or two older than me; if he had remained in the area he might have even gone to school with me. But I didn't remember him. And I couldn't find anyone named Krebs in the phone book or in any deeds, marriage certificates, divorces, deaths."

"So his adoptive parents weren't from Jasper County," said Jeremy. "Doesn't take a five-star general to figure that out."

"You're right, *Private*," I told him, pointedly. "But then I wondered something else. What if his new parents *didn't* move away? What if, instead, he—"

"Took their name," Carol burst out.

"Raht as a rainbow and just as colorful," said Gina.

"Exactly," I said. "Now who did I know who was about my age and whose first name was Joseph? Hmm?"

"It was you, Joey," furnished Gina, but Joey didn't reply. He just sat back with his lips together. He glanced at the ceiling, at Carol Frogmore, then back to me.

I continued: "I went to another part of the courthouse and looked up adoptions and legal name changes. Sure enough, Joesph Krebs had a name change to Joseph Bickley. And suddenly everything made sense. Now I knew that Joey wanted to find Carlos because he wanted to *protect* him from guys like Sadberry and Neely Burks. I'm sorry, Joey. I should have known that you were on the right side."

"But you're just so damn *ornery* sometahms," Gina piped up from her chair beside me.

Joey made an attempt to look self-righteous. "Still hot shit, aren't you, McKeown?" he said.

"*Ah* think so," said Gina.

"Barf."

"Were you in the orphanage that night?" I asked.

Joey looked at the ceiling again, then relaxed into his seat. His voice relaxed, too, and he began talking more freely. "I was there, but I was outside on the ball field. Before we even finished the game, one of the Watchers hustled me into a car and started driving. When I asked where we were going, he said it was none of my business."

"When did you find out about Allen Tilley?" I asked.

"Couple of weeks later. You know, my adoption was on the level. The Bickleys had been trying to adopt me for months, but Sadberry thought they were too old. As soon as he needed me gone, though, he called them up. I wouldn't be surprised if he cut through a lot of red tape and even waived the adoption fee. And I'm pretty sure he paid for them to take me on a little vacation to a nice little fishing village in South Carolina. But when we got back, I heard my new parents talking about it when they thought I wasn't listening. I knew what happened."

"What *did* happen?" I asked.

"Allen was a pretty boy," Joey said simply. "And he was little so I tried to protect him from the other boys." He stopped. "I need a beer," he said. "Will one of you goons get me one from the fridge?"

Col. Frogmore nodded slightly at one of the goons and he disappeared into the kitchen, returning quickly with a can of Miller Lite. Joey popped the top and took a long swig.

"What I couldn't protect Allen from was the Watchers. And from that pervert Sadberry. Allen told me that Sadberry had exposed himself once when they were alone in Sadberry's office. Allen managed to get out, but after that the Watchers were hard on him. The boys didn't wear kerchiefs back then, they wore regular ties, and the Watchers liked to grab the ends and jerk on them. I saw one of them pull some other kid up so hard that his feet left the ground. I'm sure that's what happened. They pulled too hard and Allen either strangled or his neck broke. Then they hooked the tie to the bar in the closet and 'pretended' to find him later. That's why they hustled me away. They knew that I would have found him before they wanted him to be found and that I'd know what happened."

"You never told anyone?"

"I told that other newspaper editor, what was his name, Rumfield."

"Bill Rumsford," I said.

"Rumsford, right. He was a good guy, but he died before he could get enough on Sadberry to put him away."

"You never told the sheriff?" Gina asked.

"I told the old Sheriff, but he wouldn't listen. Bastard was a friend of Sadberry's. When he retired, Marcus Sadberry gave Sherriff Anderson all the campaign donations he needed. That's why I didn't tell him about Burks trying to kill your reporter. But I knew that it was true. I thought that if I watched good enough, I could get them to slip up. Earlier, when that kid Murillo escaped, I thought maybe he'd be able to help—to testify about something he'd seen."

I stood up carefully and breathed deep. "The only thing left, then, is to catch Neely Burks. You want to do it, or shall I ask Jeremy?"

"Me?"

"That's what you've been wanting for the last twenty years or so isn't it? To bring down Marcus Sadberry?"

"Of course, but—"

"Well, here's your chance."

"But I don't know where he is."

Col. Frogmore spoke up from his chair. "We do."

"What? How? Where is he?"

Gina stood up, too. "Put yourself in Neely's place Joey. That shouldn't be too hard because you've got a lot of stalker in you."

"What the hell are you talking about?"

"Look, Joey," Gina patiently explained. "As far as Mr. Sadberry knows, Sue-Ann is the only one who's investigating him. He still wants to get rid of her and he's got Neely Burks to do it for him. So if you were Neely Burks, where would you be hidin?"

Light came into Joey's eyes like a match had been struck in them. "Let me get my pistol."

"As long as you don't shoot one of us with it," said Col. Frogmore.

"No chance," replied Joey. "I might need the ammunition."

"Would you like us to come with you?" asked the colonel.

"You mean . . . you mean you'd let me capture Neely Burks by myself?"

"You're the law. We're not, but we'll come with you if you want."

Joey stood up to his full six-foot-six height. "He's mine," he said. Then, as an afterthought, he glanced at Carol Frogmore and added, "She can come if she wants to."

And lights went on in Carol Frogmore's eyes, too.

Chapter Twenty-Three: Showdown

I was dreaming about my favorite part of the movie *Deliverance*, where Jon Voight shoots a toothless hillbilly through the neck using a Fred Bear Kodiak Magnum recurve. It was a pretty accurate scene. Voight's character was scared and may not have pulled back quite hard enough for the arrow to go all the way through the neck and into the trees beyond like it should have. I liked the idea of the arrow sticking through the neck, but I thought it would have been even better if the hillbilly could have glanced down to see it, between his nose and his chest, knowing with inevitable certainty that there was no getting out of this one.

A light touch on my arm brought me instantly awake. I was sitting in a chair against the wall in my own home. It was pitch dark, but I felt a bow and two broadhead arrows on my lap. I felt Gina's warmth beside me. "Shhhh," she whispered softly in my ear.

There was a light rattle at the front door, the kind of noise you can't avoid no matter how carefully you turn the knob. I silently nocked an arrow and stood up. The door opened so slowly that I was not sure it was opening at all. There was no moon and it was almost as dark outside as in. Still, I saw a figure—or maybe the shadow of a figure—slip into the room. Then a slew of things happened within a single second of each other.

First, Gina switched on the lights, revealing a youngish man in overalls and a John Deere cap blinking and holding a rifle pointed toward the floor. So this was Neely Burks.

I shouted, "Drop it or you're a pincushion!" He began to raise the gun anyway—don't they always?—but before he was able to bring it level, Joey Bickley had come out from behind the door and brought his pistol down hard on the man's wrist. Bones cracked, Burks went to his knees, and the shotgun rattled across the wooden floor. Luckily, it didn't go off.

"You broke my hand!" Burks cried. I was able to study his face for the first time. It was kind of a baby face. No beard or mustache, reddish hair, apple cheeks. He glanced around the room for a way out, but all he saw were people with weapons. He saw me holding my Wapiti takedown bow (I didn't own a Kodiak Magnum) with an arrow aimed at his neck; he saw Joey Bickley standing tall above him clutching his pistol; and then he saw Carol Frogmore, painted like a Samoan linebacker and dressed like a commando, cradling an AK-47 in her arms like it was her real baby, and smiling. He glanced down at the shotgun, measuring its distance.

"You got another one," Joey told him calmly. "Go for it." Burks hesitated only an instant before he did just that and tried to scramble the two feet that separated him from his weapon. No, I didn't shoot him through the neck like I wanted to. I didn't need to. Joey showed off his surprising quickness by tromping on Neely's outstretched good hand with his heavy boot. More bones cracked.

"Now you'll have to jack off with your feet," he said calmly. Carol Frogmore thought that was the funniest thing she had ever heard and began laughing giddily.

Burks curled himself up in a fetus position, both wrecked hands tucked to his stomach. He began moaning.

"You gonna kill him, Joey?" Gina asked.

"Want me to?" he asked her.

"Ah do, yeah. But not in the house. Kin you take him out in the woods where you won't get no blood on nothin?" When Joey didn't answer immediately, Gina turned to Carol Frogmore. "You'll do it, won't you, Carol?" she asked.

"You bet!" Carol responded enthusiastically.

Burks started to cry. "Don't kill me," he said. "It was Mr. Sadberry. He told me to do it."

"Do what?"

"Stop the bitches from—"

"Stop *who*?" Joey roared.

"I mean Miz McKeown and the other reporter . . . stop them from investigating Hardy. And get that kid back if I could find him."

"Why would he want to do that?" Joey asked innocently.

"He saw me . . .I mean he saw Mr. Sadberry doing stuff with one of the other boys. And he knew about the bath salts."

"What bath salts?" Joey asked.

"You know, the ones that *The Courier* wrote that piece about. We've been knowin about those things for years. Keeps the bad ones in line. Owwww. You need to get me to a hospital."

"Why?" asked Carol Frogmore curiously.

"I'm hurt. I need a doctor."

Gina strode out from behind my chair and stood over the quailing Burks with her hands on her hips. "Let me get this straight," she told him. "You trahed to blow mah head off and blow mah best friend's head off and we're supposed to care whether or not you git to a hospital? In mah way of lookin at things, you got a lot more bones that need breakin."

"No, don't do it! I'll tell you anything. Just get me to a hospital."

Carol Frogmore took a couple of steps toward Gina, cradled her rifle under her left armpit and stuck out her right hand. "You were in combat today," she told Gina. "Twice. It's my pleasure to welcome you to the club."

Gina shook her hand and said, "It's not a club ah wanted to be invahted to join."

Joey sat down in the chair Gina generally used in the evenings, keeping a watchful eye on the writhing and moaning Neely Burks. I saw Joey look Carol over the way a butcher looks over a cut of lamb. "You're probably a ladies lady too, aren't you?" he asked her.

She had to think about that for a second, but her response came quickly. "You think I'm a lesbian?" she asked. "Well, not me. They're too happy."

"What's that supposed to mean?" he asked her.

She paused for a moment. "I was happy once," she told him mysteriously. "I didn't like it."

Neely Burks had decided to take advantage of their conversation to crawl toward the door. Carol Frogmore, without even looking at him, gave him a ferocious kick in the ribs that made him scream and sent him rolling into a corner.

"I don't know what your name really is or where you come from," Joey told her, "but right now you're about as happy as a bee in a flower shop."

"Covert actions sometimes become overt actions," she said.

"And you're a philosopher, too," he said admiringly. Then his expression became steely and looked over at the captive.

"Hey, Burks, you still alive?"

"Ohhhh."

"The way I see it, asshole, you're looking at multiple counts of attempted murder, breaking and entering, damaging private property, supplying drugs to minors, and probably a whole bunch of sex crimes."

"No. I never . . . I mean, I sometimes had to punish Murillo or Fredericks or Durden if they got out of hand but I never, you know, made them do anything. That was Mr. Sadberry and sometimes one of the others might get a little on the side if—"

"What others?" Joey interrupted.

"You know, the other . . . the other guys that work there."

"The other Watchers," said Joey.

I spoke for the first time in a while. "Hardy has to be shut down now." I said.

"Yeah," said Joey, obviously turning something over in his mind. He moved his gaze to Carol Frogmore and said, "Hey, I'm thinking about going over to Marcus Sadberry's house and getting him out of bed. Wanna come help me arrest him?"

"You mean, like a date?"

"Yeah."

"Well, I'd like to go but I, um, only those that are living have official status."

"What?"

"On paper, I don't really exist right now. Nobody's supposed to see me."

Neely Burks peeked out from his arms and managed, "*I* see you. Your name is Carol something and I'm gonna tell unless—"

Instead of answering, Carol Frogmore cracked him in the back of the head with the butt of her rifle and he went still. "Loose lips can result in collateral damage," she said matter-of-factly to Burks' prone form.

This might be a good time to talk about sympathy. Seeing someone beaten up is never a happy thing. In fact, it's usually gut-wrenching. Even just seeing someone hurt at the side of the road or bitten by a horse brings out an inner panic, a need to turn away, and a relief that you are not the victim. That sounds cold, doesn't it? Most people, hearing Neely Burks' bones being broken, hearing him screaming in pain, and knowing that he was suffering would have been quick to dial 911 and a lot of them would have had to throw up first—just from the sound. But all I could think of was the fact that this coward had shot at two people he didn't even know—people who were happy and were doing something good with their lives. A shotgun blast that, if I had been even a second slower, would have reduced Gina's beautiful face and quick wit to bits of blood and bone strewn so widely around Burger King that they would have been finding pieces of her for months. My head too, by the way. So no; no sympathy there. Joey knew what kind of a man Burks was and what kind of a man he worked for. He had been nursing a grudge and a hatred of men like them for two decades and had finally found a way to avenge his friend Allen Tilley. Sympathy? None. And as for Carol Frogmore, well, she may have seen more than her share of combat in the Middle East. She was not only inured to it, she seemed to like it, almost to live for it. Now *that* was something I could feel sympathy for.

But not for Neely Burks.

But we didn't kill him.

In fact, all that was left for Gina and I to do was listen while Joey Bickley called in to his office and set up the sting. Just before the ambulance arrived to take Burks to the hospital, Carol Frogmore disappeared into the trees behind the barn in company with other shadowy figures dressed and painted like she was.

"Who figured out where Burks was hiding?" Joey asked, as the EMTs were wheeling a still-unconscious Neely Burks to the waiting ambulance.

"We all did, really. I figured that when Burks found out that he'd missed the first time he'd show up here.

But Colonel Frogmore's boss thought the same thing and—"

"Frogmore has a boss?"

"You don't want to know, Joey," I told him. "He had an idea that Burks might be hiding out near here and so he sent some commandos over to locate him and keep an eye on him without Burks knowing it. I think that Sadberry warned him away from Hardy and he's been living in his car about half a mile into the woods for most of the day."

"Why didn't they just take him, then."

"They don't exist, Joey. And I wanted *you* to be the one to make the catch."

"Why? To get me off your back?"

"Think that if you want."

"I've got to go," he said.

"Kick ass," I told him.

Chapter Twenty-Four: News in Small Towns

It was a couple of busy weeks for *The Courier*.

Hardy director arrested in abuse scandal

By Corinthia Glenn
COURIER STAFF WRITER

Marcus Sadberry, long-time Director of the H. A. Hardy Juvenile Detention Center, was arrested early Wednesday morning and charged with a laundry list of crimes, including physical and sexual abuse of the boys under his care, supplying minors with drugs, contributing to the delinquency of minors, and operating a detention center without proper licensing. It is also likely that he will be charged as an accessory to the attempted murder of not only this reporter, but *Courier* Editor-in-Chief Sue-Ann McKeown and *Courier* Office Manager Ginette Cartwright, both of whom were injured when Hardy Staff Officer Neely Burks—on orders from his boss—allegedly shot at them during a business meeting at a local food establishment.

After being captured by Sergeant Joe Bickley of the Jasper County Sheriff's Department, Burks confessed to the

murder attempts and blamed Sadberry.
Also arrested were Vic Raymond, Alfred
Spitzer, and Lollie Grimes, all of whom
have been officers or "Watchers" at
Hardy for years.

A primary witness of the abuses
perpetrated by Sadberry is a 16-year-old
juvenile, who is presently under the
protection of the Sheriff's Department.
"He saw everything," explained Sgt.
Bickley. "Beatings, strangling young men
with their neckerchiefs until they nearly
passed out, even rapes of some of the
boys by staff members."

Sgt. Bickley, who had suspected
abuse at Hardy for years, was in charge of
the operation that netted Sadberry and
his staff.

It all began just over a week ago
when this reporter made an impromptu
visit to Hardy to ask about certain
irregularities in its disciplinary policies. . .
.

Legislator favors bath salts ban
By Annie Gillespie
COURIER BUREAU CHIEF

State Representative Bryn Stevens
from Jasper County is calling for a ban
on bath salts. No, not the soothing
crystals that we put in our baths to take
the knots out of our day, but the highly
hallucinogenic form sold in small packets
at convenience stores, head shops, and
truck stops. Labeled "Not for human

consumption" to avoid breaking already-existing drug laws, these types of "bath salts" are derivatives of synthetic cathinones, and have effects similar to cocaine and amphetamine.

Labeled by some as the new designer drug of choice, bath salts—packaged under various names such as Bliss, White Snow, and Vanilla Sky—played an important role in the recent scandal involving the H. A. Hardy Juvenile Detention Center. In a news conference, Jasper County Sheriff Milt Anderson revealed that dozens of packets of the drug were found in various areas of the Center, including the desk of Director Marcus Sadberrry.

Rep. Stevens, speaking right after Anderson, held up photos taken by *Courier* photographer Rebecca Colley, showing over a dozen types of these designer drugs on the shelves of convenience stores and truck stops within the county. "This type of thing can't be countenanced," said Stevens vehemently. "It seems like we get rid of one drug and they make five others to take its place. The bill I plan to place before the members of the House will outlaw any variation of the chemical cathinone that can be packaged in such a way to entice our young people into experimenting with it."

Stevens also warned that . . .

Bath salts found
in local high school
By Randy Rivas
COURIER SPORTS EDITOR

Evidence of the designer "bath salts" drug recently discovered at the H. A. Hardy Juvenile Detention Center crime scene has also been found at Jasper County High School. Acting on a tip from Coach Jerry Jacobs, several school lockers were searched and about a dozen packets of the substance were found. The names of the students involved—both boys and girls—have been withheld.

Coach Jacobs first suspected that some type of stimulant was being used when several students in his physical education classes began acting erratically. After this reporter informed him about the existence of these seemingly benign "bath salts" packets, the coach looked into the behavior more closely and noticed that it conformed to several known symptoms, including heightened anxiety and involuntary muscle twitches.

Jasper County School Board Superintendent Artie "Poppycock" Foster said in a written statement that he would address the rest of the board in a special session set for Friday afternoon. "Anyone bringing packets of these dangerous drugs onto Jasper County campuses will be suspended," he wrote. "We're going to treat this like heroin or marijuana," he continued. "We the parents and teachers of this community have absolutely zero tolerance for this type of thing."

Although sales or possession of these drugs, which go under the various names of Purple Wave, Ivory Sleet, and White Rain, is not illegal, it is thought . . .

Homelessness a problem
for women vets
By Sue-Ann McKeown
EDITOR-IN-CHIEF

The closing of the H. A. Hardy Juvenile Detention Center and the arrest of nearly its entire staff has brought to light an even greater problem: that of the thousands of America's homeless women veterans.

Cpl. Sandra Murillo, mother of the boy whose escape from Hardy prompted *The Courier*'s initial investigation of the center (and who has given permission to use her and her son's name in this story), is a homeless veteran. She not only served her country by doing a tour in Iraq, but was awarded the Purple Heart for being wounded in a firefight outside the town of Fallujah. Cpl. Murillo, who, since the closure of Hardy, has been staying temporarily with friends, has lived in shelters, an old school bus, and even a cardboard box that once held a refrigerator.

This is not as uncommon as you might think. According to a 2003 study by *The American Journal of Public Health*, women veterans are at substantially higher risk of becoming homeless than women who are not in the military. In addition, women veterans are 2-3 times more likely to become homeless than their male veteran counterparts.

According to Volunteers of America, a charitable group who has been helping Veterans reintegrate into American society since World War I, there are over 60,000 homeless veterans on the streets on any given night and at least twice that number will find themselves homeless at least once during the year.

More soldiers who served in Vietnam are homeless than were killed in battle.

In the case of Sgt. Murillo, her homelessness was a major factor in her son's being sent to H. A. Hardy on charges of . . .

Other Hardy abuse victims come forward
By Mark Patterson
COURIER STAFF WRITER

The arrest of Marcus Sadberry and his entire staff from the H. A. Hardy Juvenile Center on charges ranging from abuse to attempted murder, has ended an era—a bad era. But it will probably be a long time before the public knows exactly how bad. In the days since the arrest, half a dozen citizens have come forward to attest to crimes that they were victims of, witnessed, or heard about from reliable sources.

Van Guerney, who read about the arrest on line in his home in Virginia, was a former resident of Hardy. He writes, "Marcus Sadberry was all smiles and law-abiding on the outside, but on the inside he was a viper. Many's the time he had his Watchers beat me half unconscious for one reason or another while he just stood there and watched."

"Hooray for Sgt. Joseph Bickley for finally shutting down H. A. Hardy," wrote a Hanson's Quarry. resident. "My son was once incarcerated there and I always wondered about the bruises I saw on his face and neck when I visited."

Others, who have asked that their names be withheld, have stated that they will be available as witnesses against Sadberry and his staff if necessary.

The abuses of boys under his care began back when Sadberry's father opened Sadberry's Orphanage in the 1970s. It is not known whether Sadberry, Sr., was involved in . . .

The stories, of course, are all longer, but most people skip the tail ends of articles anyway. If you want to read the whole stories, ask your librarian to get the correct issue from their Archives. Or you can come by *The Courier* offices between 9-4 on weekdays. Ask for Bobby DuPre.

The next few weeks brought other headlines—both major and minor—to the pages of *The Courier*.

Orphanage "suicide" case reopened

Sadberry big contributor to Sheriff's campaign

Cpl. Murillo about Fallujah: "I'm no hero."

Bickley: "No plans to run for Sheriff"

McKeown to visit Italy

My favorite piece wasn't a headline at all, but a small box ad on the back page, paid for by Red Rivers that was to run for at least three months.

> **Red River Saloon**
> Burgers, Fries, Beer
> Featuring the music of
> Ginette Cartwright
> and Roadkill
> Y'all come on out.

A couple of weeks after Sadberry had been arrested and his shop of personal boy toys closed for good, I was sitting at one of Red Rivers' solid wooden tables and hobnobbing. Rivers had gotten some of his laborers to get up on high ladders and replace burned-out florescent light bulbs with new ones, and the place was much brighter. Not that this was completely a good thing. After all, a lot of the people that frequented the saloon were shady, or used to be, and didn't particularly want to be scrutinized too closely.

But it had become a habit—like our bowling league—to dress down and go into the Saloon Friday nights just to unwind. And with all the things we'd been through, we needed it. When I say we I mean me primarily, because I loved to watch Gina perform, but many of my other acquaintances and co-workers also found it a good place to chill out. On the night I'm talking about now, I was sitting at a table with Clarence, Sandra Murillo, Red Rivers, and of all people, Joey Bickley. Among those three giants, I felt like Sandra and I were raisins among plums. It was like our table was surrounded by five pegs, but two of them—Sandra and I—had been pounded in halfway.

"I never liked that old buttfucker," Rivers said in his loud voice, disconcerting some of his ex-inmate patrons. "Heard stories about the bastard when I was at the prison—which is where a lot of his graduates ended up. I mean if he didn't just hire them to be Watchers." In fact, two of the staff members who had been arrested—including Neely Burks—were found to have been formerly sentenced there for various crimes and misdemeanors. "Bickley, if that stuff is true about you being in his orphanage, why didn't you just kick the shit out of him?"

An old inmate sitting at the next table—a sleepy-eyed old drunk—mumbled, "*I'd* have kicked the shit out of him."

"Rowser, you couldn't kick the shit out of a sock," said Rivers.

Joey was clearly uncomfortable with the question and just shrugged. "If I hadn't been adopted . . ." he began.

"Yeah, yeah. Clarence, how'd you hook up with this little lady?" Rivers asked, eyeing Sandra Murillo's fairly ample bosom.

"We ain hooked up, Mr. Bonzo," she said. "I don even like him much."

"That's good news for me, honey," he said. "Why don't you stay behind when the others leave and I'll introduce you to some of the parts of me you haven't met yet. Haw haw."

"An maybe I'll cut off those little things and make you eat em," she retorted.

"Haw haw. You got a wild one there, Clarence."

Clarence, too, was uneasy in the presence of a man so totally without couth. Yet he didn't strike back as I would have expected. Instead, he pretended to see someone coming in the door. I looked too, but the doorway was empty.

"Okay, Miz Murillo," continued Red in a more serious, slightly softer tone. "What's gonna become of your boy?"

Sandra became serious. "We donno yet," she said. "I want him to be back with me, not in some other juvie place. I may have a job now; I can take care of him like I shoulda already."

"You have a job?" I asked.

"Security at the crazy people hospital."

"In Waxahatchee?" I asked.

Red Rivers broke in. "You're in Waxahatchee right now, Sue-Ann. Sounds like a good job to me."

Clarence cleared his throat and looked miserable. He gave each of us the once-over before he began to speak. "The, um, judge . . ." he began.

"What judge, Clarence," asked Sandra.

"The, um, judge that sentenced Carlos in the first place. I talked to him today."

"Yeah?"

"He said he might be willing to commute Carlos' sentence."

"That's wonderful news, Clarence," I said enthusiastically.

"But who we have to suck?" asked Sandra.

"Well, nobody, really. I mean, unless you want to."

"What, then?" Sandra persisted.

"Judge Timmons and I had a long talk. I know him from a long time back so I trust him and he trusts me. He said that if I took responsibility for Carlos, he'd see if he could have the original charges dropped."

"But how *you* can be responsible?" Sandra asked. "*I'm* his *mamacita*."

"Well, the truth is," Clarence hemmed, "the judge mentioned something about getting married."

"And why should we care if some old judge has the hots for somebody an wants to get married?" asked Sandra.

"No, no," Clarence hastened to reply. "Not him. He said maybe if the two of *us* got married. I mean, me and you, he'd feel a lot better about the situation."

"You and me? He wants me to marry a bonzo?"

"God's melons, Sandy, why are you making it so hard? Will you marry me or not?"

"Why should I?" she asked.

"Because you love me," he stated flatly.

"Why you say that?" she asked. "Because of all that grunting you did the other night? I heard lotsa other men grunting. What makes you think you special?"

"Okay, forget it then," Clarence said dejectedly. "I'll be getting on home to mama. She probably forgot to take her medicine again." He stood up.

"Clarence," I told him. 'Sit down. Can't you see she's saying yes?"

"Can't say I do," he said. "Seems like she's makin fun of me."

"She's saying it with her eyes," I told him.

Sandra got up from her chair and walked around in back of Clarence and put her arms around him. "You don't have to bribe me with a judge," she told him. "I'm your little *chica* if you want me."

We all started clapping, although I noticed that Joey seemed a little down. His own *chicita*, Carol Frogmore, had signed up for another tour in Afghanistan.

"You're gonna have to keep close tabs on Carlos," he told Clarence. "If he gets in trouble again . . ."

"I don't think he will," said Clarence. "I want him to finish high school, then go into the Marines. After that, it's up to him, but I think he'll turn out okay."

"As long as there's no more wars," Sandra said emphatically.

But I was thinking into the future. Clarence was, like me, almost forty. I knew that he was the only logical person to take over Torrington when Ashley felt it was time for him to step aside. Sandra was a natural for Torrington. The place needed more women; more *strong* women.

More women like Sandra, but also like Gina. I wanted her there at my table with all our friends, but when she was at the Red River, it was like she was going steady with the stage. In the last few weeks, she had bonded with the old bass player, Saul Moscato, whose energy and musical knowledge had inspired her even more than her spiritual guru, Meher Baba. After the gig she had played the week before, Saul had approached her with the start of a melody, only a dozen bars or so.

"Whaddya think?" he asked her.

"About what?" she had replied.

"That melody. I just made up that melody."

"Yeah?"

"Yeeeeah. What does it make you think of?"

"Um. It's nahce. It makes me think of traveling."

"Traveling where?" he asked.

"Ah donno, maybe everywhere."

"Can you write some lyrics?" he asked.

"Me? Ah've never . . .

"Come on, babe. "You got it in ya."

And so Gina had toiled for days on the song, not only writing most of the lyrics', but finishing the melody and the bridge as well. And she found that she was pretty good at it. She was already working out another idea that Saul presented her with; kind of a forties tune, so she was insisting that we watch movies like *Singing in the Rain* and *High Button Shoes*.

But she had finished the first song, which she called "One of These Days," and she and Saul's band had been rehearsing it all week. The meaning of the lyrics were a secret, of course, to anyone except us, but they had to do with the longing we both felt to take a vacation somewhere together.

"Sorry, baby," she told me. "Ah wanted to use Florence but the only thing ah could fahnd to rhyme with Florence was abhorrence. An ah don't even use that word."

"There are some things you abhor, though," I laughed.

"A vacuum cleaner," she quipped.

And here's the song, just as they preformed it that night. Sal and Gina alternated on verses and harmonized on the choruses.

> *One of these days,*
> *We'll get away*
> *Take a vacation*
> *See other nations.*
>
> *We'll take the time—*
> *All we can find—*
> *Sleep on the beaches*
> *Turn off the speeches*
> *Of people we don't care about.*
> *We'll go on our own walkabout.*
>
> *We're all so scared we'll fail,*
> *But years go by like horses on a trail.*
>
> *One of these nights*
> *We'll see the sights*

Street life in Rio
Just you and me-o.

We'll go to Japan
And see what we can;
Museums in Venice,
Wimbledon tennis.
And if we like it there okay
We might decide to stay away.

Our lives have grown so stale,
But years go by like horses on a trail.

They all try to tell us
to stay with the crowd
But so many people, don't you know
are too loud.

One of these days
People may say
Where did they go to?
What are they up to?

We won't give a damn;
wherever we land
we'll be together,
not caring whether,
the roads are paved with people on the go.
Their heads are filled with things they have
to know.

We spend our lives in jail
While years go by like horses on a trail.
Like horses on a trail.
Like horses on a trail.

There was a lot of applause, especially from me. But I was not the only one. Smokey had brought recording equipment into the saloon a few days before and recorded the song, along with Saul's "Green Baloney." Both songs were staples on the pirate radio station. Ashley was ecstatic; he had been enjoying music for so long as an outsider that being part of the success—or even the existence—of a new song gave him renewed life.

And Gina was becoming confident at her own songwriting abilities, something she had experimented with—and despaired of—long ago.

I was glad everything was ending like it should. I was especially happy for Clarence, who deserved all good things. I had some doubts about Sandra, who he had only known for a few weeks. Yet he hadn't succeeded with women who he had known all his life, so who was I to judge.

It was hard to see Joey as sheriff if he should decide to run someday. By the same token, now that I knew he wasn't a total asshole, I supposed he would be as good a sheriff as any.

As far as the sale of Gina's house was concerned, she was only waiting on the bank to finalize her papers. She had already moved all her belongings in with me—even her photo of Meher Baba—and was talking to a builder about the small bungalow she was intent on building down the road from the farm.

The Courier was overflowing with riches—subscriptions were up almost 100 percent since we broke the story of the Hardy scandal. The big bosses—none of whom I had ever seen in person—were very pleased.

But for me, there was still a lace untied, a girth not cinched quite tight enough, a chapter missing from my own life story that had to be written.

But to write it, I had to go to Florence. And despite my desire to take a vacation with Gina, I had to go alone.

Chapter Twenty-Five: The Ending

Ten a.m. and it was already hot. Cindy McKeown, dressed in cut-off jeans, an old Mickey Mouse t-shirt I had left in my room, and rubber flip flops, wiped her sweaty brow with her wrist. She had just finished sweeping out the living room and was heading to the kitchen for a drink of water when Mike appeared, fresh from a shower. Although school was out for the summer, he still wore his faded blue slacks, a seersucker button up shirt, and lace-up shoes that were a little down at the heel. In fact, to Cindy, *he* looked down at the heel, and had been looking that way for some time. She was certain it must have been partly her fault, but it was hard to think what she might have done or not done that would have prevented it. And it was hard to care any more. After thirty-seven years of marriage, the magic was long gone.

She saw him standing there in the doorway with his hands on his hips, that exasperated expression he had adopted somewhere along the line wrinkling his features. Cindy had always expected Mike McKeown to grow old gracefully and with style. Instead, he had become kind of weasely; the beard he had begun wearing was uneven and scraggly. Liver spots were beginning to come out like large freckles on the back of his hands. A few missing teeth in back had given his face a pinched look, but he wouldn't spend money for dentures.

Cindy knew that she was no prize herself. She was ten pounds overweight and her hair was more than half gray. In her present uniform she must look like a typical hausfrau. She couldn't stand to look in the mirror any more. But all that was about to change. If she was responsible for her husband's devolution, then he had to take responsibility for hers. She put her empty glass down on the sink.

"I'm going to see a lawyer today," she said. "I'm going to tell her to get the papers ready as soon as she can."

"What papers?" he asked with a fake smile. He knew very well what papers.

"The divorce papers," she said.

"Are you still harping about that?" he said. "I thought that was a joke. And you know I won't consent to any divorce." The smile was still there.

"You won't have any say in the matter."

"The hell I won't."

"Just accept things, Mike," she said. "We have nothing in common any more. We both have to move on."

"Move on where?" he said with asperity. "It's easy for you to say. You're rolling in cash. What do I have?"

"You have a job, and that's more than a lot of people can say."

"You call what I do at the school a job?" he said. "Teaching morons to draw circles? I've sacrificed my career for you and now you want to leave me with nothing."

"You haven't sacrificed anything for me; you've simply reached your level. I'm giving you that house in Forester," she said. "It's got three bedrooms, two baths. You can make one of the bedrooms into a nice studio."

"Nothing doing. "If you divorce me, I'm taking at least half."

"Half of what?" she said.

"Half of this house, this property, and whatever other property you have. Then I'm going to sell every damn thing and get out of this fucking place."

"Have fun, then," Cindy said. "Because that house in Forester is all that's left." That was enough. She had to get away from him. Go for a ride in the woods and not have to think. She'd been doing that a lot lately. She opened the back door and walked out to the barnyard. She heard her husband's footsteps behind her, moving quickly. Then her arm was grabbed from behind and she was spun around.

"What are you talking about, that's all that's left?" he demanded.

She shook off his grasp and opened the stall door of Number 3, where her beautiful three-year-old filly was munching on hay. She put a halter on her and led her outside to the grooming station.

"I asked you a question!" he told her. He approached and Alikki put her ears back. See there, Cindy thought. Even the horse doesn't want anything to do with you.

"I put it all in Sue-Ann's name," she told him. "The house with all its acreage, the other two properties. Everything except the one in Forester. It's more than fair." Cindy was currying Alikki, getting her to relax. She put down the curry comb and picked up the brush.

"To Sue-Ann? When? How?"

"I went to the courthouse a week or two ago. I put everything in her name. Not yours, not mine, not joint. Hers."

"But she doesn't need it. She's making a ton of money."

"She's our daughter. She may need it some day."

"I need it now!"

"For what?"

"To travel around; to get out of this shithole before I die."

"Tough."

"You need to go back to that damn courthouse and change it back."

"Fuck you."

"What did you say to me?"

"I'm out of here." Cindy laid the brush carefully down on the grooming bench and stepped on the mounting block. It felt strange without breeches or boots or helmet, but she had been doing that a lot, too, lately. She wanted to be free and she wanted out of her husband's presence. Now.

And if she were standing here before me right now she would be telling me that she should have paid more attention to Alikki's ears, which were pinned almost straight back, and to her body language, nervous and prancy. Instead of responding to Cindy's leg and trotting off, Alikki began sidestepping and crow hopping.

"Girl, that's not correct," she told the filly, trying to hold the horse steady with just her legs and halter rope. But by now she realized that the horse was no longer reacting to Mike, but to her own sense of frustration and unease, her desperation. The filly was only three; had only been under saddle a few months. Cindy was struggling to regain control when Mike shouted "Come back here!" When Cindy didn't respond, he picked up the brush and threw it at her.

Cindy probably never knew that he had thrown the brush or that the horse had been hit with anything. All she knew was that Alikki was bucking and that she had no choice but to come off. What went through her head as she was flying through the air was chagrin that Mike was watching this blatantly stupid final act, that he would expect to see her get hurt and would act smug about it.

But she didn't expect to be hurt; she expected to vault right back on Alikki and ride away to a better place.

That's the way it happened, and no one would ever have known if Mike hadn't left the brush he threw in the ring for the EMT to find. Would it have been better if I hadn't found out? Maybe. But it wouldn't have been different.

The reason I gave *The Courier*'s owners for going to Italy was to make a connection with Italian newspaper editors for a kind of "sister city" exchange of news. But I really went to confront my father.

I only saw him for an hour. He met me at an expensive coffee shop called the Caffe Rivoire on the Piazza della Signoria. It was the first time we had seen one another in several years.

I greeted him without warmth and sat across from him at an outside table. Mike had never been a touchy-feely kind of guy so he probably didn't notice. A waiter that looked like a rodent in a uniform took our order for coffee and some kind of pastry. As we waited for it to arrive, Mike smiled his usual Mike-smile and asked, "Why didn't you want me to bring Maria and little Sal?"

I knew I should be glad that my father had found the new life he had been seeking, that he had built up a new family from the ruins of his old one. I was vaguely aware that I should have met his new wife and put a good face on it; that I should be eager to meet and cuddle my new half-brother. But I wasn't. Although I felt benign toward both Maria and Salvatore, I didn't have the slightest interest in setting eyes on either. And the feeling I had toward Mike was not benign at all. It was easy for me to shrug off his question.

"Why didn't you tell me what happened the day Cindy died?" I asked.

Mike's face took on a slightly puzzled expression. His smile altered a little, like a picture that slips off center when the wall it hangs on is banged. "I told you everything," he said. "And why bring that up now? I'm getting on with my life. I'm trying to forget all that."

"I'm not," I told him.

Then I proceeded to tell him my suspicions. He listened, his face hardening. He didn't interrupt. When I finished he said simply, "You don't know anything about it. What brush? And even if I did throw something, what makes you think I could have hit a moving horse? I wasn't throwing at the horse anyway, I was trying—" He stopped, totally confused at what he was trying to say and getting himself in deeper with each sentence. Then he looked at me and I saw that there were tears brimming up in his eyes. "Cindy was going to leave me," he said. His mouth had drooped, so had his eyes. His whole body looked like a vine that had been severed from its tree. "I didn't mean to throw anything. I didn't mean to. . . " He put his face in his hands.

I noticed that sometime during my speech the rodent had put our order in front of us. I sipped my coffee without tasting it and relented a little.

"Daddy," I said. "You didn't mean for any of it to happen. I know you didn't. You're not a cruel person or a vindictive one. You did it because you were stupid."

Mike looked up at me.

"How could you have lived with Cindy for 35 years and not known that something's wrong when she's sitting on a green horse without a helmet or a saddle or even any shoes? How could you think that was okay?"

"She just never shared any of that horse stuff with me."

"And you never asked her to." I responded, but before he could answer, I went on. "It's her fault as much as yours. If she didn't want you to share the most interesting part of her life, she should have left you years ago. Decades ago. And she knew better than anyone not to ride a young horse without protection. But how can I forgive the fact that almost the minute she died you cleaned out her bank account and sold off everything that she didn't put in my name? Even her books. Even the horses that she loved so much." I stopped and took a breath, then continued. "And if that wasn't enough, you trashed her computer just in case she had drafted a will leaving me the truck and the horses. Or a diary that showed how unhappy she was. Daddy, a lot of Cindy's *life* was on that computer!"

"What do you want me to say? What do you want me to do?"

"Nothing. I just wanted you to know. That I know. So I can get past it." And suddenly I flashed on the image of Mike McKeown drunk out of his mind in The Red River Saloon. "And so that you can get past it, too."

I gulped down the rest of my coffee and stood up, leaving my bomboloni or whatever it was untouched.

"You have a new life now," I told him. "Take advantage of it; make sure it's better than the one you left, because you can't come back."

I stood up and walked toward the exit, As I passed the waiter, who had been approaching with our check, I jerked my thumb over my shoulder. "He's paying," I told him.

And I walked out onto Piazza della Signoria in the bright sunlight. I had a new life, too, and she was waiting for me in a tiny little city called Pine Oak.

A List of the Songs

"Bright Yellow Gun," written by Kristin Hersh and performed by Throwing Muses.

"Buy a Gun for Your Son," written and performed by Tom Paxton.

"Hey Joe," credited to Billy Roberts and performed by The Jimi Hendrix Experience.

"A Day in the Life," written by John Lennon and Paul McCartney and performed by The Beatles.

Yesterday's Papers," written by Mick Jagger and Keith Richards and performed by The Rolling Stones.

"Ain't that News," written and performed by Tom Paxton.

"Back in Time," written by Huey Lewis, Sean Hopper, Chris Hayes, and Johnny Colla and recorded by Huey Lewis and the News.

"Are You Ready," written by Charlie Allen and John Hill and performed by Pacific Gas and Electric.

"I'm Sorry," written by Dub Albritton and Ronnie Self and performed by Brenda Lee.

"Now I Can Die," written and performed by Nina Gordon. "Green Baloney," written by Iza Moreau.

"Showdown," written by Jeff Lynne and performed by The Electric Light Orchestra.

"Rain," written by John Lennon and performed by The Beatles.

"Thunder and Lightning," written and performed by Chi Coltrane.

"One of These Days," written by Iza Moreau.

About the Author

Iza Moreau was born and raised in New Mexico, where she was introduced to Arabian horses and to the art of riding them. After a stint in journalism school, she roamed the country for a couple of years before settling down in one of the Southern states, where she has a small farm with a couple of horses. She counts Sarah Waters, Maggie Estep, and the Bronte sisters—Acton, Currer, and Ellis—among her literary influences.

Secrets in Small Towns is the third in the series of Small Town novels featuring Sue-Ann McKeown and her friends in Pine Oak, Florida. The first novel in the series, *The News in Small Towns*, was a top-5 finalist in the 2013 Next Generation Indie Book Awards in both Mystery and Regional Fiction. It and its popular sequel, *Madness in Small Towns*, are available in print and as e-books.

Although *Secrets in Small Towns* completes the three-novel sequence, there is a series of Small Town short stories featuring the same characters which will be collected in 2015 under the title *Stories in Small Towns*. Several of these are available at Amazon.com as e-book singles.

You can reach Iza at iza@blackbayfarm.com.

1

26057445R00176

Made in the USA
Charleston, SC
23 January 2014